Praise for *Bland Beginning*:

"Enough humor and good writing so that even non-suspense addicts will like it."
—*Saturday Review of Literature*

"The characters are well drawn and the technical details are interesting and authentic."
—*The New Yorker*

"Entertainingly droll characterizations in a cleverly original murder puzzle."
—*Chicago Sunday Times*

JULIAN SYMONS
Bland Beginning

Carroll & Graf Publishers, Inc.
New York

For Sarah Symons

Your three months eyes outblue the cobalt sky
And stare at depthless images that lie
Cocooned in simple webs of sleep and hunger.

Their gaze reflects a fantasy of younger
And stranger days when friendly lions residing
Within the chintzy chair roared out of hiding:

Before we knew the transverse alchemies
Corroding the bright Radicals to Tories
And turning poems to detective stories

Published by arrangement with Harper & Row Publishers, Inc.

First Carroll & Graf edition 1987

Carroll & Graf Publishers, Inc.
260 Fifth Avenue
New York, NY 10001

ISBN: 0-88184-337-7

Manufactured in the United States of America

CONTENTS

PROLOGUE—1949

I WALKED up the steps of the London Library with my mind on murder, and handed Forster's *Life of Dickens* over the counter. "Pratterstone," I said absently, and the girl looked surprised. "I beg your pardon. Symons, Julian Symons."

Pratterstone the great detective—who was Pratterstone? I wondered as I walked slowly up the stairs, almost stumbling over the wide treads and narrow risers. Pratterstone, of course, was one of the queer names noted by Dickens for possible use in books. No, Pratterstone was too comic. What else? Willshard, perhaps, or Chinkible or Glibbery? Riderhood? Dickens had used Riderhood himself, in *Our Mutual Friend*. Willshard then—I entered the reading room, stared blankly at *The Atlantic Monthly*, dropped into one of the large hide armchairs and thought about the power and hardness of man's will.

I was still thinking about man's will an hour later, after blundering like a bumble bee among English literature, isolating myself in the quiet rooms of Pamphlets and Magazines and hearing my footsteps ring on the fretted floor of History. Posit Willshard/Glibbery, the great detective, as the murderer. Commonplace? Perhaps—but let his murderous identity stay unrevealed, let him be a schizophrene making the most urgent efforts with Detectival Personality Number 1 to unravel the tangle made for him by Murderous Personality Number 2. Number 2, the wicked Glibbery, would have the edge all the time, however, on Number 1, dear old pertinacious Willshard. What a collection of red herrings he would leave around for Willshard to sniff at, down what a number of curious psychological blind alleys would the innocent detective be lured.

But schizophrenia, too, was a well-worn subject— was it not, indeed, the occupational disease of bank clerks, advertising men and artists equally? One must make an effort, after all, to inject a little shot of vigor into the flabby frame of the detective story. Injections, I thought—"Watson! The hypodermic!" Could one do anything with Sherlock Holmes? Holmes, no doubt, was a manic-depressive psychological type, like Ruskin and Dickens. Could my detective be a manic depressive—with schizoid tendencies, naturally?

My wanderings had led me near to Psychology. One left turn, one sharp right, and I was there, standing near to a man with fair hair who was staring meditatively at the shelves. I could not see what I wanted. Freud and Hirschfeld, Horney and Jung—but nothing about the manic depressive. I lowered myself with an effort to the knees-bend position and looked at the lower shelves. Psychological types, secondary sexual characteristics, the Marquis de Sade. I said aloud: "Manic depressive, manic depressive.

> The Marquis de Sade was aggressive,
> But where is the manic depressive?"

A voice said, "This might be what you want," and a hand held out to me a book which said on the spine: *Manic Depressive Insanity and Paranoia.* "The standard work—by Professor Kraepelin of Munich," said the voice. My gaze traveled slowly from the hand holding the book to the face above it (remember my knees-bend position), and I recognized with surprise my old friend Detective Inspector Bland. Fair haired, rosy complexioned, tidy as a bas-relief by Ben Nicholson, Bland might have passed for the bank clerk I had been thinking about.

I straightened myself painfully. "Bland! I was just

planning a book about a series of murders done by a manic-depressive detective."

His smile was perfunctory, and his answer apparently irrelevant. "Did you know John Basingstoke?"

"The poet and novelist, you mean? Fell off a mountain in Switzerland and broke his neck a couple of days ago? I met him at parties, Why?"

"Come with me, and I'll tell you something more interesting than tales of manic-depressive detectives." He suddenly scooped an armful of books from the shelf, and smiled slightly at my look of surprise. "I never choose books. I let them choose me. In this batch there is probably one book which has some use for a hard-working policeman. When I've looked through them all I shall find out which it is."

We stepped out of the London Library's cultured gloom into the warm bath of a June day. "I knew Basingstoke quite well," Bland volunteered suddenly. "You might say we were boys together. And you might call him the prime mover in this story." He looked up at the endless expanse of blue above our heads as we turned out of St. James's Square toward Piccadilly. "It was on a day like this that—" His eyes glazed over with goodness knew what fantasy of the past.

"That what?"

"Come and have lunch at my flat if you've nothing better to do. Mrs. Chinkible will no doubt manage something for an extra mouth—even one as capacious as yours."

"Chinkible? Her name's not really Chinkible?"

"No." Bland looked as nearly discomfited as is possible to him. "Her name's Plantagenet, but I call her Chinkible because she's so mean." He sighed. "I got the name from a list of 'available names for characters' that Dickens left—"

I broke into a hyenaish hoot that made him stare at me. "Not another word, my dear Glibbery. Onward to the Chinkible lunch."

He shook his head and said sadly, "I don't understand you." I called a taxi before his eyes could glaze over again.

Mrs. Chinkible, a square woman with a hard gaze, provided an excellent lunch of smoked salmon, mushroom omelet with a perfectly dressed salad and a continuous supply of warm toast, and gorgonzola cheese. During lunch we talked about cricket, politics, and the decline of the cinema. Afterward we sat before Bland's casement windows which almost looked out onto Gray's Inn Road, and drank our coffee. "Compare," Bland said, "compare Danny Kaye or Red Skelton, admirable comics though they are, with Chaplin, and—"

I tapped my chair arm. "What about Basingstoke?"

He turned on me the diffident smile that has deceived many criminals into trusting him. "Basingstoke, yes. It all happened so long ago that I'm nervous of recalling it. You see me now, full of years if not of honor—"

"My dear Bland, I can hardly pick up a newspaper without reading that you are actively engaged in buttressing the structure of a decaying society by hunting down psychiatric cases and getting them sent to prison."

"—and of gray hairs if not of wisdom." He touched his still thick fair hair with some complacency. "But all this happened a quarter of a century ago, when I was really rather young. And I had very little to do with any of it, except," he said with another touch of complacency, "that I happened to solve it. And then it was all hushed up, for reasons you'll understand when I tell you the story. In a way, it was my beginning, and that's probably why I remember it so well. You've heard of Martin Rawlings."

"Of course."

"He comes into the story. You'd better refresh your memory by reading the piece about him in the *Biographical Dictionary* while I look for some papers." So I sat with the *Biographical Dictionary* in front of me, reading rather idly about Rawlings while Bland looked through the pigeonholes of a walnut writing desk.

"The Larch-Rockingham forgeries," he said, "and the disappearance of Lady Vendible, Monty Montague—*he* was a queer Scottish philanthropist if ever there was one—the Pyramid Friendship League, Button and Button. You don't remember any of those affairs, I suppose?"

"No."

"All in my young time. But there are some good stories among them. The Immaterial murder case—hardly one of my successes, but amusing. Do you remember the Immaterialist art movement and its credo 'It is only the immaterial object that possesses significant form'?"

"What about Basingstoke?"

"Here we are." He produced from a thick manilla folder some typescripts, a pencil drawing of a man's head on a piece of blotting paper, and a small book of poems with the words *Passion and Repentance* on its faded blue cover. "It all happened in 1924," he began.

He talked on through the lazy June afternoon, while the taxis buzzed slowly past the door and children called in the street below and heat came up from the pavement and the shadows moved slowly across the stucco face of the house opposite. Here is the story he told; and I have introduced it to you, as he introduced it to me, through the *Biographical Dictionary*.

FROM THE BIOGRAPHICAL DICTIONARY

RAWLINGS, MARTIN (1835—1876), one of the most curious minor poets of the nineteenth century, was born on the 3rd April, 1835, in St. William Square, Belgravia. His father, the Reverend Stephen Rawlings, was minister of a Presbyterian congregation, and Martin completed his education at a Unitarian college. His father hoped that Martin would enter the Dissenting ministry, but it soon became evident that the boy had no inclination to the Church, and the family's financial circumstances made it impossible for his father to indulge Martin's wish to study at a university. For some three years after leaving the Unitarian college he lived an idle and quarrelsome life at home, and although it does not seem that he indulged in any serious dissipation, even such small debts as he incurred were of serious importance to one in his father's straitened position. Martin decided early in life that he wished to be a poet, and he wrote a great deal of verse between his eighteenth and twenty-first years. None of it has been preserved, and he acknowledged in later life that it was perhaps not worth preserving; but at the time he was indignant because his family and friends failed to appreciate his work. At the age of twenty-one, after a family quarrel more bitter than usual, he left England to live in Italy.

We have only brief glimpses of his life in Italy during the next fifteen years, as it was seen through the literary circles of Rome and Florence, who did not share his own conviction of his genius. He married Maria Tambinetta, a beautiful Italian girl, and maintained her and his young son very precariously by occasional journalism, combined with many odd occupations, such as (for a short time) that of gravedigger's mate in a cemetery. In 1868 the publication in England of *Passion and Repentance*, a series of sonnets on the themes of sacred and profane love, made him famous overnight. This fame, or notoriety was enhanced by the storm of moral indignation which greeted the book. It was denounced, in a typical phrase, as "a most indecent contribution to the school of fleshly poetry, which revels in revealing the ignobler impulses of mankind." Many famous men of letters took part in the furious controversy that followed, in which the purely poetic merits of *Passion and Repentance* remained largely unconsidered.

Although he realized that the book owed some of its success to this notoriety, Rawlings was delighted by the praise he received, and also by the improvement in his financial position brought about by the book's sales. A second son had been born to him, and his early wildness gave way to a comparatively humdrum and peaceful existence. Before the publication of *Passion and Repentance* he had been converted to the Roman Catholic faith, and his two later books, *Meditations* (1869) and *Poems Lyrical and Devout* (1871), were largely inspired by his conversion. These books were greeted tepidly by the critics, but had a large sale.

Rawlings had for some time considered returning to England; and now a fortunate circumstance made his return necessary, and at the same time placed him in a position where monetary difficulties troubled him no more. A cousin, John Rawlings, who had left England at the same time as himself to become a gold prospector in Australia, had been fortunate in his adventure. John Rawlings died soon after returning home from the Antipodes and the poet found himself the sole beneficiary of his considerable fortune in Austrialian gold and English real estate.

In 1871 Martin Rawlings returned to England, and

took up residence at a house in the village of Millingham. He showed himself a surprisingly capable man of business, and appeared to enjoy the problems involved in the management of the estate and in the conversion of the remainder of his cousin's fortune into freehold property. He lived a simple and ascetic life, was strict and even severe in personal habits, and wrote no more poetry. His wife, who had been a faithful companion in times of hardship, died in 1873, and Martin was much affected by her loss. He died quite suddenly three years later, from a heart attack, at the early age of forty-one.

There is something enigmatic in both Rawlings' life and his work. Throughout his life he had few friends; none of them knew him intimately, and we possess very scanty information about the important part of his life lived in Italy. It is difficult, also, to estimate the final worth of his poetry. At the time of their publication the sonnet series, *Passion and Repentance*, astonished many critics by its force and strangeness of epithet; today most of the strangeness seems merely obscure, and the extravagance of epithet is not pleasing to a modern taste. It is, nevertheless, on these pagan pieces that his reputation is likely to be maintained, if it survives at all. His two later books are certainly inferior to the first, although they contain one or two delightful lyrics, which have deservedly found a place in anthologies.

A brief account of Rawlings' early life and family quarrels, together with a sketch of his life in Italy, can be found in "A Turbulent Boy," one of the essays in Michael Blackburn's *Sesame Without Lilies*.

Bland Beginning

MONDAY

1924

I

WHEN ANTHONY SHELTON proposed to Victoria Rawlings, and was accepted, both his friends and hers were surprised; and although these friends differed in much else they were agreed that the marriage was in all respects unsuitable. It was not merely, Anthony's friends observed, that Victoria was the daughter of a fairly unsuccessful general practitioner (whose unsuccess had been sealed, a couple of years before the engagement, by his death from a lingering liver complaint) in the suburb of Barnsfield, while Anthony's father was known to be something, and something important—though nobody quite knew what—in the city. That might, in these regrettably democratic postwar days, be ignored. Nor was it simply, as Victoria's friends remarked, that Victoria was really awfully interested in books and writers and art and artists and all that sort of thing, whereas Anthony's capacity for intellectual conversation was known to be strictly limited. No, the serious difference between them—the yawning gap which made their suggested marriage certain, in a mixture of metaphor, to land on the rocks—touched the question of sport in general, and in particular cricket. Victoria, her friends explained, was opposed on principle (although they might have been hard put to it to say what principle) to all games, and particularly to those played with bat and ball; and if there was one game that she regarded with more distaste than another, it was cricket. Cricket, on the other hand, had always appeared to Tony Shelton, although he was not of a religious disposition, as the prime reason for the creation of man. The thing that he remembered most clearly about his years at one of England's most famous public schools was his bowling analysis; and although he spent three years at Oxford, at the end of which the university conferred no academic distinction upon him, he felt strongly that he had conferred a distinction on the university by taking nine wickets against Cambridge in his last year. He had come down prepared to settle to the serious business of life by playing regularly for Southshire. It was, Victoria's and Tony's friends agreed, obviously not a suitable marriage, and it was a mystery, besides, what Tony could possibly see in Victoria, or Victoria in Tony.

This mystery may be solved at once. What Victoria saw in Tony was abundant curling fair hair, set above a pair of disarmingly innocent eyes, remarkably wide shoulders tapering down to a slim waist and long, narrow legs. Victoria had for years proclaimed her devotion to an ideal of physical male beauty which she believed, a little vaguely, to be Grecian. This physical ideal seemed to be fulfilled by Tony's appearance; and in intellectual matters she regarded him as clay to be shaped by the potter's hand. It was not, of course, disagreeable to her that Tony's father was something in the city and it is probable that she experienced a small satisfaction from the sight of Tony's yellow Bentley drawn up outside the door of the modest home in which she lived with her mother and her brother Edward, who had assumed her father's mantle of medical failure; but still, these were not the prime factors in her acceptance of his proposal. In the diary which she kept faithfully in violet ink and a sprawling hand, she put down a vision of herself as queen of an artistic salon, always witty and charming, always making the right remark, smoothing the rough moment with a smile or wave of the hand; and Tony Shelton was an essential element in this vision. Her mots, in this salon, were famous, and rumor whispered that many great men were madly in love with her, yet none was known to be her lover. She was faithful always to her husband, not because of his genius (not even in her diary could she transform Tony into a genius), but because of his wonderful Grecian beauty. Could it be, she wondered sometimes, that she loved Tony because he was so gratifyingly impressed by *her* intellect? But she put this thought firmly away from her, and decided that it was her fatal susceptibility to a beauty that was sufficiently near to that of a Grecian statue for all reasonable requirements that had joined their fates.

Anthony's reasons for admiring Victoria were not to be found altogether in her rather unfashionably long face, her dark hair and eyebrows, her full and often-parted lips and her slightly vacant expression. Anthony *did*, in fact, admire Victoria's intellect. This admiration may seem strange in one who was viewed by his friends as essentially a cricketer, and by his enemies as essentially a moron, but behind the young man's fair, uncorrugated brow there lay, unanalysed and undetermined but still exceedingly potent, that deep sense of guilt with which many modern films, novels and treatises have familiarized us. Anthony was a victim of what, in fashionable terms, is known as a father fixation. His mother had died at Anthony's birth, and his first memories were of the small man with a nut-brown face who was his father: who talked to him so incomprehensibly, and gave him elaborate presents of fishing rods and bicycles and unreadable books; who reproved boyish tricks and jokes with a calm kindness more terrifying than any anger could have been. In the brief intervals from sporting triumphs which Anthony spent at home he came slowly to the realization that his father adhered to a scale of values in which an ability to move the new ball both ways or to sell the dummy played an inconsiderable part. Not by any word or gesture did Mr. Shelton show a lack of interest in his son's sporting achievements; yet Anthony was painfully conscious that he must be a disappointment to the old man who added to his immense knowledge of the world, and his ability to conduct business deals with the hard-faced men who sometimes came to their home, intellectual interests which were expressed for his son in his father's frequent study of booksellers' lists, and excitement over the purchases which he sometimes made from them. When he came down from Oxford Anthony was subject to a severe emotional stress in feeling that he was not worthy of his father, and to a mixed desire and distaste for his projected career as a cricketer.

Then he met Victoria—and met her, as it happened, through his father, when Mr. Shelton, who was known in the district to possess a considerable library, was asked to address the Barnsfield Literary Society on "How to Collect Books." Anthony conscientiously attended this lecture, and his attention wavered sometimes from his father's humorous description of the circumstances which induced him to break a youthful vow that he would never buy a book which cost more than half a crown. It wavered because of the knowledge that a young woman at the other side of the room was gazing at him with peculiar fixity. The young woman (whose gaze had been fixed by his Greek beauty) was Victoria Rawlings; and when she talked to him over the cups of weak tea and date sandwiches which accompanied the lecture, he was delighted to discover that she was a really well-read girl. She had written a novel—or part of a novel; she painted—or attended a School of Art; and she mentioned airily names which impressed him, even though he heard them for the first time. He was still more impressed, and even alarmed, when she said that art was in her blood, and that her grandfather was Martin Rawlings (a name which, like the other names she mentioned, was strange to him). The effect of her conversation was enhanced by the thick dark hair which she wore cut square in bangs, by her rich, yearning eyes and slightly-parted lips; and his enchantment was complete when Victoria expressed emphatically her disinterest in all sporting activities—a full life, she said, could be lived only in the mind.

She invited him to tea, and he met her brother Edward, who seemed rather disagreeable, and her mother, Muriel, who was certainly scatterbrained. Neither her mother nor brother seemed to Anthony to value Victoria at her true intellectual worth, and he said as much to her. She murmured the word "Philistines," and in a heaven of self-abasement Anthony said, "But I'm a Philistine too—I'm an awful fool, you know." Beneath the bangs, Victoria's long face looked pensive as he gasped suddenly: "Will you marry me?" Slowly and solemnly she nodded, and then said: "Not if you continue to play cricket." Gleefully, without the semblance of a sigh, Anthony made the sacrifice; and as he kissed her, he thought with pleasure of his father's delight.

When he announced the engagement, however, with the nervousness that always oppressed him in dealing with his father, Mr. Shelton showed no particular pleasure. He looked at his son for a moment or two without speaking, and then said: "You are very young."

"I'm twenty-two."

"Precisely." Mr. Shelton brought the tips of his slender fingers together. "And Miss Rawlings is a little older, I believe."

"She's twenty-four. But what does that matter?" Then, as his father was silent again, Anthony said, "You like her, sir, don't you?"

"I have always found her a pleasant girl. She is perhaps a little feather witted, but I do not regard that as a serious fault in a woman."

"Really, sir, I don't think you quite understand her." Anthony was always uncomfortable when he contradicted his father, "She's awfully clever."

"I have seen some of the paintings which she hangs around the house. They are execrable. I can understand the production of such work—there is an inferior artist in the humblest heart—but it shows a grave failure of taste to display it with apparent pride. That is a mark against her. Another mark, I should have thought, from your point of view, is her lack of interest in games. I doubt if she will enjoy watching you play for Southshire every summer."

"She won't have to," Anthony said. "I'm giving up cricket."

"My dear boy, you can't be serious." Mr. Shelton looked at his son with more sign of emotion than he had yet shown.

"I am." Anthony shuffled his feet with shy determination. "Vicky's shown me that it's all a lot of rot. All those grown men hitting a ball about—why, it's ridiculous." He laughed unconvincingly. "Poetry and painting and music and all that—they're the important things. And whatever you say about her paintings, I think Vicky's an artist. It's—it's in the blood. Her grandfather was a poet."

"I know. Old Martin Rawlings." Mr. Shelton said unexpectedly,

"I dreamed a gull whose lucent lovely wing
   Knew not the savage colors of desire,
   But waking found your body like a fire
   And never knew nor recked a reckoning."

"What's that?"

Mr. Shelton shook his head with a half-humorous pity. "You should know the works of old Martin if you want to find the way to his granddaughter's heart. Or perhaps you shouldn't—you seem to have done very well without the knowledge. Perhaps she favors these moderns who cut up their lines into all sorts of odd lengths. What do you know about them?"

"Nothing, sir."

"You are fortunate."

"But I can learn," Anthony said eagerly.

"I'm sure you can." Twice, like a neat cat, Mr. Shelton walked up and down the library. Then he slapped his son on the back. "Very well, my boy. There is one thing I want to ask you, while I say good luck and God bless you." An immense, beaming smile moved over Anthony's handsome face, a smile that vanished with his father's next words. "I want you to promise not to get married for a year. I know you won't like that, but I think you owe it to me." He spoke rather rapidly, as he saw that his son was about to interrupt. "Since your mother died, a deep responsibility has been placed upon me. I say nothing against this marriage, except that it is not the kind of alliance that I had expected or hoped for you. I am saying nothing against Miss Rawlings——"

"Vicky."

"Vicky," said Mr. Shelton with obvious effort. "I am saying nothing against Vicky. I only ask you to wait for a year so that you are both sure of your own minds."

Anthony's handsome face reddened, and his fair curls shook with his effort to concentrate. "But it's—it's ——" He drew on a not very extensive vocabulary. "It's Victorian."

His father stood smiling at him, a small brown man with a thin brown face creased in a smile. "What can you expect of a Victorian figure like me—almost an antique? After all, it's *not* what I wanted. I don't think I'm being unreasonable. Is it a deal?"

His son smiled sheepishly. "If Vicky says so."

"And you're really going to give up cricket?"

"Oh yes. Poetry and painting—they're the really important things."

"Yes, indeed," said Mr. Shelton enthusiastically, and the interview was over.

Vicky thought the old man very ridiculous, but rather sweet. "As though things could ever change for us, darling, when we're both interested in the same things." She looked thoughtful. "I'd quite like to get married this week."

Anthony's gasp was a mixture of admiration and horror. "But what about father?"

"What about him? We don't want to be tied to anybody's purse strings, do we?"

"Of course not," he said uncertainly. "But—if he cut off my allowance—I don't know what we should do. I suppose I could get a job," he said despairingly.

"We'd manage," said Vicky, and then, "but of course we don't want to hurt his feelings."

Anthony's face brightened. "No, I shouldn't like to hurt his feelings."

So the two young people were engaged, although Vicky showed her emancipation from convention by saying that she did not want Anthony to buy her a ring. An intellectual gift, Anthony understood, would be acceptable—or no gift at all, for such things were irrelevant to the marriage of true minds. He visited museums and art galleries, and expressed his appreciation of what he saw there; and if he did not familiarize himself with modern poetry, he took his father's advice as far as reading the article about Martin Rawlings in the *Biographical Dictionary*. Opinion was divided about this move of old Mr. Shelton's. Some people said that the best way of killing a cat was by choking it with cream, and that the old man was a very deep one, while others saw in it a reluctant acceptance of the changes that had come over the world in this postwar February of 1924, when the Prince of Wale⸱ was signalizing his recognition of the existence of a Labour Government by giving its Prime Minister lunch; and Mr. Howard Carter was distressing the Egyptian authorities by opening the sarcophagus in the innermost shrine of Tutankhamen's tomb; and a Hammersmith woman and her two young children were killed by falling from the campanile of Westminster Cathedral; and the Oxford Union, at its centenary, was debating "That Civilization has advanced since the Society first met."

II

Three months later Anthony came down late to breakfast, and noticed with some irritation that his father had *The Times* open at the cricket page. Anthony turned to the sports page of the *Daily Mail*. Not only was Southshire doing badly, but the report of the day's play was quite inadequate. He sipped his tea, and then rang the bell with unnecessary violence. "Janet," he said, "this tea's cold."

Janet was a tall, thin woman with a drooping nose. "If you'd come down at the right time it would have been hot enough. Ten o'clock's no time for breakfast, is it, Mr. Shelton?"

Anthony's father lowered his *Times* a little. "Don't be severe, Janet. My son is much disturbed by the political situation."

"I should think so too," said Janet. "With this Labour Government ready to murder people in their beds."

"Last night the government was saved from defeat by the Liberals," said Mr. Shelton. "A fact that I am sure you deplore as much as I do."

Janet had her hand on the teapot. "And the tea's not cold," she said accusingly.

"Nevertheless, you heard Mr. Anthony say that he would like to have a fresh pot." His smile robbed the words of sting. When she had gone c it of the room there was silence while the old man and the young man read their papers. Then Mr. Shelton said, "A bad start for Southshire. Beaten by Worcester in their first match, and now Leicestershire has scored four hundred and twenty for five against them." Anthony stuffed scrambled egg into his mouth and made no reply. "Your absence is lamented in *The Times* report. Listen. 'It is clear that the county will sadly miss Mr. A. W. Shelton, the talented university fast-medium bowler, who will not be giving the team his support this season.'"

9

Janet brought in some more tea. Anthony fidgeted with a roll. His face was red. "Why do you try to make me look a fool?" he said suddenly. "You know very well I'm not interested in politics."

The Times came down with a rustle. "Why do you behave like one? You know perfectly well that you're itching to play for Southshire. Why don't you?"

"Because I don't choose to."

"Very well." Mr. Shelton had regained his customary urbanity. "I am sorry that I was mistaken about your interest in politics. It seemed to me likely that your new-found enthusiasm for art and letters might have extended to other spheres."

Anthony was always at a disadvantage in discussion with his father, and to avoid argument he turned to the three envelopes that lay beside his plate. They were all franked with penny stamps, and on many days he would not have troubled to open them. Today he did so; and set in train a line of events that led to murder. One of the envelopes contained an offer to lend money on note of hand alone; another was a bill from a garage; the third was a catalogue of a book sale at Messrs. Bernard Lintot, Dealers in Rare Books, of Clark Street, W.1. Conscious of his father's eye upon him, Anthony turned the pages with a pretense of interest he did not feel, until suddenly his eye was caught by a name and an item:

RAWLINGS, MARTIN. *Passion and Repentance.* Letts and Ableton, 1860.
The rare first edition, seen through the press by the author, and never publicly distributed. An exceptionally fine copy, in the original parchment boards.

Anthony pondered for a moment, eating his scrambled egg. Then he looked up, his face brighter than it had been for a week. "I say, Dad, you know a lot about first editions, and all that, don't you?"

"Well?"

"What would a first edition of old Martin Rawlings' *Passion and Repentance* be worth?"

"A first edition?" His father's eyebrows were arched. "Let me see the catalogue." He looked at it and said, "It might be worth sixty pounds, or perhaps a little more. There aren't many copies in existence, and they rarely come up for sale. You know the history of *Passion and Repentance,* I suppose?" His eyes were amused under the arched brows.

"Well——" Anthony said slowly, and his father laughed.

"You should know about it. After all, old Martin was your fiancée's grandfather—a fact of which both you and she are prone to remind me. You know that it was rather indiscreet by Victorian standards?"

Anthony nodded his head like a mandarin. "I've read what it says in the *Biographical Dictionary.*"

"The story is that Martin Rawlings wrote the poems in 1860, and published them in this little private edition. Then eight years later he decided to risk the scandal of open publication, and within a few weeks the book made him famous."

"What's so scandalous about the poems?" Anthony asked.

"Why don't you read them and find out?" his father suggested, and rose to leave the breakfast table. Then he turned back, and said, "Why do you want to know their value?"

His son blushed. "Well, as a matter of fact, you know Vicky didn't want an engagement ring and said she wanted something original. I thought, you see, that as she said the other day she hadn't got a copy of the first edition of this book, she might like——"

"I see." The lines of Mr. Shelton's brown face might, for a moment, have been carved out of wood. Then he smiled and said, "You might go up to seventy. After all, it will be a family investment."

It was not until his father had left the house that it occurred to Anthony to wonder why a bookseller's catalogue should have been sent to him. He looked idly at the envelope, and saw that in fact it was addressed to *R. W. Shelton, Esq.* The letter R, carelessly written, had been interpreted by Janet as an A. His father's name was Richard William and the catalogue had, in fact, been meant for him.

III

The Bentley drew up with enviable smoothness outside Messrs. Lintot's door. Inside, Anthony felt himself to be a rather conspicuous figure in his check jacket, yellow scarf and thick brown shoes. These seemed, somehow, not to be the appropriate wear for a book sale. He held the catalogue firmly in his hand and looked round with a certain bewilderment.

The atmosphere did not seem to him that of a book sale. Some twenty men, and three or four women, were sitting round a long baize-topped table. Some of the men seemed to be asleep, while others indicated their attention only by the slightest movement of their catalogues. Other men were standing round the large room, three walls of which were lined with books from floor to ceiling, and these men, too, seemed apathetic. Some of them, indeed, were apparently so little interested that they had turned round and were looking at the books on the shelves.

Anthony had been in the room a minute or two before he realized that the sale was in progress. Then the auctioneer, a thin man with a badly fitting brown wig which did not match his gray mustache, murmured, "Lot number . . ." and his voice faded so much that Anthony could not hear the number. He tapped the shoulder of a small man standing on his left, who was wearing a bowler hat, a very tight blue suit with a red line in it, and a startling tie decorated with blue and yellow stripes. Like Anthony, this man clutched a catalogue tightly in one hand. When he turned round the man revealed a very red face which, although the room was not hot, shone with perspiration. "Whatcher want?" he asked.

"I beg your pardon," Anthony said. "Could you tell me which lot they are selling?"

"No idea, chum." As the man turned away, Anthony saw that his catalogue was marked in blue with a big cross next to Lot 85. And Lot 85 was the first edition of *Passion and Repentance*.

Anthony experienced a feeling of mingled annoyance and pleasure. It was disturbing to know that someone else had come to the sale apparently with the express intention of bidding for *Passion and Repentance*, but at the same time the thought of giving a surprise to this rude little man was positively pleasant. But surely the little man could not be a typical frequenter of book sales? While Anthony was pondering this question, a very old man just in front of him, wearing extremely tight trousers and carrying a malacca cane, leaned back and whispered, "We are now at Lot 38. Prices are low."

"Are they indeed," said Anthony, much encouraged. What a fine stroke if he could tell his father that he had bought this first edition for much less than the sixty or seventy pounds he had mentioned.

"It is a buyers' market," whispered the old man. "A first edition of *Liza of Lambeth* has just sold for five pounds." Anthony nodded uncomfortably. He had not the least idea whether this figure was low or high.

For the next few minutes he concentrated on watching the procedure of the sale. It was not really hard to follow. First of all, the auctioneer announced the lot by number, then the lot itself or a sample of it was passed round very quickly by an attendant for inspection, and then it was sold. The apathy of the bidders seemed to be simply a technique by which they tried to avoid notice. The lots were disposed of at great speed, very few of them taking more than a minute. Anthony noticed that a shrewd-looking young man seated at the table bought several of them, and he noticed also that the man in the blue suit did not bid at all. Just as he was wondering who the shrewd-looking young man was, the old man with tight trousers leaned toward him again and said, "That's Foskiss. Buys everything for the ring. Doesn't give the small men a chance."

Anthony nodded again, without any idea what the old man meant. Bidding started for a collected edition of Henry James in the Washington Square edition and Anthony, who had no wish to possess the works of Henry James, felt an irresistible desire to bid.

"Four," murmured the auctioneer. "Four-five, four-ten. Any advance on four-ten?"

"Five," said Anthony with a boldness that took his own breath away, and caused half the people in the room to turn round and look at him. The auctioneer settled his wig more firmly, and the young man at the table looked up from his catalogue, on which he had been drawing elaborate arabesques. He stared hard at Anthony, and then nodded.

"Guineas," said the auctioneer happily. "Five Guineas against you, sir."

"Six," said Anthony, staring defiantly round the room. The young man nodded. "Guineas," said the auctioneer.

"Seven," said Anthony, directing his gaze this time straight at the shrewd-looking young man, who ignored him and nodded again. At ten pounds, however, the young man shrugged, murmured something to the man sitting next to him and made no further movement.

"Made you pay through the nose for it," said the old man with enjoyment. "He's smart, is young Foskiss." He blew his nose loudly.

By the time he had given his name and address to the auctioneer's clerk, Anthony was feeling less triumphant. Whatever could he do with all those books? He suddenly cheered up as he reflected that he could, of course, present them to his father. What a surprise that would give him! He had returned to his place and fallen into a kind of daydream when he suddenly heard the auctioneer say "Lot 85." A moment later the lot was being displayed. It was carried round like a precious relic, and was revealed as a small volume with a slightly faded blue cover.

"Lot 85," the auctioneer repeated without emotion. "What am I offered? Thirty-five, thirty-seven, thirty-eight, forty. Thank you. Forty-one, forty-two, forty-three, forty-five. Any advance on forty-five?" The shrewd-looking young man raised his catalogue. "Forty-seven. Thank you, Mr. Foskiss. Forty-eight, fifty. Fifty pounds offered." The auctioneer paused.

When should he start bidding? Anthony seemed to have heard somewhere that it was wise to delay your bid as long as possible—it had a good psychological effect. On the other hand, it would be an awful thing if the lot was knocked down suddenly to the unpleasant Foskiss. While his mind was still in this state of indecision Anthony heard himself say, "Fifty-two."

Foskiss raised his catalogue. "Fifty-three."

"Fifty-five."

Foskiss now spoke for the first time. "Sixty," he said.

A five-pound raise! But that was a game that two could play. With a slight but not unpleasant feeling of nervousness Anthony said, "Sixty-five." He looked hard at Foskiss, who was creasing his catalogue pensively. A hoarse voice just beside Anthony said, "Seventy." It was the little man in the blue suit and the bowler hat. Anthony had forgotten all about him. Now the little man's head was jutting forward, and he looked both comic and menacing.

"Seventy-one," said Foskiss.

"Seventy-five," said the man in the blue suit.

"Seventy-six."

In a voice that hoarseness made almost inaudible, the man in the blue suit said, "Eighty." The auctioneer looked expectantly at Foskiss, who shook his head sharply. His face was pink with annoyance. This was the time, Anthony thought, to strike a decisive blow. "Eighty-five," he said. There was a murmur of interest in the room and the old man by Anthony's side sucked in his breath with shocked surprise. The man in the blue suit stuck his head a little further forward and said, "Ninety."

"Ninety-five," said Anthony. He was perfectly cool, he assured himself. It was true that he was far beyond the price his father had mentioned, but surely the fact that this other man was bidding showed that the book must be worth the money. Again the auctioneer settled his wig. He seemed quite bewildered by the turn of events. "Any adv——"

"A 'undred," said the little man. He took off his bowler hat to wipe his forehead, and revealed a bald red head.

"A hundred pounds," breathed the auctioneer. "Any advance on a hundred pounds?"

"Guineas," Anthony said. He had a curious feeling in his knees.

"Guineas," said the auctioneer. He was now again in control of himself and events. He gave a gray smile to the man in the blue suit and said, "Any advance?" The man jammed his hat back on his head, folded his arms and glared at Anthony.

The auctioneer tapped decorously with his hammer. "Sold at a hundred guineas to Mr. ——"

"Shelton, Anthony Shelton," Anthony announced to the world with an enormous smile. The man in the blue suit stumbled past Anthony with his head down, and went out of the sales room. There was a buzz of conversation. The old man leaned back and said, "You certainly paid through the nose——" Anthony waved him away. He felt like a book buyer of long standing, and the feeling was enjoyable. "You may think so," he said.

When he went to collect the book he was made aware that his experience as a book buyer was in fact small. It would be necessary, the auctioneer's clerk explained, to wait a couple of days for a check to be cleared. Unless, of course, he liked to pay cash.

"But I haven't got that much on me in cash."

The clerk shrugged. "Then I'm afraid you'll have

to wait, sir." He glanced at the clock. "The banks are still open."

Anthony considered. Now that he had bought the book he wanted to give it to Vicky immediately. "All right. I'll go to the bank and come back."

"Very good, sir. I'll see that they're all ready for you when you return."

"They?" Anthony said in surprise, and was embarrassed when the clerk pointed toward the pile of Henry James. "Oh yes," he said. "No. I mean—I don't want to take those. Just the other—the little book."

"Just the Rawlings," said the clerk with a look that indicated his low opinion of Anthony.

"Just the Rawlings."

Half an hour later he returned, collected the copy of *Passion and Repentance,* and gave instructions for the set of Henry James to be sent to his father.

While he ate lunch at the Criterion he thought about his purchase. The more he thought about it the more convinced he was that he had made a fool of himself. He put aside the copy of *Antic Hay* which he had been trying to read ("It is the very latest thing," Vicky had said. "It will be so good for you." But he detested it), and very carefully took out the little blue book and looked at it. "A hundred *guineas,*" he murmured. He opened the book and began to read:

When my lips touched your forehead they knew guilt.
But ah! Who does not relish guilt? Beneath
Your willing flesh my spirit laid a wreath
On hope of Heaven and—how gaily—built
Its nook in hell. So when we danced, "How sweet,"
I said, "that arabesque upon your dress."
Later I fingered each black curling tress
And knew your carcass—so much worthless meat.

Ah, bitter, fruitful, all too fruitful days!
Within the dark who knows what deeds are done
Except the Future brings all dark to light.

From youth I craved the poet's crown of bays
And still methinks that prize might have been won—
But now past sin crawls loathsomely to light.

"Too much for me, this stuff," Anthony muttered to himself. His attention wandered, and he looked at his watch. It would take three-quarters of an hour to drive out to Barnsfield in the Bentley. Vicky did not expect him until teatime, and teatime, in the Rawlings home, was five o'clock. Middlesex was playing Surrey at Lord's. He pondered these three facts slowly as he drank his coffee. Two lines of worry creased his forehead. Surely, he argued to himself, the purchase of *Passion and Repentance* represented culture and devotion enough for one day? But still he felt quite broken by the weight of the decision he was making, and the knowledge that Vicky would disapprove of it. Almost mournfully, he walked out of the Criterion, and directed the Bentley's bonnet toward Lord's. As he drew nearer to the St. John's Wood ground, however, his spirits brightened at the prospect of watching cricket. I mustn't be late to tea, he thought as he drove in. Whatever happens, I mustn't be late to tea.

IV

VICTORIA RAWLINGS' DIARY

At ten o'clock that Monday night Victoria Rawlings retired to her bedroom on the pretext of a raging headache. Her mother and brother were both inclined to resent this early departure: her mother because she wanted to enlist Vicky's aid in dealing with one of the crossword puzzles that had recently appeared in the more popular newspapers, and brother Edward because she robbed him of half the audience before which he could express his worries.

Edward Rawlings was a professional worrier; or

(to use a more modern term) he suffered from a deep anxiety neurosis. He worried about politics, about money, about his family and about his practice. He worried because the Liberal party, which he supported, did not use its Parliamentary position to defeat the Labour Government; he worried because the practice which he had inherited on his father's death showed a slight but persistent decline; he worried because his mother was an expense, and because his sister was unmarried; he worried lest his professional diagnoses should have been incorrect or his prescriptions wrongly written out. At the age of twenty-eight Edward's hair was thinning, doubtless from worry about his own health, and his bank balance was thinning too. Edward, Vicky reflected, grew more tiresome, and her mother more inconsequent, every day. How delightful it would be when she was married, and away from both of them.

When she thought of the word *marriage*, Vicky sat down at an elegant but slightly rickety writing desk in her small bedroom, that was ornamented by a rather odd collection of prints from the Medici Society, including two Holman Hunts and a luscious Tuke. Her mouth fell open and her expression became slightly vacant at the thought of marriage. She delved in the neck of her dress and fished up two small keys. With one of them she unlocked one drawer of the desk, and revealed a great red book with an imposing brass lock on it. The red book was the diary in which Vicky recorded, in a manner that seemed to her vivid and lifelike, the events and reflections of her days. It was not every day that she found material worthy of record, but tonight she was almost embarrassed because she had so much of importance to tell. She took up her fountain pen with its relief nib, turned to an open page—and paused. It was her custom to begin with some philosophical reflections before getting down to facts. What should it be tonight? Absently she scratched the tip of her nose with the nib of her pen, leaving a small violet mark on it, and then began to write in a remarkably round and unformed script:

Certain things, dear diary, have always been a mystery to me. I have never understood how so many girls, of such different kinds, could fall in love with Lord Byron. I know, of course, that he was supposed to be awfully fascinating in his manner, and very beautiful, and that would have appealed to me, though he was *fat*, I believe, which I could never have endured; but the thing is that he was *lame*. I know it's an awful thing to confess, but I've never been able to bear any kind of physical deformity. I just can't bear to look at a cripple or anyone who's lost an arm or leg, I'm almost sick at the smell of a hospital, and although I don't actually faint at the sight of blood I feel as if I could. Even the smells that sometimes come out of brother Edward's little dispensary make me feel that he must be very insensitive, or he couldn't endure to make such vile mixtures.

I've always thought that this feeling was just a part of what it means to have an artistic temperament. After all, it stands to reason if you're specially sensitive to beauty (as I am—though brother Edward is always so beastly and common about it) you'll be specially sensitive to ugliness too. I don't see anything to be ashamed of in that. And I've always said to everybody that what I love about Tony, for instance, is that he's so beautiful. Really, it makes me tremble to look at him, with those wonderful golden curls and great shoulders and perfect figure. And I've always felt that anyone I fell in love with *must* be physically beautiful. Today, though—but I must begin at the beginning.

Vicky, with her head on one side, looked at what she had written. She took great pleasure in reading the back pages of her diary, and often reflected that it was a great pity she couldn't just read it without being put to the trouble of writing. The relief nib moved over the paper.

I went to the Barnsfield Art School this afternoon to hear a lecture from Professor Lester. They say he is very advanced and I expected somebody young and dashing and altogether *revolutionary,* but he was really a dry old fellow, and kept talking about something called significant form, which I couldn't make head or tail of. I was at a loose end today because Tony had been awfully mysterious about his actions and said he wouldn't be free until teatime. I suspected that he meant to go to a horrid *cricket match*—though I did him an injustice.

But, anyway, I wasn't in a very good temper when I left the lecture, and I was really furious when I got home and found that Mother had invited Colonel Stone and his nephew to tea. Of course, Mother had asked Colonel Stone so that she could flirt with him—really it is *too* awful the way she makes eyes at this retired Anglo-Indian type (positively out of *Kipling*), who has no finer feelings of any kind. But what made me really cross was that Mother typically had told the maid nothing about there being two extra for tea, although she knows that both brother Edward and Anthony have appetites like horses. When I got home she was sitting on a sofa reading a slushy novel and eating chocolates. How she keeps her figure with all the chocolates she eats is a mystery to me. Mother saw that I was annoyed so she told me, with a kind of horrid leer to indicate that it was news which might be specially interesting to me, that the Colonel's nephew, who had come down to stay with him, was a writer. I received this information coldly.

I just had time to go up and change into a new dress (my green frock wth a pleated skirt and really *very* short, but there you are, they're getting shorter and shorter and what can you do?), and when I got down they'd arrived. The Colonel's always said to be a bit deaf, so I bellowed good afternoon to him and he got up—a bit stiff because of his corsets—and introduced his nephew, John Basingstoke. I saw as the nephew got up to shake hands that he was tall and lean and dark, and I thought from his expression in profile that he looked rather supercilious. Then he turned his head and I got an awful shock, because there was a thick white scar marking the right side of his face. It moved in a semicircle from his ear to a point just below his mouth.

And yet in spite of this terrible scar—just the kind of thing which generally I simply can't *endure*—there was something awfully attractive about him in a sort of gloomy Byronic way. And he had a beautiful voice (I'm very sensitive to voices), rich and deep and resonant.

Vicky put down her pen again and summoned that face to mind—unsmiling, slightly frightening, and yet somehow not repulsive.

I sat and talked to him about books and poetry and things until Anthony arrived, really *very* late.

She went over again in her mind those minutes before Anthony's arrival, and rediscovered her own embarrassment at the ghastly floater she had made. There was her mother telling Colonel Stone about the difficulty of running a doctor's household, tinkling a little brass bell for tea and murmuring something (on a warm day in May with the grate empty) about muffins under a silver cover, the kettle on the hob and toast made in front of the fire. There was the tea, not toast and muffins, but bread and butter and jam and little homemade cakes, coconut and plain. And there was she, saying with rather surprising timidity to this scarred young man, "Are you staying here long, Mr. Basingstoke?" and he replied,

"You must ask my uncle," and went on to explain, with a frankness almost as distressing as his scar, that he was completely broke. What a strange thing to say! The queen of the salon would have an answer to it, no doubt—but what? "I hear you write," she said, and regretted the remark as soon as it was made, especially when he responded with an unencouraging monosyllable. But having begun she must go on. "You'll think me awfully ignorant, but—what sort of things?"

He kept the good side of his face turned toward her and said gravely, "I have published a book of poems which sold exactly sixty-five copies, and I have in the press a novel which may sell a hundred and fifty."

She wrinkled her forehead. "But that's not very profitable."

"Precisely. Hence my visit to my uncle." He seemed to feel that he had been a little abrupt, and added, "I admire your grandfather's early poems."

The remark fell into a pause in the conversation, and was heard by Colonel Stone. "Poetry," he said suddenly. "Don't let this young feller start talking about poetry to you, Miss Rawlings. Talk till the cows come home, and you can't understand a word he says. Waste of time, poetry—don't you think so?" He turned abruptly to Mrs. Rawlings, but the question was beyond her. She poised the sugar tongs and said archly, "Two lumps, Colonel?"

"Thank you. When I was a young man, people used to write real poetry—stuff you could *sing*." Sitting with upright back the Colonel chanted:

"Duke's son, cook's son, son of a belted earl,
   Son of a Lambeth publican, we're all the same today.

Can't remember any of this modern stuff like that."

"Strong or weak, Colonel?"

The Colonel looked at the straw-covered mixture

in the cup and said with dismay, "That looks delightful, Mrs. Rawlings."

"I read a lot of poetry myself," Vicky said.

"Do you? Keats, Shelley and the *Rubáiyát*, with a little Rupert Brooke to bring you up to date?"

What an intolerable young man! And it happened that the *Rubáiyát* was on her bedroom bookshelf (it was so sad), and that she had shed some tears over Rupert Brooke's poems in the past. "I read the moderns."

"Oh yes. Who are they?"

She thought desperately, but every name escaped her. "Sludge," she said. "Arthur Sludge." It was the name of their butcher. "I've enjoyed his poems very much. He's probably too obscure for you ever to have heard of him."

"Not at all," he said. He turned his full face toward her, and she thought how ugly he looked. The corners of his mouth were twitching slightly. "I admire Sludge's work very much. Such a grand sweep, hasn't it? And such fervor. Such a gift of melody reminiscent of Swinburne, don't you think?" She turned scarlet and he stopped abruptly. "Do forgive me," he said. "I'm so sorry."

"Not at all." Her voice was choked, and she thought she was going to cry. She had never been so glad to see brother Edward as when he opened the door at that moment and said grumblingly that he supposed there was no tea left. . . .

She got up, poured a cup of tea and gave him a little cake which he ate in two mouthfuls. He took another, and brushed a crumb off his waistcoat. "I feel curiously hungry," he said. "I hope there's nothing wrong with me. I thought Shelton was coming to tea. Where is he?"

"How should I know?" Vicky snapped, and he looked at her in surprise. There was a cry of brakes outside, and feet pounded the steps. "There he is now," she said, and rushed outside, as much to hide her tears of humiliation as to greet him.

Her mind came back with a jerk to the diary, and she discovered that her mouth was open. All that was much too painful to put down. He had been perfectly horrid. But when Anthony arrived now . . . when Anthony arrived . . . She began to write again.

I always get a thrill just from seeing Anthony; he really looks so much like a god walking among men, so "magnificently unprepared for the long littleness of life," that it's exciting just to be with him. But today I was cross with him because he was so late for tea so I gave him a *peck* instead of a proper kiss, and I said something nasty about his great, clodhopping feet. I said he'd probably been to watch cricket and he looked guilty for a moment, but it must have been just a reaction, for then he said he'd brought me an engagement present. And he *had!* The nicest *possible* thing. A copy—a first edition!—of grandfather Martin's poems, *Passion and Repentance.* I looked at him and he looked back in that shy way he has, not knowing whether I'd be pleased or was still angry with him, and I couldn't say anything, but I threw myself into his arms and gave him another kiss, a *proper* one this time. Oh dear diary, he is sweet, and I do love him so. It was the loveliest little book, in a faded blue cover. Anthony said he'd bought it at a sale, and *that* was why he'd gone up to London.

I took him in to see them all—he'd not met Colonel Stone before, or his nephew. Mother fluttered about and poured a cup of tea, and brother Edward asked hopefully if his car had broken down. Then I couldn't resist saying that Tony had been late because he had been buying me an engagement present, and that it was a book. Brother Edward looked interested at the word *present,* but just grunted when he heard it was a book. Colonel Stone said that he thought jewelry would have been more appropriate. Then I told them it was a first edition of grandfather Martin's poems. I was specially pleased because nobody in the family has got a copy of this first edition except Uncle Jack perhaps, and I was glad to be able to say it in front of this young man Basingstoke, who had been so beastly and superior. They didn't seem much impressed by the news. Mother said grandfather Martin's poems weren't altogether nice, and brother Edward dislodged a piece of cake from a tooth and said grandfather Martin was an infernal old bore. So then I turned to the Colonel's nephew, who at least had had the grace to keep fairly quiet, and asked if he would like to see them and he smiled for the first time, really quite nicely, and said he would, very much.

I will say that he handled the little book gently, almost reverently—I don't think Tony liked it altogether, or him. And then, I don't quite know why, except that he'd been so horribly superior, I asked him if he would read one of the poems, and he looked at me hard and said yes he would. He read it beautifully. This was the poem:

Sometimes within our fleshy bouts I knew
An angel moved in you: and then my breath
Was shortened to quick gasps and I knew death
To be our dear-beloved, our sweet and true.
But other days I tuned my rampant lyre
To all the maddest music of your stringing.
Rich blasphemies and savage lusts went winging
Up on the Pegasus of my desire.
Dear lover, sweetest sweeting, lovely coz,
What if the joy we felt was transitory?
Are not our natures animal? and one
With dogs, who feel no Godhead and no loss?
Does not our goats' and monkeys' sense of fun
Reveal the farceurs of the human story?

There was a rather shocked silence, and then Mother said poetry always made her feel quite

faint, and Colonel Stone said he still preferred
Kipling to these moderns. I was just telling him
that grandfather Martin was less modern than
Kipling—he died in 1876—when there was a sudden
exclamation behind me. This young man Basingstoke was looking at my little book as though he
couldn't believe his eyes, and that terrible scar of
his was twitching away like anything. When I asked
him what was the matter, he said he thought the
book of poems was a forgery!!

There was a great hubbub. Tony was furious—I
think he wanted to fight Basingstoke—he doesn't
show to the best advantage, much though I love
him, when the situation is at all complex. Colonel
Stone kept saying, " 'Pon my soul, never heard of
such a thing." Mother was wailing that it couldn't
be true because everybody knew that grandfather
Martin wrote the poems, though she thought they
shouldn't be read aloud. I told her not to be silly,
because obviously that wasn't what the young man
meant, and Tony asked what the devil he *did* mean
then. I think Basingstoke was rather surprised that
everyone seemed so angry. He tried to back out of
it and said that he shouldn't have mentioned such a
thing, and we'd better let it drop. Then brother
Edward said, I must say rather sensibly, that he
couldn't just say the thing was a forgery and leave
it at that, and added typically that the market
value of the book must be quite high and if Tony
had paid through the nose for something that was
worth nothing he would want to know about it. So
Basingstoke looked at me (and I must say that with
the good side of his profile turned toward you he
looks *very* romantic) and asked if I wanted him to
explain. I said I did. And Tony, standing with his
legs apart on the hearthrug, glaring at Basingstoke,
said, "Let's hear what you've got to say," rather as
if the poor man were a prisoner at the bar.

It was really very simple—but awfully interesting
—and very quick of him to have noticed it. The

publisher's name on the page of the book that gives
its title was *Letts and Ableton, Beaulieu Street,
London*, and the year of publication was given
too—1860. Now, it seemed that this young man
Basingstoke is working on a history of publishing
in the nineteenth century, and to do that he's
investigating the history of various publishing
houses, changes in their policy, the time they began
and the time they ceased to publish books—if they
aren't in existence now—and so on. One of the
firms he'd investigated was Letts and Ableton—he
had notes on them which he'd left out in the hall
in his briefcase, and he showed them to us. They
were founded in 1830, and published various
books—novels, historical books and poetry mostly
but in 1857 Ableton died. Letts took in as partner a
man named Willcox, and from the beginning of
1858 all publications of the firm had on them the
name *Letts and Willcox*. At the same time the firm
moved from Beaulieu Street, which was the old
address of Letts and Ableton, to Dover Street. So
therefore, he said, any book that had on it the
name *Letts and Ableton* must be a forgery, in the
sense that it couldn't have been published by that
firm in 1860.

When he'd finished he looked round rather triumphantly. We all sat trying to work it out for a
minute or two, and then there was a storm of
objections. Mother suggested that somebody at the
publisher's had made a mistake, and put in the
wrong name or the wrong date. Brother Edward
said obviously it must be some error of that kind,
and we could clear it up very simply by asking the
publishers, and Basingstoke began to get rather
annoyed. (When he gets annoyed the good side of
his face looks very handsome.) He told us that
Letts and Willcox went out of business in 1871, and
no records of the business were available. And as
for a mistake, he said mistakes of that kind just
didn't occur. Then he hesitated, and went on: "I'm

rather sorry I raised this whole question, but now that I have, let me make the position clear. There's a presumption that these poems weren't published by Letts and Willcox, or Letts and Ableton, but were published by somebody else who just stuck the name of that firm on the book. That, if it's true, would mean that the book must really have been printed after 1871, because nobody would have dared to use a publisher's name in that way while the firm still existed. And *that* in turn, if it's true, would mean that this book isn't a first edition, but, from a bibliographical point of view, a comparatively worthless forgery."

"If this is so obvious," said brother Edward, "why hasn't it been found out before?"

Then Basingstoke got more annoyed. "It's not obvious," he said. "I simply happen to have some specialized knowledge, that's all."

Anthony had been almost bursting for a few minutes. Now he burst. He wanted to know if Basingstoke meant to say the thing was worth nothing and he'd been swindled out of a hundred guineas? He was looking splendidly wrathful, and then he suddenly realized he'd told me what he paid for the book and went as red as a turkey, and stammered incoherently. Poor, sweet Tony!

We all went on talking and arguing until I was sick of it. Tony was upset because he'd told me how much he paid for the book, and I think he would have liked to fight Basingstoke. And *he* didn't look Byronic any more, but just puzzled and rather worried, and I didn't mind him so much, even if he had been superior, and when he came over and muttered an apology to me and said that he was afraid he'd made himself awfully offensive, I told him he was forgiven. After all, he had a *great deal of charm*, and really I sometimes quite forgot about that terrible scar. Brother Edward got annoyed too, and kept saying it was a waste of good money. Colonel Stone said he disliked poetry, anyway, except Kipling, and Mother said it all made her feel rather ill. Finally Basingstoke seemed to gather himself together, and made another long speech. "I know I've been awfully tactless," he said apologetically. "Please don't think I'm trying to make matters worse if I make another suggestion. My publisher" (and then he turned to me and said, with another smile, "oh yes, I have a real publisher, Miss Rawlings") "is a man named Stuart Henderson. He may be able to help us, because he's a particular friend of a critic named Blackburn, who wrote an essay on your grandfather. Won't you both come up to London with me and see him tomorrow morning?"

Brother Edward, of course, said he certainly wouldn't, couldn't spare time for that sort of gadding about, and then Basingstoke turned to me—I believe he'd really planned it with *me* in mind all the time—and I began to feel it was all rather exciting. First of all, of course, I'd felt *madly* miserable, on my own account and on Tony's, but now the idea of going up to see a publisher and engaging in what I suppose is a kind of *quest* did seem rather exciting. And I suppose if the thing *is* a forgery it ought to be exposed. And he asked so very nicely. So I said *yes*, and then I turned to Tony, who was glowering away by the fireplace, and he said he wished he'd bought me a necklace or a brooch or something. I told him (which is perfectly true) that it was the loveliest present, anyway, but it would be exciting to see the publisher man. After all, suppose we're on the track of something really *important,* international book forgers or something like that. If there are such things, which I suppose there aren't.

Vicky viewed the last sentence with some disapproval, and then looked at her watch. It was nearly twelve o'clock. She had been writing and thinking for almost two hours and her hand felt quite stiff. She carefully blotted the last page of the diary, locked it, replaced it in the drawer and locked the drawer. Then she undressed, put on a nightdress, rolled into bed and within five minutes was fast asleep. Her almost beautiful face, with lips slightly parted, stared at the wall. Men with scars and Greek gods, both brandishing forged marriage certificates, chased each other through her dreams.

TUESDAY

I

ANTHONY TAPPED THE TOP of his egg nervously. "I say, father." Mr. Shelton lowered *The Times* a little, and arched his brows. "You know that little book by old Martin Rawlings?"

"*Passion and Repentance*? Yes."

"Is there any likelihood that it—that first edition— you know, the one we were talking about yesterday—is a forgery?"

Mr. Shelton lowered altogether his defense of *The Times* and stared at his son in surprise. "I should think it most unlikely. What on earth put such an idea into your mind? Did you buy it?"

"Well—yes." Anthony was rather reluctant. "It cost more than you said. A hundred guineas."

"That was too much." Mr. Shelton's lips were a thin line in his nut-brown face. "I should like you to bear in mind, Anthony, that it is almost always foolish to pay more than a current market price. What makes you think it may be a forgery?"

Anthony shuffled. "It's not my idea at all. There was a chap who'd been asked to tea at Vicky's—perfectly poisonous bounder he was too, took a dislike to him at once—and *he* said . . ." He recounted Basingstoke's story. "What do you think?" Anthony asked at the end of his tale. He began to open the morning's mail.

"I'm a little out of my depth in this talk about publisher's names. What I do know is that this little book has a market price. The market price has been reached only after experts have sifted all the evidence for and against its authenticity. That seems to me to make it very unlikely that—what's the matter?"

Anthony had choked over his tea, and his blue eyes were bulging slightly. He pushed a letter he had just opened over to his father. It was from Lewis & Sons, Booksellers, of Peaceful Alley, Blackheath, and said that they were given to understand that he had purchased a first edition of *Passion and Repentance* at Messrs. Lintot's sale yesterday. They were empowered to offer him the sum of £150 for this book, and they looked forward to hearing from him. They were, etcetera.

Anthony walked up and down the breakfast room, crowing with delight. "This'll show that blighter Basingstoke. Not genuine, eh. It's genuine enough for somebody else to want to pay a hundred and fifty pounds for it."

"Ye-es." His father's nut-brown face was cut into lines of concentration. "Frankly, my boy, I don't understand this."

"It's easily enough understood. Would they offer all that if it weren't genuine?"

"Would they offer that much if it *were* genuine? Think of it, Anthony. Copies of this little book usually fetch sixty or seventy or at the most eighty pounds. You pay twenty or thirty pounds more than you should have done for it. Now this bookseller, acting on behalf of somebody else, offers you twice what's it's worth. Why?"

"Some old geezer wants it badly, I suppose."

"Are you going to let him have it?"

"Good Lord, no." Anthony stared. "I've given it to Vicky. I only want to prove it's genuine to show up that chap Basingstoke. We're going to see a chap about it this morning. Man named Henderson."

"The publisher, yes," Mr. Shelton mused, tapping a finger on the table. "Be careful what you do and say, Anthony," he advised. "There's something odd about all this."

"I say," Anthony shouted from the hall. "Forgot to

tell you. I bought you a present too. Works of Henry James. They'll probably arrive today."

The door banged. Mr. Shelton repeated, "Something very odd about all this." He poured himself another cup of tea.

II

"Something odd?" said Stuart Henderson. "Why no, I don't think so." The publisher wore a beautifully cut gray suit, his features were round, smooth and slightly greasy, and he wriggled sinuously as he talked. His voice was at once gentle and petulant. "I think, John, you've been letting your imagination *run away* with you. That's always a trouble with you *creative* people."

"But what about the change in the publisher's name? How do you explain that?"

"I don't *explain* it," said Henderson with a wriggle. "But I do say that there may be many explanations without resorting to the—ah—rather startlingly improbable one of forgery."

"Such as?"

"Somebody may have made a mistake. Even in the best publishing houses." Henderson put up a white hand and coyly patted greasy blond hair, "such things *do* happen—let it only be whispered." He put one hand on his lips with exaggerated caution. "Or there may have been intimate personal reasons why Martin Rawlings made a special arrangement with these publishers. As you know, these poems were thought rather *daring* in their day—so daring that Martin had this little edition printed, and distributed it purely among his friends. The poems weren't offered on sale to the public until 1868—eight years later. And speaking of that"—he tapped his nose with one finger—"here is a possible, even a probable, explanation. Martin Rawlings goes to Letts and says, 'Will you print these poems for me?' Letts looks at them, shakes his head, and says that he can't take the risk. Martin finally persuades him to print them for private publication only, and as an additional safeguard Letts puts on his old address. How does that seem?" He beamed round at them.

"Rotten," Basingstoke said. "It wouldn't be any safeguard at all in case of prosecution unless he put on a completely false name; and no reputable publisher would do that."

"No, that's true." The publisher seemed downcast for a moment. Then he beamed again. "I see you're determined to have it your way, my dear John. But I feel sure you're wrong. You can depend on it that some comparatively *trivial* thing of that kind is the explanation. The idea of a forgery—my dear John, my dear Miss Rawlings, my dear Mr. Shelton—a forgery that deceived such experts as Michael Blackburn and James Cobb—that's a *very* romantic idea."

"What about that offer I received this morning?" Anthony asked. He felt somehow oddly disappointed now that the book was proving to be perfectly authentic, as he had known would be the case.

The publisher shrugged his shoulder. "Collectors are notoriously eccentric. If I were you, I should accept the offer." They all sat silently, and then he wriggled. "I see that you are not quite happy, John?"

"I shan't be happy until somebody gives me a satisfactory explanation of that change in the publisher's name," Basingstoke said flatly. "Will you, Miss Rawlings?"

Vicky's mouth was slightly open. She closed it firmly as she said, "No."

Stuart Henderson held up a white hand. "A thought," he said. "A thought." He picked up the telephone on his desk. "Ask Miss Cleverly to come in, please. She works on our production side," he explained, "and knows a great deal about the technical processes of book production. But she's also interested in bibliography and all that. Frankly, she *terrifies* me."

"You wanted me?" Miss Cleverly was a small girl

with a gnomelike face. Her mouth was a smear of red, she had a mass of dark, untidy hair, and her hands were dirty. "I hope it's important. I'm very busy."

Henderson pushed over to her the disputed copy of *Passion and Repentance.* "Tell us out of your *extensive* knowledge, my dear Miss Cleverly, is there *any* likelihood of this being a forgery?"

Miss Cleverly barely looked at the little book, but in her glance Basingstoke thought he saw a momentary flicker of some special interest. "Why ask me when there's a real expert available?"

"A real expert," Henderson said tentatively. "You mean—ah—James Cobb?"

"Good God, no." She made a gesture which seemed to indicate that if there had been a spittoon available she would have used it. "Cobb's in his dotage. Never sees anybody or does anything nowadays."

"Ah—Michael Blackburn?"

"A dilettante," said the small girl scornfully. "I mean Jebb."

"Jebb?" Henderson repeated, trying to animate the blankness of his smooth features.

"Jebb applies science to literature. He has some tests for the genuineness of manuscripts which are quite new, and he's applied them particularly to nineteenth-century books and pamphlets."

"Has he?" said Anthony with genuine enthusiasm. "I say, that's the stuff."

Miss Cleverly rounded on him almost fiercely. "But don't expect Jebb to welcome you. He suspects everybody."

"What of?"

"Trying to steal his ideas. Pinching them so that they can anticipate his discoveries. He's right too, as often as not. He's working hard to get a book out now and when it appears—my word—the balloon's going to go up."

"What balloon?"

"Lots of balloons," Miss Cleverly said mysteriously.

"It just depends on the mood he's in, whether he'll talk to you." She looked at them critically. "He wouldn't say anything to you," she said to Basingstoke. "Too literary. He'd think you were trying to pinch his ideas." She swung round on Vicky. "Nor to you, I think—he'd think you were a sort of beautiful spy." Her gaze rested on Anthony, who shifted uncomfortably. "I don't think he'd have any suspicions of anybody as big and blond and athletic as you are."

"Well, I don't know——" Vicky said faintly.

"Good Lord, I couldn't possible tackle a chap like that alone," Anthony said, alarmed but delighted. He added, with a ponderous attempt at guile, "Couldn't you be persuaded yourself, Miss—ah—Cleverly—to come along and lend a helping hand?"

She laughed. "All right. Jebb and I are old friends, and I haven't seen him for a week. He lives in Madderly Gardens, just off Russell Square. We'll look in on him." She settled herself on the edge of Henderson's desk and pointed a finger at Basingstoke. "I know you. Enjoyed your poems. What's the idea of this amateur scouting party?"

"Amateur scouting party," Anthony said, and chuckled. He looked at Miss Cleverly with admiration.

Basingstoke explained, and Miss Cleverly's gnome-like features showed surprise. "You must be off your heads," she said, and turned particularly to Anthony. "*You*, anyway. If you prove this is a modern forgery, you've lost a hundred pounds."

"Guineas," said Anthony automatically. He ran a hand through his curls. "I suppose that's true."

"But you still want to see Jebb?"

Anthony hesitated. He felt somehow, for no particular reason, that he was making an important decision. "Yes."

Stuart Henderson rose and extended a plump white hand. "Good luck on your exciting *chase*. This dynamic little lady knows the most interesting people.

But one thing *does* occur to me." He wriggled tentatively toward Vicky. "I should have said something about it before, but I didn't want to be embarrassing. If you really want to delve, I think there may be secrets hidden in old Martin's *naughty* past."

"What kind of secrets?" Vicky asked, but the publisher shied away nervously.

"Nobody really knows *much* about those years Martin Rawlings spent in Italy. Perhaps there's nothing to be known. I don't want to be a *scandal*monger, but if the scientific Mr. Jebb should fail you, it might be a good thing to go and see Michael Blackburn. He's written the only biographical sketch of your grandfather, and I could probably arrange it for you." He seemed to look particularly at Anthony, who shifted uneasily.

"I was going to ask you about that," Basingstoke said. He added hesitantly, "But perhaps——"

"Mr. Jebb sounds too wonderful," Vicky exclaimed, and clasped her hands together.

"Seems to have some jolly interesting ideas," Anthony observed.

"Jebb's a literary scientist, if that's what you want," Miss Cleverly said. "Of course, if you want somebody arty——"

Henderson flashed his plump hands despairingly. "Obviously it's Mr. Jebb. I shall leave you to present your fascinating problem to this little *tigress*. But if you *do* want to see Michael Blackburn, come back and let me know." He giggled and patted Miss Cleverly on the shoulder. "He may be a dilettante—but he does know a lot about Martin Rawlings."

"He's a fool," said Miss Cleverly as soon as they were outside Henderson's office. "Got time for a cup of coffee?"

She shepherded them to a café round the corner. Cups of grayish liquid were placed in front of them. "Now look here. You may be on the track of something bigger than you think. Do you want to follow it up?"

"International forgers?" Vicky asked. Her voice went up a note in excitement.

Miss Cleverly wavered. "Tell you more when we've seen Jebb. Something more than one pamphlet, anyway."

"Then let's go round and see him right away," Anthony said enthusiastically.

"I say." Vicky's voice had risen almost to a squeak. "There are a lot of old family papers in a trunk in our attic. Do you think it would be worth looking through them? Suppose we found a reference to some dealings Martin had with these publishers—or some letters or something—or a book—there's a *tremendous* lot of stuff there. It would be grand if we found something."

"Grand. Grand," said Miss Cleverly impatiently. She gulped her coffee so fast that she spilled some on her chin. "Division of labor, then. You two go off and search in an old attic, and we'll pay a call on Arthur Jebb. Then we meet and pool information."

Anthony scowled at Basingstoke. "Is that all right, Vicky? or would you like me to come with you?"

She smiled at him sweetly. "Of *course* it's all right, darling. Hasn't Miss Cleverly said that nobody except you would be able to exercise the requisite charm on the mysterious Mr. Jebb? You just go ahead and have a wonderful time"—she patted his sleeve—"and we'll poke about among old manuscripts."

Anthony's brow became corrugated. He was at sea with even the most portentous irony. "Well then," he said uncertainly, "let's meet this evening for dinner at my house. Will you be free, Miss—ah—Cleverly?" She nodded. "And you?" he said curtly to Basingstoke.

"Free as air." Basingstoke sat with his face half turned away from them, so that the two women could not see his scar. "I say—what are you going to do about that book-seller's offer?"

"Refuse it," said Anthony shortly.

"Then wouldn't it be a good thing to do so at once? Sort of force the hand of whoever made the offer—so that we could see what they do next." Reluctant though Anthony was to accept any suggestion made by Basingstoke, it was agreed that this would be sensible. Anthony went away to telephone them, and came back looking puzzled. "They didn't seem very much concerned. Didn't offer another fiver or anything, I mean. I suppose it's all right." He looked rather dubiously at the little blue book which lay in his large hand.

"Of course it's all right. Come on now; we've got no time to waste. And bring that book—we shall need to show it to Jebb."

III

"What does he do for a living, this chap Jebb?" Anthony asked as the Bentley drew up outside 18 Madderly Gardens.

"Publisher's reader," said Miss Cleverly. "And a bit of hack work here and there. Pity—he's got a first-class scholastic brain, but no money." She dashed quickly up the steps and rang one of several bells. Anthony saw that it said *A. Jebb—Grnd. Flr.* They waited, and the door shot open to reveal a large woman, who glared at them. Miss Cleverly glared back. " 'Oo are you?" the woman asked.

"I'm Miss Cleverly. Who are you?"

"I'm Mr. Jebb's char, Mrs. Upton. If it's about a bill, 'e's out."

"Of course it's not about a bill. And I know perfectly well he's in. Kindly tell him we're here. This is my friend Mr. Shelton."

"Orl right," said Mrs. Upton doubtfully. "But you'll 'ave to stay outside until——" A door along the passage opened, and a high voice said, "What is this interminable altercation?" There was a creak and Anthony saw, to his astonishment, a figure in a wheel chair. "Ruth," said the figure, "my dear Ruth, how are you? Mrs. Upton, what can you be thinking of to keep my friend Ruth on the doorstep?"

"I don't let *anyone* in to see you unless I knows 'em, sir," said Mrs. Upton. It was plain that she regarded the figure in the chair with proprietorial affection.

"Come in, Ruth, come in. But who is that I see behind you? You know how I feel about receiving strangers."

"Yes, Arthur, but I thought——" Ruth Cleverly made a gesture which was oddly ineffectual, in contrast to her usual efficiency. "This is Mr. Shelton, and he's—— Oh dear, I suppose I should have telephoned."

Anthony's face was very red. "I don't need to come in if Mr. Jebb objects," he said stiffly. The figure in the wheel chair stared at him, and then smiled suddenly and charmingly. "Do come, Mr. Shelton, and pray forgive my churlishness, if you can. My good friend, Mrs. Upton, acts as a dragon in preserving me from unwelcome visitors, and I fear I have forgotten my manners in greeting welcome ones." He wheeled his chair dexterously down the passage, and into a door on the left.

The room was a pleasant one, with a large window looking out on to the square. Books crowded the room—there were even more books, Anthony thought, than in his father's library at Barnsfield, and these books unlike his father's had an air of continual use. Some of them, indeed, were scattered about the floor, and the wheel chair moved carefully to avoid them. There was a small, neat desk, and some shabby but comfortable armchairs. Jebb himself was a man about forty years old. His eyes were bright and darting behind an enormous pair of horn-rimmed spectacles perched rather low on a large, hooked nose. His face was the color of wax, with two spots of rouge on the cheekbones. A rug covered his body below the waist.

"We've come——" Miss Cleverly said, but he held up a hand.

"Let me first of all offer you some refreshment." He wheeled his chair over to a cupboard underneath some bookshelves, and drew from it a Cona coffee percolator, coffee, and some biscuits. He put the coffee machine on a table, lighted the burner beneath it, and got out from the cupboard cups and saucers. Anthony watched these proceedings with increasing discomfort. "Can we—ah—do something to help——" he began, and then felt the warning pressure of Ruth Cleverly's arm. Mr. Jebb looked round from the cupboard with a bright smile and said in his piping voice, "No, thank you. I am very well able to manage." He wheeled his chair round suddenly, and looked at Anthony. "You will hardly be able to imagine, Mr. Shelton, in the pride of your youth and beauty, what it means to lack the use of your legs. That misfortune has been mine from birth. I will not trouble you with the abominable details. I am able to move about a little with the aid of crutches, but this chair is much more convenient. But the greatest trouble I am called on to bear, Mr. Shelton, and the one I can face with the least patience, is—sympathy." His hands moved like butterflies among the teacups. "Ruth knows this—and she is very good to me. But you, Mr. Shelton, how should you know it or understand it? How can you understand the intense envy of normality that makes me take pleasure in my very ordinary ability to make coffee unaided? I can only hope that you will bear with me in charity—and pray, while I am engaged in making coffee, tell me what I can do for you."

Haltingly at first, but with a fluency that grew under the cripple's intense and watchful gaze, Anthony told the story of the book sale, his purchase, Basingstoke's suspicions of the little book, the offer he had received that morning and his refusal of it. Jebb scribbled idly with his pencil on a blotting pad during the recital. "Miss Cleverly says that Lewis is probably acting on behalf of some wealthy client who wants this book to complete a collection."

Jebb nodded. In his high, thin voice he said, "There could be other reasons. May I see the pamphlet, Mr. Shelton?" Anthony handed it to him and the cripple held it between his thin hands, like something very delicate and precious. He examined it, paying particular attention to the title page, and looking closely at several pages of the interior. He switched on a lamp at his desk, produced a magnifying glass and examined the paper of the booklet with minute attention. Then, with an exclamation which certainly denoted excitement, but might have indicated also either pleasure or dismay, he wheeled his chair rapidly over to a bookcase, took down several books, and compared them with the copy of *Passion and Repentance*. He continued absorbed in this occupation for at least five minutes, until Anthony began to fidget. He felt a touch on his arm and saw Miss Cleverly, her monkeyish face puckered in a grin, mouthing at him the words, "Keep calm." Suddenly she said, "Arthur, your coffee is going to boil."

He looked up. "Eh? So it is. Thank you, Ruth, my dear." He briskly wheeled his chair over, took away the burner, made the coffee and gave it to them. Anthony could stand it no longer. "What do you say, Mr. Jebb? Is it a forgery?"

The cripple laughed. "You go too fast." He paused, and looked at Ruth Cleverly over his great spectacles. "What does this young man know of my researches, Ruth?"

"Nothing, except that they're epoch-making."

"Then I will make an exception, since this is an exceptional case, and tell him something about them. Bear with me, Mr. Shelton, if I seem a little long-winded. I shall reach the point of your purchase before very long. And I should like you to bear in mind that what you are hearing now is confidential." Anthony nodded, mesmerized by the earnest eyes behind the horn rims, by the eager, gesticulating hands. "Many people know me as a publisher's reader and literary journalist. Very few know me as a detective of a very special kind, a detective investigating—literary forgeries." Anthony stirred at the word, which Jebb almost whispered. "The kind of forgeries I mean are very special ones, for they involve first editions. Just how much do you know about first editions, Mr. Shelton?"

Anthony shook his head vaguely. The questioner hardly seemed to expect a reply.

"A first edition is a book which is valuable because it is just what its name calls it—the *first* of its kind. A first edition of a book by Dickens may be worth—let us say—a hundred pounds. The second edition, published in the following year, may be worth only five."

"But why?" Anthony asked, genuinely puzzled.

Jebb chuckled. "That is a question I cannot answer. Such enthusiasm, such evaluation, is rooted in human intelligence or stupidity. All I can tell you is that the valuation of first editions in a modern sense began sometime in the eighteen seventies, when people started to collect the romantic poets. It was fostered by booksellers—because, of course, it was profitable to them—and by the 'nineties it was in full swing.

"Now it sometimes happens that a previously unknown first edition turns up. When this happens, the newly discovered first edition immediately becomes valuable, and the book that had formerly been regarded as the first edition declines in value correspondingly. Very much that kind of thing happened with this little book, *Passion and Repentance.*" Again the cripple's hand reached out and lovingly patted the little blue book. "For a long time the edition of 1868 was regarded as the first. Then, lo and behold, this little edition, published in 1860, turns up and becomes the first. The 1868 edition is now worth very little, and this 1860 edition, because only a few copies are known to exist, is very valuable. Does that suggest anything to you?"

With a look of concentration on his regular features Anthony said, "Must be stupid, I suppose, but I can't say it does."

Jebb's spectacles slipped further down his nose, and

he pushed them back impatiently. "When I tell you that there were many, many cases like this one—of unknown first editions appearing suddenly—can you see then?" Anthony shook his head helplessly. "Can't you see what a wonderful opening there was for—somebody—to *create* first editions, and make themselves a fortune? It's beautifully simple. You take a pamphlet by Ruskin, or a story by George Eliot, or a poem by Matthew Arnold. You have a number of copies printed, quite privately, being careful to make no foolish mistakes. And then—the crucial point—you transform them into valuable first editions by putting a date on them which is a few years before the date of the known first edition. If the pamphlets and poems were published with the correct date on them, they would be pirate editions which were evading the copyright law, but not first editions. They would be worth nothing. By adding an incorrect date, somebody made them exceedingly valuable first editions."

Anthony was rapt. "You say 'somebody.' You mean—a master forger?"

Jebb's smile held a touch of complacency. "A master forger."

"And he's operating now?"

The cripple shook his head. "No. He hasn't operated for twenty-five to thirty years."

"But he's still alive?" Jebb nodded. "And you know who he is?"

"I think so."

Miss Cleverly said sharply, "You shouldn't say that, Arthur. You can't have any proof."

Still with that irritating smile, Jebb said, "I haven't named anybody—yet."

Anthony was listening with a kind of bursting impatience. "But what about this?" He touched the little blue book.

"I cannot say for certain—yet. I strongly suspect it of being a forgery. I should like you to leave it with me so that it can be subjected to scientific tests."

"But how can any scientific tests tell you when a book was produced?"

The upper part of the cripple's body rocked backward and forward in the wheel chair. The rug that covered his legs remained unmoved. "You are asking me my most intimate secrets," he said in his high-pitched voice. Anthony became aware that it was hot in the room. "But I shall reveal them to you, Mr. Shelton, because I like you. Ruth here knows something about them already. The application of these tests to various so-called first editions will be the subject of my forthcoming work of research—and it is upon this epoch-making work, Mr. Shelton, that I have been engaged for the past five years." He leaned forward in the wheel chair, and it occurred to Anthony to wonder, as he caught the wild stare behind those enormous glasses, if the little man was altogether sane. Perhaps something of his thought communicated itself to Jebb, for he dropped back in the chair and said, with a note of bitterness replacing the elation in his voice, "It will seem to you, perhaps, who are filled with the energy and the joy of youth, that this is a curious occupation for a grown man." Anthony, slightly dazed, did not speak. Jebb put his fingertips together and looked up at the ceiling as he went on talking. He had, Anthony saw, extraordinarily hairy nostrils.

"There are several lines of approach that can be used for testing the validity of books and pamphlets published in the nineteenth century.

"First of all, you can compare the texts. Let us suppose that Martin Rawlings made some alterations to the poems in *Passion and Repentance* when the second edition appeared, and that the forger foolishly followed the later text. Then you would get the forgery showing a different text from that of the real first edition. That, of course, would be gross carelessness on the forger's part, but it has been known. In this case it does not arise, because Martin Rawlings made no alterations in the text of his poems.

"Then there is the evidence to be obtained from the publisher or the printer. Actually, in the forgeries I have in mind a publisher's name was rarely used. The forger generally said 'Privately Printed for the Author,' or something of that sort. And all of the forgeries I have found were produced a long time ago—when Victorian first editions were becoming valuable—and few printers or publishers have records going back so far. The publisher's name doesn't help in your case, because the firm no longer exists, and it's going to be very difficult to trace the printer."

Miss Cleverly interrupted. "I suppose Basingstoke is right about the discrepancy in the publisher's name? Can you check on that?"

"Perfectly right," Jebb piped. "I have just checked. He is an observant young man."

"And was the name of Letts and Ableton—or Letts and Willcox—used in any of the other forgeries you've traced?"

"No." Jebb jerked his head down and looked at them. "But that proves nothing." he said almost fiercely. "It is one of those pieces of carelessness that I've just mentioned. Yes, he must be an observant young man, your friend Mr. Basingstoke."

Anthony grunted. He was equally annoyed to be called Basingstoke's friend, and to hear him praised for acuteness.

"There is another test—that of typography, and that is more fruitful in your case. In the nineteenth century there was a 'ring' of eight large firms of type founders who had the trade to themselves. By thorough investigation of their practice, I have been able to establish certain interesting facts. The most important concerns the queer case of the kernless f."

"The what?" Anthony asked.

Miss Cleverly's face was puckered with amusement. "Remember that you're not lecturing to an audience of typographers, Arthur. Do you need to go into all these technical details?"

"I suppose not," Jebb said reluctantly. "Well—to

put it simply, Mr. Shelton, different type faces (what we call 'old style') were used in the nineteenth century from the faces (which could be called 'modern style') used today. There are particular differences in some letters, and one of them is the *f. The letter f in your copy of* Passion and Repentance *is printed in a form which did not exist in 1860, and which in fact was not used until the eighteen eighties.* In other words," said Jebb, who had again reached a crescendo of excitement, "this book on the table, sir, is a forgery."

Anthony passed his hand across his forehead. It was slightly damp. "But a few minutes ago you said it was only a matter of suspicion."

"True, true." The cripple looked remorseful. "Excitement is carrying me away. I should have told you that I am convinced, Mr. Shelton, of all the things I am telling you. I have yet to convince other book collectors. If you went to see any bookseller, or so-called book expert, and told him what I am telling you, he would think it a garbled story, because the evidence to support it is here." He tapped his large forehead. "Until my book is published, your copy of *Passion and Repentance* will be accepted as genuine." His fingers touched the little book again, with something like a caress. "I am most grateful to you for permitting me to examine this book. I have been interested in it for a long time, but very few copies are extant and I have not been able to obtain one for testing. My inquiries have been fruitless, both to so-called experts and to the family. James Cobb and Blackburn both wrote me rude letters, and Martin's son was courteous but unhelpful." He pondered again. "There is one curious point about your book. All of the forgeries I have discovered—which are still circulating as genuine first editions—were the works of one printer, using one particular fount of type. *Passion and Repentance* is set in a different type. It is still a modern type, and still in my opinion a forgery, but it is a curious circumstance."

There was silence. Anthony sat looking round the quiet, hot room in a kind of daze. Miss Cleverly watched him with quizzical amusement. Jebb took up his magnifying glass and pored over *Passion and Repentance*. He spoke again.

There is also, of course, the test of paper. Before 1861 the raw material used for the manufacture of paper was rags. In that year esparto grass was introduced from Spain and Northern Africa, and used successfully, and in 1874 paper containing chemical wood was used. Paper tests are difficult to apply—differences are sometimes minute—and it is because they are complicated that I should like to borrow this copy of your book. Since it is dated 1860, it should, as you realize, be a rag paper. There will be a further strong presumption of forgery if it should prove to contain esparto grass or chemical wood."

Anthony seemed not to be attending. "What do you advise me to do?" he asked, and the cripple was taken aback.

"Do?"

"If what you say is right, I'm a hundred guineas out of my pocket. My father will be furious."

Jebb's high-pitched laugh was not soothing. "I am very sorry to hear that. But you are not quite correct in your statement. Say rather that you will be a hundred guineas out of pocket in two or three years' time, when my book is published. In the meantime you have a marketable commodity. You can always accept Lewis' offer."

"But that would be dishonest." Anthony was indignant. He said with a blush, "Look here, Mr. Jebb, all these things you've told me—this stuff about type faces and so on—I don't mean to be rude, but it's all a bit vague. That chap Henderson seemed to think——"

"Henderson," said Ruth Cleverly, "is not an expert on first editions."

"That's what you tell me—but he seemed awfully confident—and how am I to know what's right? I want to *know* about this thing. Isn't there anything I can do myself to find out?"

Ruth Cleverly raised her expressive eyebrows. "What about taking Henderson's advice, and· seeing Blackburn?"

Anthony looked at her with an almost doglike eagerness. "But you said he was a—dilettante."

"So he is, but he's an authority on Martin Rawlings too. He may be able to tell us something useful—eh, Arthur?"

The cripple's fingers played with the little blue book, and put it down. "Possibly, possibly. You see, Mr. Shelton, there is also the evidence of the author himself, of contemporary references he made to his own work—that kind of thing. Let us say that there is a letter in existence from Martin Rawlings, dated 1860, making reference to this first edition which I believe was produced much later—well, that would be very disconcerting. Disconcerting for me, I mean," he added with the ghost of a smile. "In most of the other cases in which I suspect forgeries I have checked author's references, presentation copies, that kind of thing—and there are remarkably few cases in which they exist. I've done no checking with *Passion and Repentance* because I haven't been able to get hold of a copy. It can do no harm for you to see Blackburn, though he wrote me an impolite letter in response to my own inquiries. But I must ask you," he sat forward again in his chair, and his eyes glared with monomaniacal intensity behind the great spectacles, "I must *insist* that you say nothing of what I have told you in confidence about my researches."

"That is understood." Anthony was stiff. "But if we are going to see Mr. Blackburn, I shall need to take this to show him." Rather nervously, he picked up the little blue book on the desk.

Jebb glared at him. "Do you mean you are not prepared to trust me with——"

Miss Cleverly laid a hand on the cripple's arm. "Arthur, this young man is a babe in the literary wood. He doesn't know where he's going. You can't blame him if he looks out for wicked uncles."

"I suppose not," Jebb said. He sank back in the chair with a curious air of being deflated. His fingers moved nervously on the desk. The spots on his cheeks were bright. He spoke faintly. "Ruth, the little brown bottle in the medicine chest on the right of the cupboard. Ten drops in a glassful of water. Down the passage." Ruth Cleverly took the bottle from the cupboard, ran to the door and came back in a few moments with a glass of water. She measured out ten drops of the liquid and touched Jebb on the arm. He was sitting back in the chair, breathing heavily. His eyes were closed, and the edges of his mouth were bluish. Mrs. Upton stood in the doorway, and commented on the scene like a Greek chorus.

" 'E's been talking too much. Works himself up like when 'e talks about 'is books." She looked round with an air of distaste. "Never did like books. Doctor warned 'im to avoid excitement—got a dicky 'eart."

Faintly but clearly, Jebb said, "That will do, Mrs. Upton," and she shrugged and withdrew. They sat and watched while his face changed to its apparently normal waxen color, and his breathing became easier. When he spoke again it was in his usual reedy voice. "She's an infernal nuisance, Mrs. U., but she's quite right. It's heart. I must avoid excitement. It would be a tragedy, wouldn't it, if I died before my book was in print." He spoke perfectly seriously.

"If there's nothing we can get you, Arthur," Miss Cleverly said, "I think we should go. But I don't want to leave you alone. Does Mrs. Upton stay with you all day?"

"She cooks my meals. Don't worry about me. These bouts are not unusual."

"Oh." Miss Cleverly hovered. It was the first time Anthony had seen her uneasy, and he was surprised by the tenderness in her voice. "Good-by then, Arthur. We'll let you know what news we get from Blackburn."

"Good-by, Mr. Jebb. And thank you for all your help." Anthony held out his right hand. The left gripped firmly the copy of *Passion and Repentance*.

Jebb's eyes were still closed, and his hands did not move from the arms of his chair. They left him in the quiet room, with the Cona machine standing on the table by his side, like an instrument of medieval torture.

IV

Stuart Henderson crossed one gray-trousered leg over the other, and looked at his two guests with amused condescension. "And what had the highly scientific Jebb to say?"

"He thinks it's a forgery," said Anthony heavily.

"Does he really? After that, Miss Cleverly here will no doubt tell us, we can do nothing but bow our heads. Does he give any reasons for his remarkable conclusion?"

Anthony was silent. How could you talk about conclusions unless you gave the train of reasoning? And he had promised not to do that. Miss Cleverly had returned to her usual brusqueness. "He said something about the type faces being wrong period."

"Rather a *slender* basis for such a *vast* conclusion, isn't it? Is this Jebb, by the way, the same man who writes chit-chat for the *Peoples' Literary Weekly*? And does odds and ends of reading for publishers? He is?" Mr. Henderson dabbed his damp lips with a handkerchief. "My *dear* Miss Cleverly, as you know, I have the utmost respect for your *terrifying* perspicacity, but I should hardly have thought the view of such a man should be preferred to that of somebody like Michael Blackburn."

Ruth Cleverly rubbed her nose with a dirty hand. "All right then. Let's see Blackburn. You said you could arrange it."

Henderson trilled musically with head thrown back, and then smiled coyly and confidentially at

Anthony. "Excuse me, Mr. Shelton. I'm sure Miss Cleverly regards me as a terrible dilettante myself, so I can't help feeling, a *teeny* bit pleased that the cold hand of science has referred this question back to the—more *elegant* touch, shall we say—of the dilettante. But just let me see if I can arrange this little matter for you." He picked up the telephone and asked for a number. "Would you be free for tea today?" Anthony nodded. The publisher left him almost dumb. "*Hullo,*" said Mr. Henderson, and his rather podgy features seemed almost to melt, and his voice became extremely girlish. "Michael? Guess who. This is Porky Henderson. Yes, *Porky.* How *are* you, you old sinner? I so much enjoyed that piece of yours in the *Spectator* the other day—it was one of the most beautiful things you've ever done. Oh yes, it was. Listen, Michael. A young friend of mine here has a problem which I think will fascinate you about that old scoundrel Martin Rawlings. Oh, a literary problem, of course. Yes, he's fascinating, too." He smiled archly at Anthony, who had gone very red. "I wondered if I might bring him along to talk about it. Today? Oh, Michael, are you sure? That *is* sweet of you. And may I bring a dragon as well? A female dragon, I mean—if there *is* a female of dragon. She works in my Production Department, and has the most *terrifying* technical knowledge." The sound at the other end of the line was not enthusiastic, but it was apparently not wholly condemnatory. "About half-past four then. So nice of you. Bye-bye, Michael." Mr. Henderson spoke these last three sentences on a dying fall, so that his "bye-bye" was hardly audible. "Half-past four in Hampstead," he said to them. "You'll love Michael. Will you pick us up from here at about four o'clock? I can't help regarding this, Miss Cleverly," Stuart Henderson said with a wriggle, "as a triumph of Art over Science."

Anthony breathed a sigh of relief when they were outside Henderson's door. "I say, are you free for lunch?"

"Yes," said Miss Cleverly without hesitation. "Five minutes."

He noted with admiration that she rejoined him in four minutes, and after one look at her more womanly, and almost demure, appearance, decided to take her to Scott's. He presented a grim profile to her at the wheel of the Bentley. "How on earth do you put up with him?"

"Henderson? He's really not bad to work for." She added slyly, "You bring out the worst in him, you know."

Anthony was startled. "Do I? Why?"

She said maliciously, "Because he thinks you look like Shelley or Rupert Brooke. Know what Rupert Brooke looked like? A young Apollo, golden haired, dreaming on the verge of strife. That's the kind of thing Henderson thinks of when he sees you."

"Good Lord, does he?" Anthony was genuinely alarmed. "And what about this chap Blackburn? Will he be the same?"

"Don't know him, but I shouldn't think so. Don't be deceived by my calling him names. He's really a well-known figure, written three or four books of essays and gossip about books and authors. You know the kind of thing—how Henry James patted him on the head when he was five and said, 'I hope, my dear young friend, that you will always retain your present fine awareness of simple, and in fact incommunicable, emotion which it is the endeavor of a lucky few, quite simply, to communicate.'" Anthony listened, completely bewildered. "Sorry," she said. "You *don't* know the kind of thing. Lucky you. You're A. W. Shelton, aren't you? Played in the university match last year?"

"Good Lord, yes. I say, how on earth did you know?" Anthony was astonished. "I say, don't tell me you're interested in cricket."

"Certainly I am."

"I say, that's absolutely splendid." In his enthusiasm Anthony took hold of her arm as they went through the doors. "We should have won that match," he said as they sat down at table. "But old Parker set such a damned silly field for their tail-enders that half the catches didn't go to hand." He stopped. "I say, I must be boring you. It's so good to have someone to talk shop with, you know."

She raised her thick eyebrows. "You're not playing this year?"

"No. Vicky—she's the girl I'm engaged to, Vicky Rawlings, you know—doesn't like cricket, so I've given it up. Waste of time for a grown man, she thinks. I expect she's right."

"I didn't know you were engaged to her," Ruth Cleverly said. She added, apparently after some thought, "I saw one day of the match last year. Thought you bowled awfully well."

"Oh, did you." He was delighted. "But I practiced a bit in the winter, and I think I've developed in some ways."

"Have you now?" said Miss Cleverly.

"When I had the new ball I used to make it go away for slip catches, and occasionally bring one back from the off. Now, I've been experimenting with a ball swinging the other way—toward the leg side. Supposing you had a ring of fieldsmen on the leg side—but I say, this is awfully complicated for you."

"Do go on," she said, and Anthony went on, through soup and lobster Newburg. When they reached dessert he looked at his watch. "I say."

"Yes," said Miss Cleverly, leaning forward a little.

His face was radiant. "We've just got time to get down to Lord's and watch some cricket for an hour or two, if you'd like to."

She sat back. The expression on her monkeyish features was enigmatic. "I believe you think I don't do any work. I've got to get back to the office and see a printer. Sweet of you to ask me."

"Work? Oh yes," Anthony said disconsolately. "Then we shall have to think about this thing again." He tapped the briefcase containing *Passion and Repentance.* "I say, I have enjoyed this lunch, Miss——"

"You'd better call me Ruth." She smiled, and showed white, even teeth. "All my friends do—like poor Arthur Jebb."

"I'm awfully sorry I upset him. I didn't mean to, you know—about leaving this thing with him. But hang it, I did pay a hundred guineas for the thing, and I gave it to Vicky too, so it's hers really." Anthony wrinkled his fine, straight nose. "But I didn't mean to upset him. I'm sure he meant to be helpful and all that, but I didn't much like him."

"Arthur? You should feel sorry for him. He has no power in his legs—they're no larger than a child's."

Anthony stared at the tablecloth. "It seemed to me he was awfully anxious to get hold of *this.*" He tapped the briefcase again.

She stared at him. "Of course—so that he could make the paper test."

"I suppose so. But he seems a bit obsessed by it all, doesn't he? Got a bit of a kink, I suppose. Those ideas about a master forger—things like that don't happen, do they?" His face brightened. "It would be fun, though, if Vicky turned up a lot of things about forgery in her old attic."

Her face was quite blank. "I must go back to work. Thank you for a nice lunch."

"I say—I say." Like a great protesting puppy, Anthony rose from his seat in alarm. "I haven't upset you too, have I, with what I said about old Jebb?"

With the same frozen face she said, "Not at all. Just that you've got a suspicious mind. You can't help it."

Anthony bumbled across the room after her as she rushed along, throwing remarks over her shoulder. "I suppose you thought I'd take you along to somebody who'd steal your damned book. Jebb's a research worker—you wouldn't understand that. To the pure all things are impure." At last he caught her up, and she turned to him a face no longer frozen, but suffused with color.

"Look here, I'm most terribly sorry. I don't know what I'm saying. It's just that I'm out of my depth in all these theories about type faces and publishers' names. And even experts don't seem to agree. And he is a bit odd, you must admit, your friend Jebb. Please forgive me."

She gave him a sad monkey smile. "I forgive you. Poor Anthony. You'd be more at home with a ring of fieldsmen on the leg side."

He threw back his head in a great roar of laughter. What a grand girl she is, he thought as they walked out of Scott's. And, he noticed as she walked in front of him, she had very nice legs.

Anthony did not, after all, spend the afternoon at Lord's. He telephoned Barnsfield, learned that his father would be out to dinner, and said that he was bringing home three guests. Then, moved by an impulse he could not have explained, he went to several booksellers in and round about Piccadilly, and asked for a first edition of *Passion and Repentance.* His inquiries achieved no results, except to assure him of the rarity of the little book that he carried in his briefcase. He looked forward with apprehension to meeting Michael Blackburn—suppose he should turn out to be another Henderson?

But Michael Blackburn was not in the least like Stuart Henderson. Something over fifty years old, and more than six feet in height, he presented to Anthony an upright figure and a fine head with a halo of gray hair, a strong nose and mouth and a weak chin. He treated Henderson with an amused but not unfriendly condescension which, Anthony felt, was too kind to the antics of that little man; he spoke to Anthony as to one on terms of warm equality, and to Ruth Cleverly with a slightly exaggerated deference which she seemed not altogether to relish.

Blackburn lived with his mother in a small house

on the edge of Hampstead Heath. She was a splendid old lady with white hair who poured weak tea into delicate china cups, gave them thin bread and butter, and made small talk about the iniquities of the government, and the recent visit to England of the King and Queen of Italy. They drank their tea on a tiny but perfectly kept lawn at the back of the house; and, whether because of the unaccustomed mental strain to which he had been subjected during that day, or because of the warmth of the May afternoon, Anthony found himself lulled into a kind of waking daydream in which the tinkling cups and the smooth, gentle, cultured voices formed an undisturbing pattern. A kind of film formed over his mind, and behind the film it seemed to him that he was about to discover the secret of his questionable first edition, a secret that had something to do with Miss Cleverly, and with the thin hands of Jebb and the scarred face of Basingstoke. The secret was just about to be revealed when the film over his mind broke at the sound of his own name. Blackburn, leaning forward, was suggesting that they should go inside the house, and his mother, rising from the table, said with a benevolent smile, "Now that I have dispensed my duties as hostess, Michael, I shall return to *The Dolly Dialogues.*"

Blackburn laughed as he led the way into the house. He addressed Henderson, but his hand was placed, like a feather, on Anthony's arm. "Can you believe, my dear Stuart, that my mother has never read a work of fiction published after 1900? I assure you that is the case. Upon her fine nineteenth-century taste the lists of present-day publishers beat in vain. How horrified you must feel, Stuart, and you too, Miss Cleverly, ruthless modernists that you are, by this confrontation with one to whom H. G. Wells is an outrageously new author."

"Old novels are so much more interesting, I find," said Mrs. Blackburn. "But I can't expect you to agree with me, my dear," she said to Miss Cleverly.

"I have read some books published before 1900," Ruth said rather acidly, and Henderson rushed in to cover a moment of awkwardness.

"But I think that's perfectly *splendid*, Mrs. Blackburn. I only wish I had time myself to go back more to the classics and read less of the trash that's written and—whisper it only—*published* nowadays. Dickens, Trollope, George Meredith," he sang, as though he were intoning a psalm. "Ah, we can't match them now."

"I'm sure you are right," Mrs. Blackburn said placidly. "But personally I prefer Anthony Hope and F. Marion Crawford." She left them a little disconcerted.

Another book-lined room, Anthony thought gloomily as they settled down in what he supposed was Blackburn's study; but the tasteful and ordered luxury here contrasted very pleasantly with Jebb's untidy workroom. Here the curtains were of heavy red velvet, and gilt frames on the walls enclosed pictures of a rich brownish shade. They were offered cigarettes from an oddly carved mother-of-pearl box which Blackburn mentioned casually that he had picked up for a few shillings in Florence. It was all very pleasant, and very restful. The only unrestful sound in the room was Henderson's voice.

". . . so I told your young friend that he was on a wild-goose chase, but he was so *anxious* to consult you, Michael, because he had heard that you were *the* authority on Martin Rawlings——"

"And how does Miss Cleverly come into this?"

Miss Cleverly spoke truculently, "I took Mr. Shelton to see a friend of mine named Arthur Jebb. He believes that this so-called first edition is a forgery."

"Jebb?" Blackburn said, and raised his eyebrows.

"Somebody of *no* importance—a literary journalist, Michael." Henderson giggled and straightened his tie. "But now we have come to the fountainhead."

"Are you an expert on nineteenth-century literature, Miss Cleverly?"

"Not at all. Don't claim to be. I know something about production, made a special study of the nineteenth century, that's all." It seemed to Anthony that Blackburn and Ruth were like two cautious fencers.

"That is most interesting." The light shone on Blackburn's halo of gray hair. "I myself can lay claim only to amateur status." He waved away Henderson's protest. "I am not being modest. I am merely expressing my incapacity for the kind of pertinacious scholarship that is becoming fashionable nowadays. I am also a little doubtful of its use. You place a piece of paper under a magnifying glass, you subject a book to a test like a piece of litmus paper, and then you pronounce, like Jove, your verdict. Those are your Mr. Jebb's methods, are they not? Forgive me if I cannot believe that the literary critic needs to wear the deerstalker of Sherlock Holmes. No doubt I am growing old." He paused. "And I am certainly digressing unforgivably."

Henderson broke in like the tide rushing up the shore. "Miss Cleverly here said Jebb thought the type face too *modern*."

Ruth said vaguely, "Not quite right for 1860."

The copy of *Passion and Repentance* was a blue spot on the oak table in the middle of the room. Blackburn picked it up and looked at it, and said with the gentlest scorn, "*Not quite right for 1860.* How I envy Mr. Jebb his ability to make such a claim with such confidence."

Anthony was following it all with a puzzled stare. "He seemed very certain—"

"I'm sure he did," Blackburn responded with a sigh. "It is a pleasure to see a man so full of certainty in this normally dubious world. It happens that Mr. Jebb is known to me and that we maintained for some little time a correspondence about other Victorian first editions, in which he has shown the same enviable certainty that they are forgeries. I have not been able to agree with his conclusions. I think he ignores the healthy wood in his frantic search for individual dead trees. I regard him, in fact, as a crank." Miss Cleverly moved slightly, and Blackburn said even more gently, "But, as I say, I speak as an amateur. In that capacity, Mr. Shelton, I am not competent to answer abstruse queries about the particular year in which a type face was introduced. I am a literary critic, and not a compositor. The point about the publisher's name is a curious one, but I do not feel that it is incapable——"

Again Henderson rushed in. "I'm surprised you didn't notice that yourself, Michael, for you know you really *are* being modest. I mean you *do* know an awful lot about Martin Rawlings' work, don't you."

With a condescension that was becoming slightly strained, Blackburn said, "You are too kind, Stuart. But it happens that a copy of this charming first edition is not in my possession."

"But you *had* one, hadn't you—because you showed it to me once."

There was a pause. Blackburn's hands were clasped together tightly. Knotted and lined, they were the hands of an old man. When he spoke, his voice was as gentle as ever. "I had a copy, true. I sold it about a year ago, when a bookseller made what seemed a rather extravagantly good offer for it."

"What bookseller?" Miss Cleverly asked bluntly, and Blackburn frowned slightly although his voice, when he spoke, was unchanged.

"I believe they are a long-established firm. Their name is Lewis & Sons, and they are situated at Blackheath."

"Good *Lord!*" Anthony said, emerging suddenly from a kind of waking sleep. He showed Blackburn the letter he had received that morning. "Isn't that odd?"

"Not, perhaps, as odd as you think. It is very possible that Lewis' act for two or three collectors of Martin Rawlings' work. I assume from the presence of this little book that you have decided not to sell."

"I've refused this offer. But I don't see that I could

accept it, anyway, until I know if this is genuine, and worth that much money."

Blackburn smiled charmingly. "Such scruples do you credit. But you need have no doubts on that score. If Mr. Jebb had been less concerned with proving a case, he might have found time for some commonplace, and not excessively fatiguing, investigations into literary history, which would have shown him that he was on a wrong track." He went to the shelves and took down a book. "This is *Sesame Without Lilies*, a small collection of my own essays, published in 1905. Perhaps I may read you a page or two from one of them. It is called 'A Turbulent Boy,' and is a brief biography of Martin Rawlings. I shall not need to weary you with more than a page or two."

"Such a *perfect* piece of prose," Stuart Henderson panted. "Won't you read it *all*?"

Blackburn waved him away, and began to read from the essay in his gentle, uninflected voice.

A few years ago the first edition of *Passion and Repentance* came to light, and book lovers and bibliographers learned with surprise that these love poems, which were first offered to the public in 1868, had in fact been written, and privately published, nearly ten years earlier. The full circumstances attending their composition and private publication have not yet, I think, been told; but it seems that there can now be no possible indiscretion in telling a tale which must already be known to many of the poet's friends.

I have said something of young Martin Rawlings' wild life and of the reasons, alcoholic, financial and literary, that led him to renounce his native country in 1856, when he was twenty-one years old. Almost penniless, and with a grudge both against his family and against the society that showed no sign of appreciating his rather Keatsian Odes, he left England, as he thought, never to return.

Italy was a natural home for this young man, who found in himself a strong temperamental kinship for the hot sunlight, the aching blue skies, the sharp division into sun and shade, that may be found in the life, as well as in the climate of southern Italy. This was the country of Michelangelo and Cellini, of Dante and Petrarch; it was also a country where life was lived with a joyousness that seemed to him unknown in colder climes. He had ceased to correspond with his family in England, and there is no record that he troubled to keep in touch with his few English friends; but the wild, erratic young man who was convinced of his own poetic genius found a welcome in the English literary circles of Rome and Florence. Few regarded seriously his claim to literary talent, but all were impressed by his strange and wayward beauty.

Although he mixed with these circles, however, he was not of them. He would vanish for months at a time to reside in some tiny fishing village, where he lived the life of a peasant, fishing and swimming, and writing lyrics, sonnets and odes, most of which were destroyed almost as soon as written. Little is known of this period in his life; and this little would be even less but for the observations he made to a great friend a year or two before his tragic early death. It is to this friend that we owe the story of the astonishment with which those same literary circles greeted the young poetic buccaneer when he returned from one of these expeditions accompanied by a young and beautiful Italian wife, who was unable to speak a word of English, and by their child, Cæsar. He brought with him in his pocket also a draft of the book that was to bring him fame.

Martin took up again the life of riotous and indiscriminate enjoyment that had marked his bachelor days; and, not doubtful of his achievement but moved by a feeling of pride and resentment toward the literary society that had accepted him but slighted his work, he kept these poems still in his pocket. One day the literary critic, Garth Mansell, who had always been friendly toward him, exclaimed laughingly that young Martin's muse was uncommonly silent. The poet then showed him the manuscript, now much worked over and revised. Mansell read it, and was convinced immediately that these were pieces of exceptional power; but he saw also that such fiery descriptions of physical passion, touched though they were with a repentance which at this time was purely verbal—for Martin's conversion to Catholicism did not take place until 1865—would be likely to cause a storm of protest on moral grounds, when they were published.

Martin was elated by Mansell's good opinion, but, with a prudence that foreshadowed the caution of his later years, was unwilling to run the risk of prosecution. It was agreed finally that a very few copies of the poems should be printed, privately, and that these should be circulated among a chosen few. Accordingly, a small octavo volume was produced in 1860; but there is no record that those who read it thought it other than a chaos of disordered images and violent sentiments. The author had to wait another eight years for open publication, and fame.

Blackburn closed the book. Henderson wriggled in his chair and said triumphantly, "There you *are*. I'm ashamed to say I'd *forgotten* that passage, Michael."

"Jolly clear," Anthony said. He did not know whether he understood it all or not, but these were the words that seemed expected of him. "Jolly clear."

The sunlight shone on Blackburn's strong face and halo of gray hair. "I am so glad if I have helped to solve your problem, for I feel that I am already in your debt."

"Debt?" Anthony asked dazedly. His mind failed to make any connection. Was Blackburn making an offer for the book, or something like that?

"You have given me so much pleasure on the cricket field that I feel it a poor recompense to offer a little amateur literary knowledge in exchange."

"The *cricket* field." Stuart Henderson charged in again. "But how exciting. You must look simply *wonderful* among all those stumps and pads and things."

Anthony scowled at the publisher. He felt dislike of him growing with every sentence he spoke. Perhaps Blackburn sensed this, and it was for this reason that he turned to Miss Cleverly and said, "And is our severest critic satisfied?"

"Can't say I am." Her small jaw was thrust forward aggressively. Henderson held up his hands in comic despair. "That's not evidence. It's just something told you by someone else."

Blackburn was playing with an ivory paper knife. "Surely the same observation might be made about every statement made by every biographer—except those unfortunate enough to be directly known to their subjects, who can be accused of plain untruths."

The girl's voice was thin. "Your story is based on what Martin Rawlings told 'a great friend.' Who was the friend?"

There was another pause, and this time it was obvious even to Anthony that it was a painful one. Blackburn tapped the paper knife on his palm. He seemed to be considering what the girl had said. "You are a confirmed materialist, Miss Cleverly, are you not? But still, I see no reason why I should withhold the name of my informant. The story came to me through James Melton Cobb."

Cobb? Where, Anthony wondered, had he heard the name? From Henderson's little pant of astonishment it was obviously an important one. Ruth Cleverly sat still in her chair.

"If you wish to pursue your investigations still further—though I really can't understand why Shelton here should be so eager to prove that he owns a forgery—I must leave you to do so through James Cobb. I am sure that he will acquit me of any deception—or should I say, with a cautious legality that you will appreciate, any *intentional* deception. Further than that——" He did not shrug his shoulders, but he gave the impression that only good manners caused him to refrain from adding some scathing observation.

Henderson was on his feet. "But Michael, Anthony and I are altogether convinced—aren't we? *Of course* we are. It's been so good of you, Michael, to——" He backed sinuously to the door, and the others followed him.

"Very good of you," Anthony said. He did not really know at all what had been going on.

"And of Mrs. Blackburn to make tea for us," Ruth added.

"I dare not disengage her from *The Dolly Dialogues*, or I would ask her to come down." Blackburn's hand rested again, lightly, on Anthony's tweed jacket. "Do remember, my dear fellow, if you are playing at Lord's this season, that I shall be watching you enviously."

Anthony mumbled incoherently. There seemed no need, after all, to say that he was not likely to be seen at Lord's that season.

From the back of the car Henderson kept up a stream of reproaches against Miss Cleverly for her rudeness to Michael Blackburn. "He asked me if I was satisfied, didn't he?" she said at last.

"Yes, but really——"

"At least we know who to approach next," she said thoughtfully. "But Cobb may be difficult."

Henderson squeaked. "*Cobb*? You can't mean to say you want to get in touch with Cobb?"

"That's your pigeon," she said to Anthony, and he moved his broad shoulders uneasily.

"I've said I'm satisfied." For some unknown reason, however, he felt extremely dissatisfied.

There was silence until they reached Camden Town. Then Henderson said, "You can put me down here. Thank you very much. Don't let this girl's wild theories lead you away, Anthony." Anthony shook his head, resenting the use of his Christian name. "And do come and have lunch one day when you're in London. Remember—I shall be watching, too, when you're playing at Lord's."

Anthony drove on, and there was another silence. Miss Cleverly's small nose was wrinkled with distaste. "Isn't he a beastly man?"

"Appalling. Don't know how you can bear to work for him."

"Not Porky Henderson. He's just foolish. I meant that man Blackburn. There's a snake in the grass for you. No doubt about that."

"He seemed to me quite charming. I must say I thought you were rather rude to him."

They approached Regent's Park. Her monkey face was slightly puckered. "Look," she said, "you'd like to call off this dinner party, wouldn't you? I mean, there's no point in it now you're convinced that little book's genuine, is there? Call it off, then—that will be all right as far as I'm concerned." As she spoke these last words her voice suddenly rose to a wail. Anthony was alarmed.

"Miss Cleverly—Ruth——" Her face was covered by an enormous white handkerchief, into which she was sniffing. He was painfully conscious of the appearance they must present. "Please," he said in agitation, "don't cry here in the street." She wailed again.

"You've been so awful—agreeing with that snake— about everything. I hate you." Her wail was changing to a roar. Reluctantly he drew the Bentley to the curb, and patted her shoulder. He gently drew down the handkerchief from her face, and saw the marks of tears. "Why," he said with an unhappy jocosity, "I didn't know you were the sort of girl who cried."

"Well, you know now. Take me home, please."

He put in the clutch obediently, and then said, "I don't know where you live."

"Red Lion Square, Holborn." She remained huddled in the opposite corner from him, a small and sniffing figure, for the rest of the journey. Anthony's mind was a maelstrom of emotions, in which a confused tenderness seemed to be uppermost. When they pulled up outside a dingy block of flats he said, "I say look here old girl—Ruth—I'm terribly sorry. Please come to dinner. It won't be the same without you." She sniffed, and to his dismay Anthony heard himself stammering as he said, "Do c-come—p-please."

The sniffing ceased. She looked at him alertly. "You must give me fifteen minutes to change, and I can't ask you up because it's a one-room flat, and it's in an awful mess."

Anthony beamed. "I say, that's wonderful. Look here, old girl, if you aren't down in fifteen minutes, I shall come up and fetch you."

He did not have to go up.

Was it her change of clothes, he wondered, when she came back (she was wearing a simple black evening dress with a cameo brooch), or her added touch of color, that made her seem so different, that made her talk so vivaciously?

She told him her uneventful history. She was the third of four daughters of a country solicitor who had married, surprisingly, a chorus girl. The marriage had not been altogether successful, because her father had been given to drink, and his practice had always been a struggling one. He had been disappointed that his wife had not borne him a son, but his daughters after all had not been a burden on him. "Nobody ever called us the beautiful Miss Cleverlys," she said with some complacency, "but we've not done badly." Margaret, the eldest daughter, had been old enough to be a V.A.D. in the war, and had married a colonel whom she nursed back to health. "Romantic," Ruth said briefly. Ellen, the second daughter, had married a rich boot manufacturer in Northampton, and two months ago Claire, the youngest, who was only just twenty-one, had married the son of a neighboring squire. "He has expectations," she said. "Dad's very pleased. I'm the black sheep."

"You're not married?"

She flashed her ringless left hand. "You're an unobservant ox, Anthony Shelton."

"Nor engaged?" She shook her head. "I'm engaged," Anthony said with a slight sigh.

"I suppose you're rich?" she said, and he was rather taken aback. "Don't ask me why I think so," she went on hurriedly. "Anyone who can afford to buy books for a hundred guineas is rich to me. I live on my income and a pound a week which Dad allows me. Not that he always sends it."

"I suppose I *am* well-off." He pondered deeply. "Do you know, I don't know what my father does, except that it's something in the· city. Something to do with stocks, I mean." He pondered again. "I must ask him. Does money mean a lot to you?"

"Not really. I'm sick of living in one room, that's all. I long for a little luxury—just one or two mink coats, and a necklace dripping with diamonds. Like all poor girls, I'm vulgar at heart."

"It's funny," he mused, "Vicky doesn't care about money." She made no reply, and he said, "Who's this chap Cobb? I've heard something about him, but I couldn't quite place it."

"Don't you remember Henderson mentioned him as an authority? He's an old, old man."

"What's he an authority on?"

"Bibliography—that means pretty well everything connected with books except the writing of them. Friendly with Swinburne, Browning, Tennyson. Used to correspond with them about their first editions, all that kind of thing."

"Is he more important than Blackburn?"

"You can't quite put it like that. Blackburn has a reputation as an essayist—pretty inflated one, if you ask me. He happens to know a lot about Martin Rawlings because he wrote an essay on him. But he isn't an authority on first editions. Cobb is. If he tells us Martin Rawlings told *him* that he had that booklet printed in 1860——"

She paused. Anthony grunted a query.

"I suppose we should have to accept it. Though it still wouldn't explain about the publisher's name being wrong."

Looking straight ahead, Anthony said, "Let's go and see him tomorrow."

She laughed. "Easier said than done. He's incredibly old, supposed to have been at death's door for years. And he lives in complete isolation. Won't be interviewed by the press or anybody else. Besides, I thought you were convinced about the book. Hullo, what's this?"

A man was standing in the middle of the road, waving his hands. Anthony came to a stop. The man was youngish, and a dark mustache made a thin line across his upper lip. His eyes flickered quickly over Anthony, Ruth and the Bentley. He said in a Cockney voice, "Could yer lend a hand, chum? Sorry to bother yer, but we've just ditched our car up a lane."

"Right-oh," Anthony said. He got out of the car. The lane was a few yards up the road. By the side of a large car three men were lounging. They straightened up when Anthony and the man with the dark mustache turned the corner. The face of one man seemed vaguely familiar to Anthony. The car was a gray tourer, and it was not in the ditch. Anthony turned to the man by his side and said, "I don't——" Then he saw the raised black jack in the man's hand and threw himself to one side so that the blow landed on his shoulder and not on his head. Even so it forced him to his knees. He caught the man's leg, jerked him to the ground, and put a fist in his stomach. The other men were running up. A voice—and again it had a familiar sound—said "I'll take 'im." Anthony moved up and away, but he was too late. A vivid flash of lightning seemed to split his skull, and then there was blankness.

When he regained consciousness an electric hammer seemed to be at work in his skull. He was lying on the grass by the side of the road, and Ruth was shaking his shoulders gently. "Do you feel all right?" she asked. "You've got a great lump on the back of your head."

Anthony stood up and the electric hammer began to work faster. "I think I can walk to the car," he said faintly.

"There isn't a car. They've taken it. But that's not what they were after. They've got the book. Now perhaps you'll believe me when I say there's something fishy about—oh, you poor darling." Anthony, overborne by this news, and by the electric hammer, had sunk down again onto the grass, and was holding his head in his hands. He was conscious that he did not present a positive heroic figure.

"Just sit there. I'll stop a car," she said, and within five minutes she had done so. She seemed to have told the driver, a facetious commercial traveler, a tale about a lover's quarrel, for he kept casting glances at them in the back and roaring with laughter. When they had been driving for half a mile Ruth suddenly said, "Stop." There, driven just off the road, was the Bentley. "There's our car."

The commercial traveler looked bewildered. "But you didn't say you had a car."

"Didn't I? Well, we have. I hope it's in working order." She got in, sat in the driving seat and let out the clutch. The Bentley moved. "Splendid. Come along, Anthony." Slowly and painfully, Anthony made his way over to the Bentley. "We just left our car here," Ruth said airily.

"You did?" The commercial traveler looked at her with his mouth open. "But then why did he—I mean why did you ask for a lift?"

"You wouldn't ask a sick man to walk all that way, would you?" Ruth asked indignantly, and he was abashed. "But thanks very much, anyway," she said as she moved past him in the Bentley.

"How far are we from Barnsfield?" she asked. "You'll have to guide me."

"About ten miles. Right turn at crossroads."

"Do you want to call in and see a doctor?"

The electric hammer, which had quieted down, started up again fiercely as Anthony thought of his head being probed by Edward Rawlings' unsympathetic hands. "No."

"Right. We'll talk when we get to your place." Anthony grunted.

Sitting in an easy chair from which her feet hardly touched the ground, Ruth told her story while Anthony reclined on a sofa with a wet towel round his head. The man with the dark mustache had come back to the car with another man. He had shown her a blackjack, and the other man had shown her a revolver. They had told her to get out of the car, and she had done so. The dark man had seen the briefcase, looked inside it, and said, "Let's go." They had got in the Bentley and driven it away. She had run round the corner into the side lane, and there found Anthony.

"There can't be any doubt about it. They were after the book."

Anthony raised his hand to his aching head. "Why should they want it if it's a forgery?"

She shook her head. "There's something funny about it all. You don't knock people out to steal a book worth a hundred guineas." She continued with excitement, "And how did they know you had the book? They must have been trailing you. Did you recognize them?"

"I thought I knew one of them, but I'm not sure. My head aches," he said peevishly, and looked at his watch. "It's a quarter-past seven. Where on earth can Vicky and that awful chap have got to?"

"He's worth two of you, Anthony Shelton." Anthony made a movement of the towel, intended to signify dissent. "He couldn't have made a much worse show at stopping those toughs."

"At least I was knocked on the head. I didn't just get out of the car because a man pointed a gun at me. Probably an unloaded gun. He wouldn't have dared to use it in a place like that."

"Next time I'll watch you take the gun away from him by jiujitsu," she said placidly. "In the meantime, what are you going to do? Sit holding your head in your hands?"

The telephone bell rang. Anthony crossed the room and took off the receiver. "Anthony?" It was Vicky's voice. The line was faint, and she sounded breathless. "We've had such an afternoon, darling. So exciting."

"Where are you? I thought you were coming to dinner."

"We're at Peaceful Alley."

"Peaceful Alley?" Anthony repeated, and remembered. "Oh, that bookseller. What on earth are you doing there?"

"Detective work. I haven't enjoyed myself so much for ages. John's been wonderful."

"*Who?*"

She sounded surprised. "You know, John Basingstoke."

"Now, look here, Vicky——"

"You sound awfully peevish. I'm sorry we're late, but we're coming back straightaway. In Edward's car."

"I've been hit on the head."

"What?"

"By thieves," he said in a martyred voice. "They stole your present."

"I can't hear you. This line's awfully bad. I thought you said you'd been hit on the head. Just a minute." There were clicking noises. Anthony suddenly felt furiously angry. "Look," he bellowed into the telephone, "I *did* say I'd been hit on the head." He heard Ruth Cleverly laugh behind him.

Vicky's voice was cold. "Can I help it if you've had an accident? There's no need to shout."

"It wasn't an accident. It——"

"John's found out something much more impor-

tant than that. He's found out that the first edition
was forged, along with lots and lots of others, and
he's found out the name of the forger."

A desire to throw the telephone across the room
warred with an insistent curiosity in Anthony's mind,
and curiosity won. "Who?"

"John says he's extremely well known—in literary
circles, of course." Vicky's tone was one of unctuous
superiority.

"What's his name," Anthony yelled, and was quite
surprised when he received a clear and cool reply:

"It's a man named Cobb."

V

When Vicky and Basingstoke left their companion
investigators they returned to Barnsfield by train.
There were no other passengers in the carriage, and
on the way down Basingstoke told Vicky the story of
his life, as Ruth Cleverly had told hers to Anthony,
but at much greater length. They sat facing each
other, and he looked out of the window occasionally,
when he thought she was staring at his scar.

His father, he told her, had been an Irishman and
a professional boxer, a huge man with enormous
physical strength; his mother a pretty variety singer
with the brain of a mouse, who had run away from
her respectable middle-class home to go on the stage.
The family severed relations with her, with the single
exception of her brother, Gilbert Stone, who had
retained an affection for his pretty, silly sister, and
sent her small presents of money from time to time.
Behind Colonel Stone's bluff exterior, Basingstoke remarked parenthetically, was hidden a romantic heart.

His father first met his mother at one of the sec-
ond-class halls where she sang her sentimental songs—
her voice, although pleasant, was never good enough
to take her into the best halls, or even to the top of
the bill at lesser ones. Their attraction was that of
opposites; his mother had told him how much she

admired the brutish strength of the handsome Irishman who seemed always to be bursting out of his
suits, and the boxer must have been drawn to all that
was mouselike about her.

They were happy together for two or three years
although they did not live with each other more than
a small part of that time. She had her engagements,
and he had his fights, and although he wanted her to
give up singing she would never do so. She felt, in
some obscure way, that she was justified when he
came home drunk one day after losing a fight—"They
were both essentially second rate, I fear," said Basingstoke, again in parentheses, looking out of the window—hit her in the jaw and knocked out two of her
teeth. From that day she was terrified of his occasional drunkenness, not on her own account, but because
she feared that in a violent mood he might harm the
baby, John.

The relations between them worsened whenever
they lived with each other for more than a couple of
days. His own memories of childhood were of a suc-
cession of shabby lodgings in provincial towns, and
he was vividly impressed by the terror his mother
showed whenever his father was coming to stay the
night. When his father was sober he was generally
friendly, but when he was drunk (and he was drunk
increasingly often, for he lost many fights through
careless training and easy living) he would strike her,
and he would always threaten on such occasions to do
something to the boy, saying that this thin, puking
child was none of his. At last one night he knocked
her down and branded the boy's face with a hot
poker. Rather dramatically, Basingstoke turned
toward her. "As you see, the mark has remained."

Green fields and toy houses flashed by. Vicky stared
at him with horror and fascination. His scar was
rapidly assuming the quality of Byron's lame foot in
her imagination. "What happened then?"

"She got a separation from him. Then he met her
one day in the street, and threatened her with a

knife. He was arrested, and although she didn't want to give evidence against him, her family persuaded her to do so—she was always easily persuaded. He got twelve months, and she never saw him again. He couldn't get any more fights, and became a chucker-out at a public house. He was knocked over by a taxi and killed when I was ten years old." Basingstoke paused. "My mother was very sorry. I think she always loved him. She died two years later from T.B."

"How awful," Vicky said. She meditated. "Nothing like that has ever happened to me," she said regretfully, and then, "What happened afterward?"

"Afterward?"

"I mean—who brought you up—all that kind of thing."

"Oh yes. Thanks chiefly to Uncle Gilbert, the family stepped in. They sent me to boarding school, and paid for my education. I came out of school into the Artists' Rifles, and I was training when the war ended. Since then I've done all sort of jobs—librarian, tutor, journalist—anything to avoid asking them for money. Just at present"—he rattled coins in his pocket and gave her the sidelong smile that appeared sinister or romantic according to taste—"you find me at an exceptionally low ebb until my novel is published or something else turns up."

"I see," said Vicky. She gazed in a kind of trance out of the carriage window.

"I tell you all this," Basingstoke said, "because I was so atrociously rude to you yesterday." She waved a hand, a great lady deprecating mention of an occasion so trivial. "My background is, I think, partly responsible. I feel a disinterested curiosity to see how people will react to the unexpected and embarrassing. When you laid yourself open to attack, I couldn't resist probing like a surgeon. Curiosity, I often think, is the most debased of man's instincts. What is it, for instance, that moves us to delve into the secret of this small literary scandal?" Dumbly, Vicky shook her head. "The most ignoble and beastly curiosity. Or, at least, that is at work in my own case. What will your oafish lover do when he finds out that he has paid a hundred guineas for a forgery? What effect will it have on your relations with him? What human secret is hidden behind that modest discovery of mine about the falsification of a name or a date? Something mean, you may be sure, something shameful or terrible. For there is always something shameful behind the façade of respectability and routine. Move a stone, and the worm of deceit emerges. I am fascinated by the shape it takes." Looking out of the window again, he said, "Such fascination is unhealthy."

What extraordinary—and what romantic—things to say! What a lot there would be to note down in her diary. She occupied herself in building up a situation round the secret of old Martin's book, in which she would play a romantic and heroic part. Perhaps there was something astonishing hidden among those dusty papers in the attic. Dimly she thought of an unopened box and a great worm coming out of it. . . .

The train stopped. "B-a-a-rnsfield," the porter mooed like a cow. Vicky sprang to her feet. "Come along. Let's go to the attic."

Just inside the front door they met Edward, who looked at Basingstoke with surprise. "You're back from London quickly," he said, and added with a kind of gloomy glee, "all a washout, I suppose?"

"Not at all." Vicky's cheeks were glowing with pleasure and anticipatory excitement. "Anthony is making investigations there. We have come back to look at the attic."

"The attic?" Edward stared at her.

"Papers—masses of old papers up there. We're looking for a clue. Is the attic locked?"

"Certainly it is; and Mother's got the key," Edward said. "I've got more important things to think about—

Mrs. Curtis has some curious pains in her chest—but Vicky, I'm bound to say I can't approve——"

Halfway up the stairs she turned and put out her tongue at him. He went into his surgery, and slammed the door. Basingstoke was hovering at the bottom of the stairs. "Perhaps I shouldn't be here. I don't think your brother was altogether pleased to see me."

"Don't be ridiculous," she said. "Come up. Mother, where are you?"

The door of a room on the first floor opened. "If it's something to do with dinner," Mrs. Rawlings said, "I have a bad headache. I spent all the morning arguing with cook about lunch and then she misunderstood everything I said and it was really quite uneatable." She peered over the dark stairway. "Why, Mr. Basingstoke, how do you do? I had no idea you were there."

"He's come to help me look in the attic, Mother. Have you got the key?" Vicky asked.

"I expect so, my dear," Mrs. Rawlings said placidly. She produced a large bunch of keys and fumbled through them. "This is the padlock key for that iron coal bunker we sold, and this is the old key to the front door before we changed the lock, and this is the key to the surgery cupboard—though why I have that I can't think—and this is the key to the attic, and this Yale—now, whatever can this Yale be for."

"Mother," Vicky said, "it's just the attic key we want."

"Oh yes, of course." With a seraphic smile, Mrs. Rawlings took the attic key off the ring and gave it to her daughter. "But whatever is Mr. Basingstoke going to do in the attic?"

"We think there may be something about that book."

"Do you?" Mrs. Rawlings looked doubtful, and then brightened. "If you find a pair of black kid gloves, bring them down. I can't think where they have got to, but they may be in the attic."

"Yes, Mother." She gestured impatiently to Basingstoke. "Come on."

They went up another flight of stairs, and then up a stepladder into a loft. "The attic's a separate room at the end," she said. "Mind your head." Suddenly she screamed, flung herself into Basingstoke's arms and just as suddenly moved out of them again. He was left with a disturbing recollection of a womanly scent. "What was that?" she asked. Her eyes were wide.

"Probably a mouse," he said, though in fact he had heard nothing.

"I'm terrified of mice," she said, and indeed she was shivering. "Stay close to me, won't you?"

"Yes." He put his hand on her arm, and felt it warm but quivering. "How far ahead is the attic?"

"Here it is." Basingstoke struck a match, and she put the key into a small door. The key creaked as it turned. By the flame of his match, Basingstoke saw a switch just inside the door. He pressed it, and a dusty lamp lighted up a collection of books, broken furniture and china, a rusty bicycle, several pictures and two tin trunks. She pounced on one of these, and opened it. "Look," she said dramatically, and Basingstoke saw a great mass of papers underneath a film of dust. "We'll both take a handful," she said eagerly, and, sitting on the other tin trunk, began to leaf through a collection of bills, theater programs and letters, muttering to herself as she did so in a way that Basingstoke found slightly reminiscent of her mother. He sat by her side, rather precariously, on a three-legged stool.

"Bills! Bills! Goodness knows why we keep them. How the price of everything has gone up. Bourbon biscuits—I used to love them when I was thirteen years old, and now the very sight of them makes me sick. *Elementary Studies in Human Pathology*—that must have belonged to brother Edward when he was studying, don't you think? Yes, here's his name in it. Here's a program for *The Maid of the Mountains*—

that was a wonderful show." She looked at him suddenly, and then said, with the mantle of the literary lady assumed again, "I used to think so long ago. Of course, we were very young then. Uncle Jack took us to see it. It was a great treat." She tossed back a strand of dark hair that had fallen over her eye. "Uncle Jack. We ought to see Uncle Jack.

"Who is Uncle Jack?"

"His names's not really Jack, it's Cæsar, but we call him Jack because Cæsar's such a ridiculous name. He was Papa's elder brother, and he inherited the estate and money when Grandfather Martin died. Papa quarreled with him terribly because he thought he should have had half the money. I expect grandfather Martin would have left him some, but he died without making a will. Uncle Jack wanted Papa to have some money, but he wouldn't accept anything less than half. He thought that was his right. They had a frightful quarrel, and kept it up for years. In fact, Papa never made it up, and Edward hasn't really either—he's awfully cantankerous, you know, very much like Papa in many ways—but I sometimes go over and see him. Uncle Jack, I mean. He's sweet, and I know if he can tell us anything he will." She stared at him. "I say, what are we looking for, really?"

"Some papers to do with that first edition." Basingstoke lifted the package of letters from her knee. "And if we're going to find out anything we'd better ignore theater programs and bills for bourbon biscuits." He began to go through the papers methodically, putting any personal letters on one side. Vicky was not restrained from occasional indistinct mutterings, but for the most part they worked in silence. Most of the letters were to Vicky's father, Edward, and it was apparent from a casual glance that his financial position had been insecure. There were letters asking for payment of accounts for medical equipment and supplies, and a whole series that seemed to consist of a protracted argument about payment for life insurance. Vicky sighed as she read these—sighed in the manner of the grand lady. "Poor Papa. He had no head for money. None of our family has ever had any head for money. Even brother Edward hasn't. We're too artistic." Something in Basingstoke's look prompted her to add hurriedly, "But something always turns up. Or else Uncle Jack helps us out. He's done that two or three times when we were in an awkward spot, but nobody gives him credit for it." She dug into the bottom of the trunk. "These look older. Yes, they are—I say, here are some letters that begin 'My dear Martin.' But they all seem to be notes from friends." She looked through them rapidly and dug further. "Look, here are some letters from publishers—but it's not the firm you said—it's somebody called Winster, Marlow & Company. Who are they?"

"They were your grandfather's publishers—that is, they published the 1868 edition of *Passion and Repentance* that caused so much fuss, and his later books too."

"These are all letters about the later ones," Vicky said, turning over the yellowed sheets. "Oh, here are one or two about the first book. They don't tell us anything, though, do they, because they're the wrong date—1868."

"No, they don't—yes they do, though. This one does." Basingstoke tapped one of the sheets excitedly with his forefinger. "Listen to this—dated November 30th, 1867—'We shall be pleased to publish your sonnet series, *Passion and Repentance,* on the terms already agreed. We understand that none of these poems has previously been published, either in book form or in periodical publication. We shall be glad if you will let us have formal confirmation on this point.' Do you know your grandfather's handwriting?"

"No. Why?"

"Because there's a note on the side—look. It says, 'Wrote 7 December '67 and gave the assurance required regarding publication.'" Basingstoke put down the letter. His face was twitching slightly on the scarred side. "Could your Uncle Jack tell us about the handwriting? Or your mother?"

Vicky moved on her tin trunk. "Better to ask Uncle Jack, I think. He'd be certain to know—and he might be able to tell us something else. I say, it's rather exciting, isn't it?" Her mind moved in a whirl of forgers and midnight chases.

He said in his rich, deep voice, "Where does Uncle Jack live?"

"About thirty miles away, at a little village called Millingham. You'll like him—he's a sweet old boy, and intelligent too. Doesn't like brother Edward, but he's very fond of me. He says I'm the beauty of the family. Do you think so?"

"Yes," Basingstoke said. He kissed her awkwardly on the side of her cheek and nose. "I think you are much more beautiful than your brother."

She looked at him in a contemplative way, and he wondered what thoughts were moving in her mind. He would have been surprised to know that she was wondering whether she should make a note of his kiss in her diary. "Come on," she said. "I expect the car's in the garage." It was, and they stood looking at it. "Edward should have finished his rounds by now. I think we'll just take it."

"But supposing somebody wants him urgently?"

"He can use his bicycle. The exercise will be good for him. He uses the car too much. I'm sure half his worries are caused by indigestion." As they drove away Edward's startled face could be seen at a window. "Onward," said Vicky, taking her hands off the steering wheel and narrowly missing a dog. "Onward to Uncle Jack."

VI

They found Uncle Jack chopping logs in his garden. He was a small man in his sixties, with a round red apple of a face, and a rather extravagantly fierce manner. He greeted Vicky warmly. "Nice of you to come and see an old fogy like me." He drew a handkerchief across his brow.

Vicky was slightly flirtatious. "You aren't an old fogy, Uncle Jack, when you can chop up logs like that. This is my friend, Mr. Basingstoke. A writer," she added after a moment's thought.

"How do you do, sir. You from London?" He spoke as though London were five hundred instead of thirty miles away.

"Why, yes."

"And what's the news in the clubs, sir, eh? When's this government going to be out?"

"Mr. Basingstoke hasn't much connection with politics, Uncle. He's a poet," Vicky said, with surprising promptness.

"Ah," Uncle Jack said. He looked at his watch. "I must just finish these logs. Exercise, you know—must have an hour every day. MacDonald—Snowden—Henderson——" he said as he resumed the rhythm of log chopping. "Ruin of the country. Got to get rid of 'em." Chips of wood flew in all directions. "Not a question of being interested in politics—just plain common sense. Do you know what the farmers are saying about this government?" A storm of blows prevented them from hearing what the farmers were saying. Uncle Jack threw down his ax and contemplated the pile of logs with satisfaction. He turned to his niece.

"You've got a look in your eye I don't like, Victoria. There's something you're wanting, I can tell that. You've not come over here just to see *me*. But you're in for it now." He showed them a barn converted into a gymnasium, an elaborately laid-out rose garden, and beyond it the new asparagus beds. Then he stopped and stared at Basingstoke. "A poet, eh, sir. My father was a poet."

"I know his works, of course."

"He lived the last years of his life here. Used to sit writing on this lawn." They came to a small, perfectly kept lawn at the end of the path. "He sat out here with his chair and table—always put it just here, where he could see the house." Through a hedge they saw clearly the back of the square Georgian house. Uncle Jack shook his head. "This hedge was thicker in those days. How's Edward?" he asked so abruptly that Vicky was taken aback.

"He's very well, really. Worrying as usual."

"He's got something to worry about now. Didn't help to put 'em in, did he?"

"You know Edward's a Liberal, Uncle Jack."

"Liberal, indeed." He hacked fiercely at a dandelion. "And what are the Liberals doing? Keeping 'em in. If Lloyd George gave the word, they'd be out tomorrow. But there—a little Welsh lawyer—I never did trust him. Hope you're not Welsh, sir?" Basingstoke shook his head. "Very glad to hear it. Always putting my foot in it. Have done ever since I was a boy by saying just what I thought." The red-apple face broke into a laugh, revealing fine false teeth. "Come in and have a cup of tea."

He led them into a comfortable sitting room. A large picture hung over the mantelpiece. "That's your father, isn't it, Mr. Rawlings?" Basingstoke asked.

"Ah. Millais' portrait of him after he came back from Italy. He was thirty-six then." Behind the traditional growth of beard and side whisker the painter had seen a sharp and handsome face. The hair was thick and brown above a low forehead, the eyes glowed somberly, the mouth was a thin line. The face was powerful, and also in some way sinister, and even menacing. Basingstoke stared at the portrait, lost in some obscure conjectures of his own, until his host coughed. "I'm at your service, Victoria, my dear. What can I do for you?"

Vicky explained and Basingstoke, silent, watched the changes on Uncle Jack's mobile, red-apple face. At first an expression of incredulity showed itself, but this was succeeded by a rather comic look of intense concentration as she recounted the evidence re-

garding the publisher's name, and finally produced
the letter from Winster, Marlow.

"Certainly been to some trouble, haven't you?" Uncle Jack said, only half jovially. "Blessed if I can
understand why. There's your young man up in London seeing this Jebb fellow, and you're down here.
What are you trying to do, besmirch your old grandfather's name?"

"I don't think that's in question," Basingstoke said.
"Obviously, if there is a forgery, Martin Rawlings
wouldn't have been a party to it."

"How do you know?" Uncle Jack said fiercely.
"Quite the contrary. He might 'a done anything
when he was a young man. Let me see that letter,
Victoria, my dear, will you?" He looked at the anno-
tation on the letter. "That's your grandfather's hand
right enough, no doubt of that. Neat and crabbed.
Can't mistake it. Hum. Mind if I smoke a pipe?" He
took out a pipe, filled it methodically, and lighted it.
"Takes me back, all this does, takes me back a long
way." He began to make a sucking noise with the
pipe. "I don't take much stock of this so-called evidence of yours. Take this letter here. My father—rest
his soul—was wild in his youth and uncommon respectable and churchish after he came into money."

"When *did* he come into money?" Basingstoke
asked. Uncle Jack was not best pleased at the inter-
ruption.

"In eighteen-seventy-*one*, sir, when my father was
thirty-six and I was twelve years old, my father's
cousin John died out in the Antipodes. John had
been a wild man himself, but he'd made a pot of
money out of the gold mines there. He got back to
England, bought himself this estate, and was just
settling down to enjoy it, when—pfft—he went out
hunting one day in filthy weather on a roan mare
and she threw him. Broke his neck on the spot. Never
trust a roan mare. Does that answer your point, sir?"
Basingstoke nodded.

"But we're speaking now of eighteen-sixty-*seven*. At

that time my father was poor, struggling and bitter—bitter because he was unrecognized. He'd never had anything published except this privately printed edition. Now, when he got a chance of publication he must have been mad with excitement. It is likely that when these people, Winster, Marlow, offered him publication and asked him to certify that his poems hadn't been published before, he'd bother to tell them about this little privately printed edition? I can tell you, sir, remembering my father, that he wouldn't."

Basingstoke's scar was twitching slightly. "Do you mean," he asked, "that you remember the existence of that privately printed first edition from your own childhood?"

Uncle Jack took his pipe from his mouth and snorted. "Good God! No, man; o' course not. I was only a year old when it was published, and it was little enough I saw of my father before we came to England. I'm only telling ye what *may* 'a happened, or what *probably* happened. I don't remember any copy o' this little book from my childhood, but then it isn't likely that I should." He put back his pipe, sucked hard on it, and continued. "Now about the publisher's name—there you've got me foxed. But I'll make a guess—may be right or may be wrong, but it's as good as the next man's. You said just now, Mr.—uh—Basingstoke, that my father wouldn't have been a party to a forgery." He smacked a hand on his knee. "There you're wrong. When he was young, my father would 'a done anything to make his name known. Now, he was living in Italy at the time. Why shouldn't he 'a got this little edition printed himself, and stuck an English publisher's name on it to lend a touch of distinction. And it 'ud be typical of my father," he said with a chuckle, "to get the name a bit wrong. How's that?"

"Not good," Basingstoke said. "It wouldn't lend any distinction to put a publisher's name on a privately printed book and, anyway, your father was in

Italy and would have had to arrange it all with
somebody in England. Frankly, Mr. Rawlings, I get
the impression that you don't believe this yourself,
and that you're trying to cover up something or somebody." Vicky gasped, and waited for the explosion
that Uncle Jack's manner seemed to presage. But a
great gale of laughter came instead, that swelled the
apple cheeks and showed the white false teeth.

"Ah, you're a man of the world, sir, and a typical
man of the younger generation. Skepticism—infernal
skepticism everywhere. I like it in you, though, mark
you. I think it's healthy. Perhaps it *is* a thin story.
But my father, to be frank, was such an engaging
scoundrel in his youth—and such a sanctimonious
hypocrite after he was converted to Catholicism and
came into money—that I could believe anything of
him. I was a man of the world myself, sir, in my
youth, and a traveler——"

"Uncle Jack was an officer in the South African
War," Vicky said with a touch of malice. He waved
the remark aside.

"That was nothing—what any decent man would
do for King and country. I'm speaking of a time
before that, when I was a regular globe-trotter as they
say. France, Spain, the Austrian Tyrol, Italy. Ah, my
boy, I spent a glorious year in Italy when I was
young." Uncle Jack stared contemplatively into that
glorious year of the past. "Italy, Italy. What was I
saying? About my father, yes. When I was in Italy I
revisited the little places he stayed at years before—
sort of a pilgrimage, y'know. Didn't find many who
remembered him, but those who did had a name for
him all right—mad Englishmen. That'll tell you what
they thought of him. Don't look shocked, Victoria,
my dear, you know it's true. But the joke's on you,
Mr. Basingstoke, because I'm not covering up anything, but simply trying to find an explanation of
something I know to be true. You see," he confided,
"I have positive proof that the 1860 edition was genuine."

"What's that?"

Uncle Jack cocked his head on one side like a bird. "Will you accept as proof a presentation copy, signed by my father? Anyway, you shall see it." He trotted with a quick and nervous step to a walnut bookcase. "You think me a rustic now, but I used to be interested in books too—collected first editions, all that sort of thing. Got no patience with these modern writers, though. Can't understand 'em." He fumbled with a bunch of keys on a chain attached to his trousers. "I tell you, the world's going to pot. Would you be one of these modern young men, now?"

"I suppose I would."

"No offense meant," said Uncle Jack, undisturbed. "And none taken, I hope. Ah, here's the key." He unlocked the cupboard. "You can judge for yourself —" He stopped short and then said, swinging round on them with a ferocious expression. "By God, it's gone!"

"Do you mean someone's taken it?" said Vicky rather foolishly.

"How the hell do I know?" snapped her uncle. "I beg your pardon, my dear. Look for yourself."

There, by the side of Henley and Kipling, stood the work of Martin Rawlings.

"But there's *Passion and Repentance*," said Vicky, pointing to a book bound in red.

"That's the 1868 Winster, Marlow edition," said Basingstoke.

Uncle Jack was dancing with impatient fury. "Of course it is. *That's* where it was, next to the 1868 edition—and all these books were signed by my father. It *must* be here—it must be." He took out the other books on that shelf, and peered behind them. There was no sign of the missing book "It was here a couple of weeks ago. I remember seeing it."

"It must have been stolen," Vicky exclaimed.

"Nonsense, nonsense," he said pettishly. "Who would steal it?" Darting across the room, he pressed a bell. It was answered by a stolid, middle-aged woman.

"Mrs. Holroyd, have you seen this bookcase open in the past week?"

She looked surprised. "No, sir."

"You've got a key to it, haven't you? Has that key been out of your possession?"

"No, sir."

"Sure of that?" He glared at her, but she remained unruffled.

"Quite sure, sir. Here it is."

"All right, all right. It must be mislaid here somewhere." Uncle Jack turned back to the bookcase, and Basingstoke coughed. "May I ask a question, Mr. Rawlings?" Uncle Jack nodded impatiently.

"You have a key so that you can open the bookcase and dust the books, I suppose, Mrs. Holroyd?"

"That's right."

"And when did you dust it last?"

For the first time something approaching emotion showed on Mrs. Holroyd's broad, smooth face. "Tuesday I always do this room, and Tuesday I do the bookcase."

"That means you've dusted it today?" She nodded. "Did you happen to notice a slim book in a faded blue cover—it would have been next to that red one."

Her face had resumed its customary blankness. "Oh no, sir. I shouldn't notice anything like that."

Vicky had been bouncing on her seat with excitement and eagerness to ask a question. "Mrs. Holroyd, has anyone called in the last few days to read the gas or electric meters—or to look at the drains—or tune the piano? Anyone like that?"

"There was someone, Miss Rawlings—the gas inspector."

"Ah!" Vicky cried. "He was a new man, no doubt?"

"Not at all, miss." The bovine placidity of Mrs. Holroyd's face remained unchanged. "I've known Joe Thomas for five years or more."

Uncle Jack gave a sudden whoop. He had been examining the cupboard door. "Scratches here. Might be some dirty work after all."

Basingstoke went over and looked at them. "They don't seem to be very new scratches, sir," he said doubtfully.

"No more they do," Uncle Jack agreed. "Probably made 'em myself one day after I'd had one or two. That'll do, Mrs. Holroyd, that'll do."

"Do you mean to tell me that somebody's *stolen* that book?" said Uncle Jack incredulously, when she had left the room. "What the devil for? And why should they want to steal it if it's a forgery?"

Basingstoke nodded. "That's just what Shelton said about the high offer made for his copy. Was there anything special about your copy of the book, sir?"

"It was a presentation copy my father gave to Garth Mansell—the literary critic, y'know. Mansell had a row with my father afterward, and he must have sold this copy. At least," said Uncle Jack with a sudden doubtfulness, "I suppose he must. All I know about it is that I bought it from a bookseller more than twenty years ago, because there wasn't a copy of that edition in my library."

Basingstoke was triumphant. "Isn't it remarkable that your father hadn't got a copy of this edition himself?"

"Not very. I've told you Martin was a damned careless chap when he was young. Never even had a copy of the 1868 edition. Look'ee here." He pulled down the red book from the shelf and showed them an inscription written inside, in a flowing hand: *Martin Rawlings from James Cobb, in friendship, and to fill a surprising gap on his shelves. May, 1872.* This Cobb's a big man in the book world now, I hear. Wasn't then, I can tell you. Glad he was then to come here and see my father and drink a glass o' wine and say, 'Yes, Mr. Rawlings, no, Mr. Rawlings,' and pat me on the head, while he wormed a bit of information out of father. But that's neither here nor there. Point is, y'see, father hadn't even got a copy of this 1868 edition, so it ain't strange he hadn't got the earlier one." They nodded. "But how do *you* explain, my lad, the fact that it was a presentation copy? Wouldn't 'a presented a forgery to Mansell, would he? And damme, what am I doing?" he roared suddenly. "I must get on to the police."

"The police," said Vicky and Basingstoke together. The words seemed to take the affair out of the atmosphere of a lighthearted joke, and lend it an unwelcomed seriousness. They were silent a moment, and, then Vicky shivered a little and said impulsively, "Oh, don't do that."

"And why the devil not? Why shouldn't the police do something for the money they take from the taxpayer? Not that they'll do any good now that they're under the thumb of these Labour men."

"Just leave us to investigate a little longer by ourselves," Vicky pleaded. "We were having such fun. Don't call in the police. Think how wonderful it would be if we were able to get back the book for you."

"Little I'll get out of the police, sure enough," Uncle Jack grumbled. "And I wouldn't be wanting to spoil a bit of sport. I was one for a bit of sport myself when I was younger. What are you going to do?"

"We're going to see a bookseller named Lewis. He's the man who made Anthony an offer for his copy. We can ask him the name of his client," said Vicky boldly.

Uncle Jack looked at her keenly. "Lewis? Man at Blackheath? Queer thing. I had some dealings with him years ago. Matter of fact, he was the bookseller I bought that presentation copy from."

"The one that's been stolen?" Uncle Jack nodded. "That's too much. There must be something funny about it all—don't you agree? Oh, please say you agree and let us go and see this man. Don't call in the police yet."

He pinched her cheek. "All right. I won't spoil your fun for—what shall we say? Twenty-four hours?"

"Forty-eight hours. Forty-eight hours to find the forger," she said gleefully.

"You're a smart girl, Victoria." He looked at them with his head cocked on one side. "And this young poet's got his head screwed on the right way too. Off you go then—hot on the trail. But keep in touch with your old uncle. And don't forget, Mr. Basingstoke, *you* may be interested in tracking down a literary forgery, but *I'm* interested in getting my book back, forgery or not."

Basingstoke emerged out of a long silence. "Speaking of that book, could one of your personal visitors in the past few days be the thief? Have you left any of them alone in this room?"

Uncle Jack stamped his foot on the floor and roared with laughter. "Didn't I say he had his head screwed on right? Well now, my young poetic Sherlock, it may seem queer, but the same thought had already come into my thick old skull. I can offer you a choice of the vicar, General Brett, who's been settled down here as a gentleman farmer for several years, Mrs. Pemberton, who came to tell me about a Pound Sale next month, and Dick Spendrell, who called to ask me to go fishing. Those are the *only* people who have been in this room in the last week, and even in these days I'd be prepared to swear none of 'em is a thief."

"What about the servants? Isn't Mrs. Holroyd a bit too good to be true?"

"Maybe. But you'll not convince me that a woman who's been with me for years is a thief. And Ellen, the maid, has been with me ten years too."

Basingstoke was lost in thought. "Really, it's very odd. What about windows——"

"Oh, come *on*," said Vicky. "It's past four o'clock now. If we don't start soon we shan't get to see that bookseller." She pecked her uncle's cheek. "Good-by, Uncle Jack. You never gave us that cup of tea, but I forgive you. We'll keep in touch, and let you know when we've tracked down your book and caught the forger, won't we, John?"

Basingstoke looked at her half-ironically. It was the first time that she had used his Christian name.

VII

Lewis' bookshop in Peaceful Alley, just off Peaceful Vale, Blackheath, was not impressive in appearance. It had a fairly large frontage with an outside stall containing books priced from *2d.* to *6d.* More expensive books were in the window—but not very expensive ones; *Napoleon and Prince Eugene* priced at half a crown, volumes of the Mermaid poets, books of nineteenth-century memoirs, the collected works of Charles Lever and Lord Lytton. The shop looked faintly incongruous among the fruiterers and grocers which surrounded it. A bell clanged when Basingstoke pushed open the door.

Was imagination playing tricks, he wondered, or was it really exceptionally dark inside this shop? He blinked his eyes and saw books arranged on the shelves, and piled untidily on the floor. There seemed to be no one inside the shop, and he took a step forward. As he did so, Vicky screamed, not loudly, but with a certain penetrating power. A black cat, with a protesting miaow, jumped onto a pile of books by her side, and the figure of a man became apparent, standing at the door of an inner room. A voice, soft but with something like an amused purr in it, said, "Did March frighten you?"

A light was switched on, and they both blinked again at the very fat man who waddled forward to meet them. Although he was little more than five feet in height, he must have weighed more than fifteen stone, and the phrase, which is so often casually used, "He was as broad as he was tall" was almost true of him. His fat was not firm, but drooping. Balls of fat hung down from his cheeks, his ears seemed pulled down by a weight of flesh, his chin merged imperceptibly with a short, thick neck, and the enormous paunch he carried before him drooped visibly downward. He was wearing a dirty pair of flannel trousers, and a greasy waistcoat which had lost most of its buttons. His shirt was collarless, and he wore no jacket.

"What do you mean—March?" Vicky asked faintly, and his face quivered with amusement.

"This one of my cats I call March. I have one for each month of the year. They will not disturb you. Can I be of help to you?"

"We should like to see Mr. Lewis," Basingstoke said, and the fat man's face quivered again. His voice was high and thin.

"There has been no Mr. Lewis since twenty years ago, when I bought this shop from him." He made a movement of the head and shoulders that might have been interpreted as the ghost of a bow. "Jonathan Jacobs at your service."

Vicky jumped nervously again as a whistle sounded, sudden and shrill. The fat man turned and waddled toward the curtained recess from which he had come. "My kettle. Will you join me in a cup of tea? I think it is time to close the shop now. I do not like to be disturbed at teatime." He waddled past them again to the door. There was a click as he turned the key. He clapped fat hands. "Come, March, April, May. Tea is ready." They followed him behind the curtain and found themselves in another smaller room filled with books, Here, however, there was less attempt at arrangement, and more books were lying piled in heaps. A Siamese and a blue Persian cat lay asleep on two of the piles, but they woke up when he said, "October, December. Tea is ready." He spoke to them as he might have spoken to human beings, not with the changed inflection which most people use in talking to animals.

In the middle of the room stood a rickety table. On it were half a dozen pink-and-white cream cakes, a teacup and a large empty bowl. The fat man got two more cups while the cats moved round his legs, purring and rubbing against him. He poured nearly a pint of milk into the bowl, sat down heavily in an old armchair, and with a visible effort put the bowl of milk on the floor, where the cats lapped it greedily. He poured three cups of tea, pushed two toward them and sank again into the armchair. Vicky, looking rather prim (the pursuit of forgers led into such strange ways!), sat on the edge of a dusty kitchen chair, and Basingstoke sat down on some books. With a sigh the fat man said, "A cake perhaps?" When they refused he did not press them, but took one himself, and ate it in two gulps. The blue Persian cat, purring, jumped onto one arm of his chair. "Tell me now, what can I do for you?"

"We are looking for a copy of *Passion and Repentance*," Basingstoke said. He was conducting the interview on lines that they had agreed on in the car.

"Passion and Repentance," the fat man said. Below his fleshy forehead small eyes were alert. "I think I have a copy."

"We are looking for the *first edition*." Basingstoke spoke with what he hoped was peculiar emphasis, and Vicky looked at him a little uneasily. A white cat sprang up on the other arm of the fat man's armchair and stared at her.

"Oh burning, burning," the fat man said in his squeaky voice, and both of them looked at him in surprise. He continued:

"Oh burning, burning! That red sky at night
 And the hot mind that's ashes in the morning,
 Nor ever hope that any bird of dawning
 Can put the record of past sin to flight.
 I dreamed a gull whose lucent lovely wing
 Knew not the savage colors of desire.
 But waking found your body like a fire
 And neither of us recked a reckoning."

With some care, the fat man selected another cream cake, and Basingstoke said in his solemn baritone, like an actor taking up a cue, "All that is past—

All that is past. Now within quiet gardens
My spirit feels the silken air of rest
And is no longer torn. Not torn? A quest
Goes on within me that must make the worst
Of mankind shudder. The spirit quivers, hardens.
No pietistic God can stop its thirst."

Sitting uncomfortably on her dusty kitchen chair, Vicky felt slightly sickened by the smell of cats. Then she realized that they had been quoting from one of the sonnets in *Passion and Repentance*. The realization brought relief, and she cried, "Why, that's grandfather Martin's poem."

"Precisely," said Basingstoke, and looked annoyed. It had been agreed that they should not mention Vicky's relation to Martin Rawlings. The fat man heaved with pleasure.

"I am honored by your presence, ma'am. And may I compliment you, sir, upon your memory? I was brought up in days when a man of culture read poetry aloud. Those days are past, but my memory—I say it in all modesty—is still prodigious." He sighed, brushed crumbs off his waistcoat, and seemed to dismiss the question. "And so you are looking for a first edition. If I can find one, how much would you be prepared to pay for it?"

"Anything up to a hundred pounds."

"Not enough." He broke another cask into segments, and put a small piece into his mouth, but did not eat it. The piece remained pursed between thick violet lips until the blue Persian stretched forward delicately and took it. Basingstoke did his best not to seem disconcerted by this procedure, which was rendered more curious by the fact that the bookseller looked steadily at him while the cat took the piece of cake.

"It's well above market price."

"No, sir." The bookseller's great egg head moved gently from side to side. "I have a client who is prepared to pay a hundred and fifty pounds for a first edition. I know where one is to be found, and I offered a hundred and fifty pounds for it. The offer was refused."

"You know of one," Vicky said excitedly. "Oh, but so do——" She stopped in mid-speech with her mouth open, remembering that the copy which had been refused to the bookseller must of course be Anthony's. ·

Basingstoke continued without glancing at her. "I think you know of two." Vicky admired the venomous note in his voice.

"Two?"

"Some years ago you sold a copy to Mr. Rawlings of Millingham."

"Ah!" Jacobs crumbled another piece of cake and placed a piece in his mouth, where it was taken by the white cat. "That copy also is for sale?"

"Come now, Mr. Jacobs, you know as well as I do that that copy has been stolen." Basingstoke spoke harshly, and the scar on his face stood out.

"Nonsense," the fat man said calmly.

"And you know as well as I do that this so-called first edition is a fake."

For the first time the fat man seemed disturbed. He shifted uneasily on his seat, and pulled at his jowl with a fat hand. The blue Persian cat moved its face forward to him, and he absently pushed it away. "That is a bold word, sir. By what authority do you ask these questions?"

"I am a private investigator from Scotland Yard," Basingstoke said. "Miss Rawlings here has applied to us for assistance."

The fat man returned his stare with a look that was at first hostile, but softened slowly to a smile. The smile broadened, and he began to laugh. As he laughed, his body shook all over. Even the calves of his legs, Vicky noted with disgust, wobbled under his dirty trousers, and the chair in which he sat vibrated with the movement of his body. The cats, alarmed, jumped off the arms of the chair, and one of them ran out into the shop. The laughter moved up into the high well of this room, and rebounded from the book-lined walls to die away in a menacing silence. Vicky looked from the fat man's wobbling face to Basingstoke's ugly scar and shivered suddenly. The fat man was speaking.

"Impudence, my young friend, is an admirable quality. It achieves results not always obtained by the most judicious and intelligent of men. Impudence, as La Rochefoucauld would undoubtedly have observed if he had happened on the phrase, is the wisdom of the young. Now, Mr.—what is your name?"

"Basingstoke."

"Transparently a pseudonym, but we will let it pass. You come here, you introduce to me rather clumsily a young lady as the granddaughter of Martin Rawlings who very possibly has no connection with him at all——"

Vicky moved indignantly on her dusty chair, but a fat hand asked for silence. "And you make this outrageous pretense that you are an emissary of Scotland Yard. It happens that years ago one of my best friends was a police inspector. What I saw of the police force at that time makes me certain that you do not belong to it. Do not interrupt me. I do not know, then, Mr. Basingstoke, who you are, except that the credentials you present are false. I do not know, either, what your interests are in this matter, or whether they are identical with mine. Would you care to elaborate your case against *Passion and Repentance*?"

"No," said Basingstoke. He added, "It is true that I am not a Scotland Yard man myself, but I have friends there. I shall certainly get in touch with them if you don't give satisfactory answers to my questions. I want to know why you've had so much to do with selling copies of this book, and the name of the client who is willing to pay so much for it."

The fat man's stomach heaved in a sigh. "You make things very difficult. Youth is always impetuous.

But how I envy you that impetuosity. It is time you went out," he said, and they understood after a moment that he was speaking to the cats. He opened a door leading to the back of the house and six cats walked obediently out of it. It was as if, Vicky reflected with another shiver, he did not want them to hear what he had to say. They heard him walk down a passage and open another door. While he was out of the room, Vicky and Basingstoke did not speak to each other.

"What would you think," the fat man said when he waddled back into the room, "if a descendant of Charles Dickens asked you to dispose privately of the manuscript of a complete unpublished novel by that writer?"

Basingstoke said sharply, "I should think the book was a forgery."

"Just so. But let us suppose that the person who offered it to you was beyond reproach, and that he assured you of the book's authenticity?"

"I don't know." Basingstoke was impatient. "Do you want me to say that I should have accepted the manuscript and sold it? I suppose I might have done."

"Just so," said the fat man again. He sat back placidly, feeling, apparently, that he had gained a point. "Twenty years ago, soon after I had taken over this bookshop from Lewis, I was approached by a respected figure—I might say *the* most respected figure—in the world of bibliography. I am prepared to make no mention of names. We will call this figure Mr. X, if you please. Mr. X asked me to dispose of first editions of certain works of Victorian authors on his behalf. I did so, through my list and in sales rooms. I was paid a percentage, and thought no more of the matter. The only uncommon thing about the transaction was that Mr. X stipulated that his name must not appear—and even that, after all, was not so very uncommon, for he naturally did not wish his name to be linked with the sale of books.

"I was a little surprised, however, when a few months later another batch of first editions, some of them the same titles and some fresh ones, came to me from Mr. X with the same instructions as before. And during the next few years these instructions were repeated again and again, and again and again I carried them out.

"Had the vendor of the books been anybody but Mr. X my suspicions would have been aroused regarding them, although I should have suspected not forgery, but theft. But his name, as I have suggested, is above reproach, and I had no reason to suppose that the books, which fetched very good prices, were anything other than the first editions they pretended to be. It was not until two years ago that any doubt about the authenticity of some of these books as first editions occurred to me. I was approached then by a Mr. Arthur Jebb——"

"Jebb!" cried Vicky, and the bookseller looked at her with his small, shrewd eyes, but made no comment.

"Not until then did I have any suspicion that I might have been an unwitting agent concerned in imposing frauds upon book collectors."

"And did you write to Mr. X?"

"I wrote to him two years ago—courteously, I hope. I put forward some of the observations which had been made to me—not, I may say, about *Passion and Repentance*, but about other books. I received no reply—and since then I have had no more of these first editions for sale."

"Have they gone to any other bookseller?"

"I do not think so. To all appearance," said the fat man slowly, "the supply has dried up."

Vicky had been afraid to speak, in case she earned another venomous glance from Basingstoke. Now she said, in a voice that had turned into an unhappy falsetto, "Why are you telling us all this?"

He moved enormous shoulders. "It is difficult to say. You may call it a salve to conscience. I have found Mr. Jebb rather—excitable, shall I say? in our correspondence. We have never met, but I understand he is writing a book and I think he suspects me of trying to obtain some of his ideas, so that I can write one myself."

Vicky pursued her remark. "If you think these things are forgeries, why don't you say so? Or why don't you force Mr. X to give you an explanation?"

"You are very beautiful," the bookseller said with a touch of exaggeration, "but very young. Why, after all, should I stir up muddy water? I should certainly be splashed. And in any case what would my word be worth against that of Mr. X?"

"What about this client who is prepared to pay a hundred and fifty pounds for a first edition?" Basingstoke asked.

"He is nothing more to me than a name—a name which I do not propose to reveal. I see no reason to suppose that he is anything other than a collector, who will pay a good price for what he wants."

"And you won't confirm any idea I may have of the identity of Mr. X?"

"You are persistent, sir." His great shoulders heaved again with silent laughter. "I hope it is in a worthy cause." The pudgy fingers were laboriously tracing outlines on a piece of paper. "I am sorry that I cannot accede to your request. I shall now leave you, to go and look after my twelve months. I shall not return for a few minutes, and during that time I shall expect you to make your departure. The outer key is a simple Yale." The piece of paper fluttered from his hands to the ground. He rose from his chair with an effort. "Miss Rawlings—if that is really your name—you have irradiated this gloomy room with sunshine. I must thank you for it. To you, sir, my respects. I wish you both luck in your quest." Slowly the fat man shuffled his bulk out of the door, and went down the passage. Vicky sat with her mouth open, looking after him, until Basingstoke said impatiently, "Come no." They stumbled through the outer shop, unlocked the door, and came out into the sunlight of a fine May evening.

"My goodness!" Vicky said. "What a horrible place—and what an awful man. Ugh—those cats."

"The eighteenth-century actor Lun," Basingstoke observed pontifically, "had twenty-seven cats with whom he drank tea. One ate toast from his mouth, and another licked his teacup." Vicky looked at him suspiciously, but he seemed perfectly serious.

"I don't know about that," she said, "but I know I felt all the time as if a goose was crawling over my grave. And how mean of him not to tell us the name of Mr. X."

"He did tell us the name," Basingstoke said. "He wrote it on that piece of paper, and then dropped the paper on the floor. I picked it up." He held it out to her, and she read, in a florid and straggly script, the name, *James Melton Cobb*.

WEDNESDAY

I

ON THE FOLLOWING morning, Victoria Rawlings dressed with more than her usual care in a red silk blouse, embroidered on its round collar and cuffs, and a short black pleated skirt. One of her habits was to talk to herself when she was alone, and she told herself, aloud, that she was dressing for Anthony. Then she muttered, "I think you know of two" in an unintentional parody of the threatening tone Basingstoke had used to the fat bookseller. Her thoughts rambled to Ruth Cleverly, and with a tolerably accurate mimicry she said savagely, "We ought to see Arthur in the morning."

That had been the sum total of the deliberations carried on from the time when Vicky and Basingstoke arrived back at Anthony's house, to find him sitting on the sofa with a bandage round his head drinking Bovril, while the little monkey-faced girl sat watching him. The idea of dinner had been abandoned, and they ate chicken sandwiches and exchanged stories, all of them talking at once and expounding their own theories. Out of the tangle of conversation two or three points emerged.

First, somebody was collecting, by orthodox methods when possible, and otherwise by force, copies of the first edition of *Passion and Repentance*. Basingstoke was inclined to think that two people were collecting the book, one forcibly and the other by paying cash, and that they were in competition; but this idea seemed to be negated by the fact that Anthony had remembered that one of his assailants on the Barnsfield Road—the one whose voice seemed familiar when he said, "I'll take 'im"—had been the little red-faced man who bid against him at the sale.

Second, the first edition was a forgery, and was probably one of a whole mass of forgeries. All of them were convinced of this, except Anthony; and he, fingering the bump on his head, reiterated that it was a queer kind of forgery that people were so anxious to obtain that they knocked you on the head to get it.

Third, Cobb must be asked to explain himself: The trails all led back to him. Vicky thought that he was obviously the forger. Miss Cleverly and Basingstoke found it hard to believe that such a famous scholar would stoop so low. Anthony did not express an opinion, but under pressure was persuaded to write a letter to Cobb, explaining that he had bought a copy of the book and had doubts of its authenticity, and asking for his advice. "I hope he doesn't ask me to produce the book," Anthony said wearily, and Ruth pointed out that if he did then that would at least give them a chance to see him and ask him questions.

Fourth, they must all go to see Arthur Jebb. "He said he knew who the forger was," Anthony observed, and Ruth nodded her monkey head. "Arthur's not reliable—he bound us to secrecy, but he's been in touch with almost everyone we've talked to. He believes it's Cobb, but I can't think he's right." Her face puckered up in a laugh—and Vicky, imitating it to herself, made a hideous grimace to the mirror—and she said, "I don't know what he'll think of you, Anthony, when he finds out that you've lost the book you wouldn't leave with him because you were afraid he'd steal it."

That was as far as they got. None of them could think of a reason that would prompt anyone to be so enthusiastically criminal in collecting these first editions, whether they were genuine or not. They spent some time in argument, and then Mr. Shelton came in and seemed, in his ironically courteous way, to be

pleased to see them. They told him a little of their
story, but he appeared only mildly interested, and
after a few minutes went to bed. Anthony recovered
sufficiently to be able to drive the Bentley. He drove
them all over to Vicky's house, and then (she
frowned) took Miss Cleverly on to the station. He
dropped John outside her house, too, and John had
recited one of his poems before saying good night.
She couldn't understand a word of it, but of course
didn't say so. She had come indoors at twenty-past
ten, and had written in her diary for an hour after
that.

"Vicky, Vicky." Her mother's head looked round
the corner of the door. "Anthony is waiting for you
downstairs, and so is that disagreeable young man.
Really it's all too much for me."

"Brush me at the back, will you? What's too
much?"

"The cook has given notice—she says there are too
many people giving orders in the kitchen. I'm sure I
never wanted to give orders," said Mrs. Rawlings
tearfully. "And Edward has been very disagreeable
about your taking the car. You were wise not to come
down to breakfast. He has been reading a new American textbook, and feels sure that I have stomach
ulcers."

"Tell him he is looking exceptionally pale—that
should upset him. Ring up the Labor Exchange
about the cook. I must go."

"But where are you off to? All this coming and
going is too much for me."

"I'm on the trail of the Rawlings forger," said
Vicky, and closed the door as her mother was asking
if they had found her gloves in the attic.

On the way up to London Vicky kept up a flow of
conversation which received little support from her
companions. Basingstoke sat in the back seat, and
seemed preoccupied. He wore the same shabby dark
suit, but had put on a clean shirt. Anthony was pale,

and said that he had slept badly. "I had a dream," he said. "And I never dream. It must have been that hit on the head." Vicky asked him to tell her the dream, and he did so, not turning to look at her, but keeping his gaze on the road ahead.

Anthony had dreamed that he was in an enormous room, and that something very important to him was at the other end of it. He tried to walk toward it, but made no progress. He could not understand why this was so, until he saw that the floor beneath him was moving as well, so that the greatest effort of which he was capable left him stationary.

"Like Alice in Wonderland," Vicky said, but Anthony seemed not to hear her.

In the meantime, he was aware that this thing of value was being carried further and further away from him. He increased his efforts to move forward, and—it was as though springs holding him to the ground had been released—found himself swimming gently through the air, a few inches from the ground. The object he was pursuing was at first a speck in the distance, but it gradually increased in size, and was revealed at last as a cloaked figure scuttling crabwise over the ground. The efforts that Anthony made now were prodigious, although they seemed not perceptibly to increase the speed of his motion. He felt the thudding of a heart, but it seemed to him, curiously, that the heart was not his own. He placed a hand upon the figure's shoulder, but it slid away from him like quicksilver, and the ensuing chase was complicated by the fact that it was governed by rules which Anthony did not understand, but which nevertheless he observed.

Vicky was bored. "What happened in the end?"

"That was the horrible thing." Anthony did not turn his gaze away from the road. "I caught the figure in the end, and took off the mask it was wearing so that I could see its face. And the face was my own, but it was all battered and bloody."

"Perhaps you should see a psychologist," Vicky said

hopefully. "I'm sure interest in cricket is a sign of fetishism."

They picked up Ruth Cleverly at her office. Even at this early hour in the morning her face was slightly smudged and dirty, and she looked rather like a schoolgirl playing truant as she ran down the steps. "I'm supposed to be seeing the printers. Henderson thinks we were convinced by snake Blackburn. He'd be furious if he knew I was off to see Arthur again."

Basingstoke roused himself. "Did you tell Jebb we were coming?"

She shook her head. "Better to call on him. He might be rude on the telephone."

There was an air of liveliness about Madderly Gardens this morning. Two motorcars were drawn up outside Number 18, and as Anthony brought the Bentley by their side Vicky said, "Look. There's a policeman."

Outside the door of Number 18 a blue-coated policeman was in fact standing. Ruth Cleverly ran up the worn steps and the man in blue said stolidly, "Yes, miss."

"I want to see Mr. Jebb."

"Yes, miss. Just wait a moment, will you?" He opened the door, spoke to someone inside, and came out again.

"What's happened?" Ruth asked shrilly. He made no reply. Anthony said, "Won't hurt you to answer a civil question will it, constable?"

"I've got my orders, sir." Ruth stamped her foot on the ground. The door opened again and a sergeant said, "Come in, please." As they went in they heard the sound of weeping. They went down the passage and were just about to enter the door to the left into Jebb's room when Ruth screamed and pointed to the room on the right. It was the kitchen and in it Mrs. Upton sat, crying drearily. In it also stood Jebb's wheel chair; and it was at the sight of this empty wheel chair that Ruth screamed and cried, "Where is he?" At that moment the door of Jebb's room opened, and a tall man with white hair stood in the doorway. He said, "If you mean Mr. Jebb, he is dead."

Ruth was still staring at the wheel chair. Anthony patted her clumsily on the shoulder. They went into the shabby room where Ruth and Anthony had seen the cripple on the previous day. "I am Inspector Wrax," the man with white hair said. "Are any of you related to Mr. Jebb?"

"None of us are relations," Ruth said. "I was a friend. None of the others knew him. He—had—a brother, I believe."

"His brother lives in Edinburgh, and has already been notified. Such formalities have received attention." He sat down in Jebb's chair and looked at them placidly. Ruth and Basingstoke spoke at once. Ruth said, "Where is he?" And Basingstoke, "Was it suicide?"

"His body has been removed, and he was murdered," Inspector Wrax said. "Why did you want to see him?"

There was a silence. Basingstoke said hesitantly, "That's rather a long story."

"We have all day."

They were silent again. Then Anthony took a breath and said, "Two days ago——"

Inspector Wrax listened without impatience to the stories which all four of them told. At last he said, "What time did you separate last night?"

"I drove Miss Cleverly to the station at Barnsfield," Anthony said, "and put her on the ten-thirty to London. Then I went home."

"Jebb was killed between eleven o'clock last night and two o'clock this morning," the white-haired man said pleasantly.

"Now look here, my man," said Anthony hotly. "You have no right to make insinuations of that kind."

"Keep your hair on, Mr. Shelton," the inspector

said. "And what beautiful golden hair it is, too. Which chair did you sit in yesterday morning?"

Anthony stared at him. "I can't see that it matters, but I sat in the one by the fireplace."

"It's very natural, then, that one or two golden hairs should be found upon the back of that chair, isn't it?" His voice became sharp. "It would be very curious, you'll agree, if they were found on any other chair in this room."

"Very curious," said Anthony boldly.

The inspector's eyes were dark and greedy. "What would you say if I told you that these were found on the chair in which I am sitting?" He took from an envelope two thin golden hairs.

"I should say it was damned nonsense," Anthony said.

The inspector laughed pleasantly. "I am happy to say that they were found in the chair you sat in, Mr. Shelton." He looked at the hairs in the envelope and said musingly, "I have known as small a thing as this hang a man. And now, since you have been so frank with me, let me be equally frank with you, and tell you some of the things you want to know."

Mrs. Upton, he told them, had come that morning at half-past eight, and had let herself in as usual. Sometimes Jebb got up early and made his own breakfast, but otherwise she knocked at the door of his bed-sitting room and asked him what he would like to eat. She did so this morning, and when she received no reply she opened the door. As soon as she did so she saw his body in the wheel chair, screamed, fainted—and called the police.

Investigation revealed that Jebb had been killed by several blows from some heavy object, which had broken his skull. They had no need to search for the heavy object; one of his crutches was lying on the floor, spattered with blood and brains. Since he was unable to rise from the wheel chair without crutches, the inspector pointed out, he would have been at the mercy of anyone who took them away. The murderer had ransacked the room and, as they could see for themselves, had done it thoroughly. He had lighted a fire in the grate and burned a considerable mass of paper, taking care to pound the ash to a pulp afterward. He had then, presumably, left the flat.

Questioning of the tenants in the other flats revealed nothing. They were all used as offices, and were empty at night. Medical evidence fixed the time of death between eleven o'clock at night and two in the morning. A telephone call had been made to Jebb's number just after eleven o'clock from a call box near Charing Cross.

Inspector Wrax stopped, and regarded them with a smile which somehow lacked benevolence. "Perhaps you think we have gathered rather little information. But we have grounds for believing that the murderer was a man known to Jebb, that he was right handed, and that the crime was unpremeditated.

"Consider, first, that eleven o'clock is a curious hour at which to pay a call. It's unlikely that Jebb would have made an appointment in advance for a meeting here at eleven o'clock at night. Probably the appointment was made through the telephone call from the murderer; and again we can assume that Jebb wouldn't ask somebody to come and see him at that hour unless he knew them. The murder was clearly unpremeditated, in view of the weapon used, and the direction of the blows indicates that they were struck by somebody right handed."

His greedy eyes moved to Vicky. "Did you say something, Miss Rawlings?"

Vicky's voice was a squeak, and she lowered it hastily. "I was only going to say that it might not have been someone he knew. Miss Cleverly here has told us"—she squeaked again and coughed—"that he was very keen about his book. Supposing whoever it was rang up and said they had some terribly important information about it—and supposing it was somebody Jebb knew by name—some famous person—he'd have seen him. Wouldn't he, Miss Cleverly?" She finished rather out of breath.

"I think he would," Ruth said. "Nothing else mattered except that book. He'd been so neglected, done so much hack work. He was so sure it would make him recognized as a fine scholar. And he meant to keep it a secret, but he talked about it to so many people. Poor Arthur." Two large tears rolled down her cheeks, and she blew her nose hard. The inspector watched her appreciatively.

"Are many of Jebb's papers missing?" Basingstoke asked.

"There are *no* papers connected with the book to which Miss Cleverly refers. Presumably they have all been destroyed. Or almost all." From his capacious inside pocket the inspector took yet another envelope, and extracted a sheet of blue paper from it. "I shall get myself into trouble for showing you all these things," he said amiably. "I'm too good natured. This was under the blotter on the desk."

"It's the kind of paper he made notes on for his book. He was always making notes," Ruth said.

"I see. This seems to be a note connected with your researches. It's a pity perhaps that his visitor wasn't five minutes later. This is what the note says:

MARTIN RAWLINGS

The case of the forged edition of *Passion and Repentance* (dated 1860) is in a different category from the other items. I am inclined to think that the secret here is not solely a matter of pecuniary gain. A study of . . .

It's a pity he didn't live long enough to say a study of what." His eyes were on Ruth as he added, "It's true that in a way this adds a spice of interest, for now we have to find out."

Ruth Cleverly sobbed and Anthony's fair face went very red. "Damn you, Inspector, how can you be so infernally callous? It's just a blasted game to you, isn't it?"

"You're very much concerned for Miss Cleverly. I thought you were engaged to Miss Rawlings?"

"You said that just to torment her, and you know it," Anthony cried. "Can't you see she's upset? Why don't you do something useful for a change, and get after the murderer?"

"Who is the murderer, Mr. Shelton?"

"Why, this chap Cobb, of course. It's as plain as a pikestaff."

"Isn't it obvious?" Vicky cried. "He knew that Jebb was going to expose him. Cobb's the forger, so he must be the murderer too."

"You have a straightforward mind, Miss Rawlings," the inspector said. "What do you think, Mr. Basingstoke?"

The side of Basingstoke's face twitched. "I suppose what you're getting at, Inspector, is that you haven't enough evidence."

"*Enough* evidence," the white-haired man said contemptuously. "I haven't any evidence. What does it amount to? You tell me a complicated story about a first edition which you think is forged, although apparently experts don't agree with you. You don't even possess the book, because it's been stolen from you. You tell me a story about a bookseller in Blackheath, which tells me no more than that the bookseller is eccentric. Miss Cleverly says that this man Jebb was preparing a book which would tell the story of a whole lot of forged first editions—and there is no sign of the book here. Everything you have told me may be true—but there is uncommonly little proof of it." He looked at them with a bright and frightening light in his greedy eyes. "What I am sure of on your own admission is your own connection with this man. That interests me profoundly."

"I say," Anthony said. "What's that?" He pointed to the blotter. "It wasn't there when we were here yesterday morning. I remember because I noticed him making that sketch of Ruth—Miss Cleverly—and the rest of the blotter was blank then." They crowded round to look. On the blotter was a firm pencil drawing of Ruth's head, encircled by what looked at first like a simple scroll, but was seen at second glance to be heads of corn. "Ruth amidst the alien corn," Basingstoke said. A little below and to the left of this was another drawing, a kind of medallion showing within it a face in profile, a remarkable, long-nosed intellectual face, with curling hair running back from a high forehead. "Portrait of the murderer," Basingstoke added.

The inspector raised his eyebrows, but made no other comment.

"Are you sure, Mr. Shelton, that this little sketch was not there yesterday morning?"

Anthony was dogged. "I tell you the blotter was blank until he began to draw on it."

"And none of you recognize it?" Nobody spoke.

The inspector put the sheet of blotting paper carefully into his briefcase. "The question is a formal one, but I suppose that you, Miss Rawlings, did not go out again after you went indoors. What time did you say that was?"

"Just before half-past ten. I went straight to my room."

"And to bed?" The inspector's little eye was predatory.

"I—why, no. I had some letters to write." She would not for the world have said that she was writing in her diary. Suppose he asked to see it—with such a man one really never knew!

"Letters?" His raised eyebrows and scornful glance made it clear that he thought she was lying, even before he said with an offensive drawl, "Rather late for writing letters, Miss Rawlings, wasn't it? I should have thought you would have been tired."

"I—I——"

For the first time since she had known him, Basingstoke appeared genuinely annoyed. "This is insufferable," he said sharply. "You've no need to answer him, Vicky."

Anthony and the inspector spoke at once, and then the inspector said, with his lips drawn up over his teeth in a snarl, "I am so sorry to have interrupted you, Mr. Shelton. Were you saying that Mr. Basingstoke should mind his own business? Do tell me."

Anthony muttered something inaudible, and the inspector resumed gratingly. "Passing over the subject of your letters, Miss Rawlings, which Mr. Basingstoke feels so strongly should not be disclosed, perhaps you would not mind telling me when you finally—um—turned out your light and sought repose?"

Vicky's mouth was open, and she closed it with an almost audible snap. She was both alarmed and confused. "About half-past eleven."

"So you were writing letters for an hour. What an interesting correspondent you must be, Miss Rawlings. And what about you, Mr. Basingstoke?" The inspector spoke deliberately. "You did not permit late hours to interfere with your—beauty sleep, I trust?"

In the dull flush of Basingstoke's face only his disfiguring scar stayed white, but when he spoke his voice was low and deliberately controlled. "I am staying in Barnsfield with my uncle. You heard when I left Miss Rawlings. I got indoors about half-past ten, talked to my uncle for half an hour, and went to bed."

"Where God, I trust, saw to it that you slept soundly after your busy day. And Mr. Shelton, you kindly saw Miss Cleverly to the train—did you wait to see her off, by the way?"

"Yes."

"I take it that you went straight home and to bed, and slept peacefully? What a blessing sleep is to be sure, knitting up the raveled sleeve of care as it does. But then you had no sleeve of care to be knitted, had you, but only a bump on the head to go down?"

"I felt all right." Anthony's brow was fiercely corrugated. "I drove straight home."

"Did anybody see you come in?"

"My father said good night to me when I was going upstairs."

"What time was that?"

"How the devil should I know? I don't look at my watch every five minutes. It was sometime round about eleven."

"Time, Time, how the spirit of youth denies you," the inspector said with unbearable archness. His voice was sharp again as he said, "Miss Cleverly, what time did your train reach Charing Cross?"

"Three minutes to eleven."

"A servant of Time's sickle, like myself. The telephone call made to Mr. Jebb from a call box near Charing Cross Station was, by an odd chance, made just after eleven o'clock. You are sure that you didn't make it?"

"Yes. I went straight home to Red Lion Street. I walked," she added suddenly. "It was a fine night. I wanted to think. I got in about half-past eleven, or just after."

Inspector Wrax shook his white head with a ghastly playfulness. "Nobody yet added a cubit to their stature by taking thought. But perhaps you did not wish to add a cubit to your stature. What were you thinking about?"

"Nothing to do with this case," she said, and blew her nose violently.

The inspector looked at them all deliberately. "I have no further questions for the moment. There will, of course, be an inquest. I will notify you if your single or collective presences are needed."

They looked at each other, and Basingstoke spoke for them all. "Look here, Inspector, aren't you going to see Cobb? You can easily check what that bookseller Jacobs told us. Surely he's your obvious suspect."

Inspector Wrax put his fingertips together, and stared at them from behind Jebb's desk with cool unfriendliness. "What is an obvious suspect? A police investigation involves the casting of an enormous net which gathers in all sorts of material. It includes such items as fingerprints, forged or genuine first editions, telephone calls, a hold-up on the Barnsfield Road, relatives in Edinburgh, and many other things. Those items are sifted. The probable is weighed against the possible. Some items are rejected, others appear more and more important as fresh evidence appears. Let us assume, for example, that our routine investigations reveal that Jebb left a considerable amount of money, that it was inherited by a near relative, and that this relative was seen entering this flat last night. It would then immediately become apparent that your adventures are a red herring."

"But that's all conjecture," Basingstoke protested. "We're presenting you with facts."

"So you tell me. But they exist only upon the evidence of your word, and if I choose to disbelieve them, they make *you*"—he jabbed forward a finger— "individually or collectively my suspects. I might, for instance, if I wished to be unfriendly, ask why you did not inform the police that you had been attacked and robbed, Mr. Shelton."

Anthony ran his hand through his hair, and winced. "Didn't want to seem a fool, I suppose."

"Perhaps. Or perhaps you have invented the whole story." They looked at him, startled. "If I may offer you a word of advice, my young friends, it is to abandon your search for this stolen first edition, and leave the police to their pedantic but effective investigations. The mills of God, you remember, ground slowly, but they ground exceeding small. Let the mills grind—or, not to lose our previous metaphor, let the net be gathered. And then when the right time comes we shall have the murderer"—he cupped his hands together, and a curiously complacent expression showed on his face—"like that."

Anthony and Vicky drove home in almost complete silence. Once or twice he turned to her, looked as if he were about to speak, and sighed heavily. Vicky also seemed absorbed by completely private thoughts. When they reached her home Anthony said, "Vicky, I must speak to you. Let's go into the garden."

The garden of the Rawlings' Edwardian Tudor house was neat and small. Behind a hedge at the bottom of the semicircular gravel path a rather uncomfortable garden seat was placed, hidden from the house. "Shall we sit down?" Anthony said, and she sat down obediently, like somebody in a dream. "What are you thinking about?"

She turned her dark eyes toward him, and seemed to bring him into focus. "I was thinking what I would buy if there were a reward offered for the murderer, and I won it."

"Really, Vicky, you're too callous for words. That poor little cripple battered to death like a fly——"

"You don't batter flies to death. You squash them."

"It's all the same. I think it's horribly callous. Look here, Vicky. I've got to talk to you." Anthony hesitated like a swimmer on the edge of the bath, and then plunged. "I want to play cricket this year." She made no reply, and he repeated, "I want to play cricket."

"Yes. Do you think something you said when you saw Jebb yesterday morning could have made him get in touch with the murderer? Perhaps some phrase you let drop. Can you remember what you said?" Her dark eyes were earnest.   .

Taking Vicky by the shoulders, he shook her vigorously. "Look here, old girl, wake up. You know you don't want me to play cricket. We agreed I shouldn't. Now I'm telling you I want to."

With a devastating return to rationality, she said coldly, "There's no need to shake me as if I were a doll. I suppose you mean you want to break off our engagement because of that sluttish little Cleverly girl with her dirty face and crafty ways."

"She's not crafty."

"She certainly is—and 1 shouldn't be at all surprised if she had a great deal to do with that attack on you—and with the murder. How did those people know you'd be going home by that road? Somebody told them."

"They'd probably been following me all day. But look here, old girl——"

"And I suppose it's a coincidence that she happened to be at Charing Cross at the time that telephone call was made." Vicky was magnificent. It was a scene for her diary. "Since you prefer a murderess to me, here is——" She stopped, remembering that she had neither ring nor book to return.

"I didn't mean that at all." Anthony was almost wailing.

"Then why did you say you were going to play cricket? You know I hate the beastly game. I had to play it at school."

"I don't believe you've ever seen a first-class match."

"Don't be ridiculous."

"And you talk about me, but what about you and that fellow Basingstoke? You seem to be jolly thick together.."

"We have artistic interests in common." Feet sounded on the path.

"*There* you are," said Mrs. Rawlings. "I saw the car outside and knew you must be somewhere about. You are naughty young things to hide yourselves on a love seat. Youth, youth," sighed Mrs. Rawlings, in a kind of unintentional parody of the inspector. "Rosewhite youth, passionate, pale—how does the song go? You'll come in and have a cup of tea, Anthony, won't you?"

"No, thank you, Mrs. Rawlings," Anthony said in a choking voice. "I must be going." The garden gate slammed behind him.

"The manners of the young are *not* improving," sighed Mrs. Rawlings. "Where has he gone?"

"Off to play cricket, I expect."

"Oh yes. But *need* he have been in such a hurry? How did you find the man you went to see this morning?"

"We didn't find him. He was dead."

"Was he really?" They walked across the lawn. "Well, in the midst of life, as they say. I rang up the Labor Exchange, and they are sending a new cook tomorrow."

As they reached the house the telephone bell was ringing.

III

Basingstoke had announced his intention of spending the afternoon at the British Museum, and had arranged to drink a cup of tea with Ruth Cleverly at a local café. As soon as she pushed open the swing door she saw his tall, untidy figure, with the disfiguring scar running across his face. He looked up with a smile.

"The only difference between the tea and coffee here is that one is brown and the other gray," he said. "You look as if you need a cup. It's so horrible that it will certainly drive other troubles out of your mind. What's the matter?"

Her lipstick was smudged. She gave him a watery smile. "Had a conference with Henderson all afternoon—planning books for winter. Very trying." She stopped, as though doubtful whether to go on, and then said, "Can't get poor Arthur out of my mind."

"Did you tell Henderson about it?"

"He wasn't much interested. Nobody will be." A tear dripped down her cheek and she pushed it away impatiently with a small, grubby hand. "Did you know him?"

"I met him once or twice at the *New Arts Magazine* office. He came in for some books."

"Poor Arthur. He was a good scholar, though nobody recognized it because he did so much hack work to keep himself alive. And now nobody ever will. It's a damned shame." She gulped a mouthful of liquid. "How did you get on at the B.M.?"

"I did a few odds and ends of research. There's a copy of our little pet edition of *Passion and Repentance* there. It's been presented to them—and can you guess who presented it? None other than our friend, James Melton Cobb."

Ruth smacked her small hand on the marble table top. "That damned inspector—I don't believe he took any notice at all of what we told him. Oh, why did God make policemen so stupid?"

"He's not stupid. I think he took a good deal of notice of what we said, or of what *you* said. After all, you were the only one of us who knew Jebb well, weren't you? And you *were* at Charing Cross when that telephone call was made."

She stared at him. "But that's damned silly. Why should I——? No, he can't think that. It's too ridiculous."

"You may be right. But why shouldn't we do something about Cobb ourselves?"

"Well—Anthony has written that letter. And everyone knows Cobb's eccentric and won't see anybody."

"He won't answer the letter, or he'll refuse to give any information. If we could see him we might do something. I have a plan." His thin face was eager as he bent over the table toward her, and she drew back involuntarily as she saw the thick whitish scar at close range. At once Basingstoke sat back in his chair, and Ruth, who prided herself upon a considerable sensitiveness to the feelings of others, cursed herself for clumsiness. With no perceptible change in his voice, Basingstoke went on: "I don't think we shall get to see Cobb by any ordinary means. We shall have to appeal to some special interest."

"But we don't know his interests."

"Simple enough to find out—with the aid of *Who's Who*. Do you play chess?"

"I know what the men are called." Her monkey face looked alarmed. "Why?"

"Because unless I'm much mistaken chess is Cobb's Achilles' heel. Listen to this—it's an extract from the piece about him in *Who's Who:*

> *Recreations.* Has found during a long life that most of the activities labeled "recreation" are infinitely less interesting than those characterized as "work." The single exception to this is the noble game of chess, of which he has been for years an enthusiastic but incompetent exponent.

That shows you," said Basingstoke parenthetically, "what a pompous old fool he is. Now, we know that he won't see anybody in the ordinary way, but he might see someone interested in chess. A reporter from *Chess News and Views,* who wanted to get an interview called, let's say, 'A Bibliophile Looks at Chess.' First of all a telephone call to make the appointment, with a delicate suggestion that *Chess News and Views* has heard of his interest in the game, and would very much like to have his views on it. Has the training in accurate examination of texts demanded by bibliography a value when carried over into the game of chess? Does he analyse the games of the great players as he analyses the structure of a book? And so on. I think he'll fall for it. Then, once past the barrier, face to face with the old rascal, it must surely be possible to get something out of him." He was glowing with enthusiasm. Ruth's face was screwed up thoughtfully.

"Suppose he won't speak to you when you ring up?"

"Then tell his secretary, and hang on for an answer."

"Suppose he says, 'All right. I'll send you an article.' "

"No good. We must have the personal touch. But there's nothing lost, even if he does refuse."

"No, I suppose not." She considered it again, looked at his delighted face, and gave him a reluctant smile. "I think it's a very good idea."

"That's the first time I've seen you smile today. You'll do it, then."

"*Me?*" She almost fell off her chair. "You didn't say anything about me. I thought you were going to do it."

He said dryly, "My appearance doesn't inspire confidence. And he's much more likely to talk to a woman than a man."

"Then why not Miss Rawlings?"

"She doesn't know anything about books."

"I don't know anything about chess."

"That isn't necessary," he countered impatiently. "I'll do the telephoning and arrange the appointment. Once you're in there's no point in keeping up the chess pretense for more than a couple of minutes. Then come straight out with the story of Jebb's murder, and ask if he won't help the cause of justice."

"Suppose he just turns me out?"

Basingstoke's face twitched slightly. "Don't expect that you'll be able to unveil him dramatically as the murderer. The point is this—we may be altogether up the wrong tree with Cobb. He may have some perfectly good and reasonable way of accounting for his connection with this book, and if that's so we ought to know it." She still looked doubtful. "What's the matter?"

"I don't know. All this is such—musical-comedy stuff. It seems so beastly to be doing it when Arthur's dead."

He pushed his cup away. It rattled a little as he did so. "All right. Don't do it if you don't want to. I thought Jebb was a friend of yours."

Her face was puckered in thought. "I'll do it."

Half an hour later Basingstoke telephoned her at

her office. His voice was gay. "It's all fixed for ten-thirty tomorrow morning. You're from *Chess News and Views*." She heard the glee in his voice as he said, "Do you think you'd like to wear a disguise?"

"Did you speak to Cobb himself?"

"I talked to his secretary first of all, then to Cobb. I must say he sounded rather quavery—not much like a murderer. But he's looking forward to your visit." He chuckled.

"What's the matter?"

"It's just that I said you'd watched all the important chess congresses of the last five years."

IV

Vicky crossed the hall to answer the telephone, feeling the curious foreboding of evil that had oppressed her at times ever since Uncle Jack had suggested calling in the police because of the theft of his book. It was an effort for her to lift up the receiver, and when she did so she was in some obscure way relieved to hear Uncle Jack's voice. But whose voice had she expected to hear, and what words would it have been saying?

"Hello, hello," said the voice. "Vicky. Thought you were going to keep in touch with me."

"Hello, Uncle Jack."

"Why didn't you tell me that chap Jebb had been killed? Never heard of such a thing in my life."

"I'm sorry—everything's been so confused. How did you know?" she said curiously. "Is it in the papers?"

"Know, indeed!" Uncle Jack's bellow was so furious that Vicky held the receiver away from her ear. "Just had a damned policeman to see me. Wax, or some such name."

"Wrax." The inspector had not told them that he might go down to see Uncle Jack. "Whatever did he want?"

"What *didn't* he want. Asked me a lot of damnfool questions about that book. Where was it? Who could have stolen it? All that stuff. Asked my housekeeper a lot of things too; good as called her a liar, and made her snivel. Nasty type. I didn't like him." Uncle Jack's bellow suddenly loudened. "I said to him, 'Look here, Inspector Wax or Waxy, or whatever your name is, do the Reds pay you to make servants cry?' That gave him something to think about."

"I'm glad you stood up for the servants."

The front door slammed. That would be Edward back from his rounds. Mrs. Rawlings had wandered into the kitchen, and now she wandered back. "Is that your uncle? If he's lost a servant, he should ring up the Labor Exchange."

"And how's young Sherlock what's-his-name?" asked Uncle Jack.

"He's all right. We think we know the forger's name. Who does the inspector think it is?"

"He suspects everybody, from me to old General Brett." An enormous sigh came over the telephone. "If I weren't an old man, I'd do some Sherlocking myself. Matter of fact, I've got a few ideas about this thing. How's your other young man—young Shelton? Waxy tells me his copy's been stolen too. You're a fine reporter, not telling your old uncle about that."

"Oh Lord, Uncle Jack, I *am* sorry. I simply forgot. Everything's happening so fast——" She thought of her quarrel with Anthony and found herself in a flood of unexpected tears. She hiccuped "Sorry" into the telephone, and wept into a handkerchief as she thought of the decisive click of the garden gate. A series of confused noises indicating distress came through the receiver. When she picked it up again Uncle Jack's voice was gentle.

"Look here, Vicky, don't let an old fool like me upset you." He paused, and then said, "Come out and have tea with me on Saturday, eh, my girl? Bring young Shelton and Sherlock too, if he's free. Give your old uncle a treat. Who knows—he may be able to help you."

"That would be lovely." She sniffed. "Don't take

any notice of me. I don't know why I'm crying. What about Mamma and brother Edward?"

"Oh, bring them by all means—if they care to come." There was a noticeable lack of warmth in Uncle Jack's tone. "But tell Edward not to say that I'm looking my age. May be true, but it ain't tactful. Good-by for now, my girl. Don't forget—Saturday."

"Good-by." Her mother called out from the drawing room and asked what Uncle Jack had wanted. Vicky said miserably, "He asked us all over to tea on Saturday."

"Can't go," said Edward immediately. "Can't leave the practice."

"Don't go, then," Vicky said. "I'm sure I don't care. He's asked Anthony and Basingstoke and all of us, but you needn't come if you don't want to. I don't think he particularly wants to see you."

Edward swallowed the last half of a bun in one gulp, ran his hand through his thinning hair, and assumed the anxious manner which patients found so unconvincing. "That's as may be, but I want to talk to you about something else, Vicky." He tapped the early edition of the evening paper at his side, and read, " 'Crippled Journalist Murdered. Mystery of Missing Papers.' You shouldn't have got mixed up in this disreputable affair."

"Oh, don't be such a fool, Edward. How could I help getting mixed up in it?"

"I am the head of the family now," said Edward. He got up and stood with his back to the empty fireplace, a man prematurely old with anxiety. "And I think you should pay my words the respect due to that position. You will remember that when the young man Basingstoke raised this whole question——"

"An odious young man," Mrs. Rawlings murmured, sipping her tea.

"—I was much against the idea of pursuing it. You insisted, however, on making these investigations. I don't suppose they will reveal anything at all, but if they do we can be sure it will be something undesirable. As a result of this nonsense, a man has been killed; there will be an inquest and a great deal of publicity." Edward drew himself up to his full height—he was not very tall—and said, "It will be bad for the practice."

The words "bad for the practice" were familiar. It had been bad for the practice when Vicky decided to attend art school, it was bad for the practice when she came home late from dances, it was bad for the practice when she was seen at work in the front garden. And these words, never pleasing to her ear, were altogether unbearable in her present mood.

"Bad for the practice," she cried at the top of her voice. "Damn you and your practice—if you were a better doctor you wouldn't have to worry so much about it."

Mrs. Rawlings put down her cup. "Pray don't scream so, Vicky. It goes through my head like a knife."

"You are overwrought," said Edward, slightly alarmed, but persistent. "Nevertheless, I shall say what I think it my duty to say, and leave you to reflect upon it. I do *not* think it desirable that there should be any more of this ridiculous detective work. The police should be left to deal with a matter which they can perfectly well handle. I must ask your assurance that there shall be no further attempts to anticipate police activities."

"You must, must you?" said Vicky. She advanced upon Edward threateningly. He tried to step back, but was prevented from doing so by the fender. He retreated toward the door. "You are overwrought," he repeated. He jumped out of the way just in time to miss the book that she aimed at his head, got out of the door, and closed it after him.

Mrs. Rawlings was unperturbed. "Now you've lost my place," she said.

Vicky stood for a moment with her arms swinging

loosely. Then she ran out of the room, up the stairs and into her bedroom, where she lay sobbing on the bed.

V

Anthony got into the Bentley and drove away from the Rawlings' house with a furious disregard for traffic conventions. He drove toward his own home, but changed his mind as he reached it, and went past the gateway. He needed action of some kind, he decided, but he found himself brooding instead on Vicky's conduct. Who would have thought that a girl would fly off the handle like that just because a chap wanted to play a bit of cricket? Was he to consider their engagement broken? And did he want it to be broken? Could it be that she was in love with that odious Basingstoke? "Damned unwashed artist," Anthony muttered, which was rather unfair, for Basingstoke, although he might be shabby, was certainly clean. And why the devil had the fellow ever been there to cause this trouble in the first place? Why couldn't it have been a straightforward gift from a chap to the girl he was in love with?

By an obscure process, his thoughts moved to Ruth Cleverly. *There* was a girl for you—clever and all that, but still understood that a chap might want to play cricket. Interested in the game herself, and knew something about it too. Couldn't compare with Vicky in looks, of course, but attractive in her own way, and seemed to like him. She'd been jolly sporting when he'd been knocked out—he certainly hadn't shown up very well over that. If only he had that same chance again—if only that little red-faced man came his way . . .

Anthony slowed down as he came into London. He still had no idea of what he should do, except that he might telephone Ruth, but driving and brooding had made him thirsty. He stopped outside the "Goat and Compasses" on Whitmore Street, and was just about to enter the Saloon Bar when he noticed a gray car drawn up a few yards down the street. He blinked and looked again. There could be no doubt about it. It was the car which had been used by the men who had knocked him out, and in the driver's seat was a figure wearing what looked like a very familiar bowler hat. As he watched, this figure got out of the car and went down a dark alley by the side of the "Goat and Compasses." Anthony watched him enter a door marked *Gentlemen,* flattened himself against the wall and waited until footsteps tapped again on the cobbles. Then he stepped out. It was the little man of the salesroom and the Barnsfield Road encounter. Anthony gripped him firmly by the collar, and a round red face glared up at him.

" 'Ere, 'ere," said the little man. "Whaddyer think you're doing? Let me go."

"Not likely. We're going to have a little talk."

"I could 'ave the police on to yer for this. Do you know what this is? It's assault."

"Nothing I'd like better," Anthony said. "Let's go and see Inspector Wrax now, shall we?"

With a brisk wriggle, the little man freed himself from Anthony's grip, gave him a well-placed and painful kick on the shin and darted down the alleyway. It would be too great an indignity, Anthony thought desperately, if the man escaped after being literally in his grasp. He made a Rugger tackle and brought the little man down with a crash on the cobbles. When they got up the man's face was streaming with blood, and Anthony was alarmed until he saw the cause of the trouble. The little man's nose was bleeding, and a few drops fell on his tight blue suit.

"You shouldn't 'a done that, mate," said the little man. "You might 'ave 'urt me bad. I never done you any 'arm." He noticed the drops of blood on his trousers, and added indignantly, "And look what you done to me suit. And me 'at." He picked up his bowler hat, and dusted it with his sleeve.

Anthony's look was fierce. "I know you. You were bidding against me at the book sale, and you were one of the gang of thugs who knocked me out on the Barnsfield Road. You can either talk to me or to the police—make up your mind which."

"Oh, all right," said the little man sulkily through the rather dirty handkerchief he was holding to his nose. "I knew it was a bleedin' silly idea to 'ave me in on that party yesterday. Let's 'ave a drink. And you needn't try to break my arm. I ain't going to run away."

Rather to his bewilderment, Anthony found himself following the little man into the empty public bar of the "Goat and Compasses." His companion sat down on a wooden bench and put his head back. "'Aven't got such a thing as a key to put down my back, I suppose? Stops the bleeding. Ask Jimmy be'ind the bar if 'e's got one. And I'll 'ave a large whisky."

Anthony's bewilderment increased. The situation seemed to have passed out of his control. The key was obtained and applied externally, the whisky was applied internally, and presently the bleeding stopped. The little man sighed. "I'm out of training, and that's a fact. Couple o' years ago you wouldn't 'a been able to bring me down like that, big though you are. Nice work, though," he said judicially. "S'pose they teach you that at the old public school playin' what'd'ye call it—Rugby football."

The conversation seemed to be moving on quite the wrong lines. "Look here," said Anthony desperately. "What's your name?"

"Call me Flash," said the little man easily. "'Cause me clothes are smart, see."

"Why did you rob me?"

"Damned if I know, mate. Did we pinch anything? I was only carrying out instructions, like I always do."

"What do you know about Jebb's murder?" Anthony said fiercely.

" 'Ere. Don't speak so loud. That's a nasty word. I never 'ad anything to do with that. Nothing like that for yours truly."

"Robbery with violence is one thing, I suppose, and murder is another," said Anthony sarcastically.

"You said it, chum." The little man straightened his dazzling tie. "What'll you 'ave? The same again?" He bought two more drinks, and while he was at the bar Anthony collected what seemed to be scattered wits. "Best of 'ealth," said the little man, raising his glass. He put it down in alarm as Anthony said, "I'm going to call the police."

"Don't do that, mate. Don't do that. Won't do you any good. I shan't say a bleedin' word to 'em. Whaddyer want to know?"

"Why were you bidding at the sale? Why did you rob me? What's this thing all about?"

The little man's piggy eyes looked at Anthony speculatively. "If I tell you about it, you won't call the cops?" Anthony nodded, against his better judgment. "I'll take the word of a gentleman for it," said the little man handsomely. He stared thoughtfully at his whisky, and began to talk.

"Well, I'm a member of an organization, see. What you might call a business concern, same as any other. I ain't sayin' what we does or what we don't do, but we 'andles pretty near anything, see. Some of what we do is legitimate, but sometimes we 'andles the other thing."

"Who's the head of this organization?"

"Ask old Wraxy—'e knows," said the little man unexpectedly. "Now, one of the jobs we was asked to do was to go to that sale and buy the book you got 'old of. We 'ad a commission like—see—from a client. Nothing wrong with that, is there?" he said rather defiantly.

"Who was the client?"

"I dunno. I ain't the boss—but I don't know if the boss knows, either. I think some bloke just gets on the wire and asks 'im to carry out these little jobs. Any-

way, I was told to go along to that there book sale
and bid up to a 'undred pounds for that book. Which
I did, and, 'avin' no instructions to go no 'igher, I
stopped there. But when I got back there was 'ell to
pay when this bloke rang up and talked to the boss."

"Are you sure it was a man who rang up?"

"I wasn't on the wire—'ow should I know?" the
little man said testily. "But the boss creates, and says I
ought to 'ave 'ad sense enough to go on bidding. So
then 'e says, ' 'E's making one more try to get it legit,
and if that won't do we'll 'ave to try the other way.'
And then the next day the boss says, 'All right. We're
going to get that book.' So we did."

Anthony pondered this story. "And where's my
book now?"

"You can search me. The boss sends 'em on and
——" He stopped, took off his bowler hat and wiped his
red, ridged forehead with a silk handkerchief. "I
don't know, chum. And I don't like you tryin' to mix
me up in any murder business, neither. I've 'ad noth-
in' to do with that, so 'elp me."

Anthony ruminated again. He felt a great surge of
indignation against the people who had stolen his
valuable book, and raised a lump on his head. "I
want you to take me to your boss," he said.

The little man looked at him openmouthed. "You
must be off your 'ead. What divvy will you get out o'
that?"

"I want that book back. You people have got to be
made to understand that you can't do things like this
in England, and get away with them," said Anthony
firmly.

Amazement, admiration, indignation and perplex-
ity were mixed in the little man's piggy stare. "All
right," he said. "Come on." He got up to go out, but
swayed, and clutched at Anthony. "Feel a bit faint,"
he muttered. Anthony lowered him, not very gently,
onto the wooden bench, and he sat for a moment
with closed eyes. "It's loss of blood," he said. "You
wouldn't think it, but I'm delicate. Anemic, the doc-

tor says." He led the way out into the street, but when Anthony moved to get into the Bentley the little man shook his head. "Better park that. I'll get the bird if I take a posh car like that down where we're going." With a mounting sense of adventure, Anthony put the Bentley in a car yard, and got into the front seat of the gray car. What would Vicky say if she could see him now.

They went through Holborn and down the Commercial Road, into a part of London that Anthony hardly knew, where women looked at them with hostility from open doors of houses, and children played ball in the gutters. A kind of hush prevailed in these streets, as though an inner, secret life persisted under more obvious activities. Was there something menacing about this hush? Anthony wondered for a moment, and then his spirits moved upward again in the excitement of the chase. "Don't suppose you come down 'ere much," said the little man, and when Anthony signified that he did not, added, "You're wise."

They turned off the East India Dock Road toward the river, and Anthony lost his sense of direction in the series of twists and turns which the little man executed. They passed through mean street after mean street, each one apparently a duplicate of the last. Finally the gray car came to rest in a cul-de-sac which seemed to be composed of deserted warehouses. "Here?" Anthony asked, and felt a twinge of misgiving.

"Rahnd the side," said the little man. He drove the car into the yard and pointed to some iron steps that ran up the side of the warehouse. They got out of the car. "Come on," said the little man again. Anthony clutched firmly the pipe in his pocket, which he intended to point as a revolver.

Their feet clattered on the iron steps, a door opened at the top of them and a thick, moronic face peered out. " 'Allo, Flash," said the face. "Oo's this?"

"Friend," the little man said briefly. "Where's the boss?" The door was opened wider, and they stepped inside. They were, Anthony supposed, somewhere above the warehouse. A dank smell was in the air. A naked electric lamp swayed slightly from a cord and revealed dirty and discolored walls and, above them, a great expanse of darkness. "Half a jiffy," said the little man, and opened a door in front of them. The moronic figure, who was perhaps six feet six inches in height, looked at Anthony, and Anthony looked back at him.

"Come on in and meet the boss," said the little man. He held open the door and, with a sense of disappointment, Anthony saw, sitting behind a desk, the youngish man with the thin, dark mustache who had accosted him on the Barnsfield Road. The man was smiling. "So you've found us out. Sorry for that bit of unpleasantness yesterday."

"I want my book back," said Anthony.

"Sorry. I haven't got it," said the youngish man. His smile did not change, but his eyes were watchful.

Anthony put his hand in his pocket. The pipe looked quite credibly like a revolver. "Put up your hands," he said. Neither of them moved. "Put up your hands," Anthony said again.

Half-pityingly, the little man said, "You ain't got a gun, chum. I frisked you while we was in the pub." Anthony had a premonition of danger. He swung round just in time to grapple with the vast, moronic figure who had come in after him. He ducked and heard the swish of air as a hamlike fist swung past, and then he was caught by the moron's rush. They were on the floor together, and he could smell the moron's sweet breath. He pushed the great, thick head backward and away, and then heard a voice say words that seemed to come out of another time, "I'll take 'im." Anthony moved up and away, but he was too late. A vivid flash of lightning seemed to split his skull, and then there was blankness.

THURSDAY

I

JAMES MELTON COBB was a man of legend. His exact
age, even, was unknown; for although in *Who's Who*
he obligingly gave details of his liking for chess, he
remained silent about the year of his birth. His
origins were obscure. It was rumored that his father
had been an artisan and that Cobb kept this fact
secret because he was ashamed of it. The first thing
publicly known of him was that in the eighteen-
sixties he had owned a bookshop; and it was assumed
that he had ridden to fortune on the crest of the
wave of interest in first editions that marked the
eighteen-eighties and nineties. He had been an in-
veterate correspondent with the great writers of the
time—Swinburne, Tennyson, Stevenson, Browning,
Henley, and others—and some of them had roundly
denounced as a public nuisance this figure who worried them about publication dates of their first editions, and asked for details of the exact form in which
their books had been bound. "This Cobb," wrote
Swinburne to a friend, "is one of those parasites who
pesters poets in our decadent day. Genius for them
shines with the glitter of gold, and they are making a
merry monetary meal off an art they cannot appreciate." But it is rarely that persistence goes unreward-
ed, and as the artists who despised him died Cobb
became recognized as an authority on their works in
that mysterious world where the worth of books is
estimated less by their contents than by their physical
condition, and their date of publication. He made bibliographical discoveries, and published notes about the

poets and prose writers whose calligraphic company he had assiduously courted. The impatience and indifference of those who had corresponded with him was forgotten, while the letters in which they had more or less patiently answered his queries remained. He amassed an enormous library of first editions (he ceased to be a bookseller in the eighteen-eighties), built a curious home for himself in Clapham Park to house it and became more and more a recluse, coming into public life only to snap occasionally in *The Times Literary Supplement* at the incorrect conclusions or assumptions of younger bibliographers, upon whom he bore down with the weight of one who had actually known the writers about whom they were speculating. His irascibility (which was said to be tempered occasionally by a surprising generosity), his dislike of interviewers, and his love of sweetmeats were all well known to Ruth Cleverly and many of her friends.

What would such a man expect a woman reporter from a chess paper to look like? Ruth felt that her appearance should surely be a little dowdy. Rising to what she conceived to be the spirit of the occasion, she put on old flat-heeled shoes and a pair of rimless glasses, fitted with plain glass, which she had worn in a school play, and screwed her hair into a bun. In spite of these precautions, she felt a little uneasy when she moved out of the neat, busy, comfortably suburban atmosphere of Streatham Hill into the wide and empty roads of Clapham Park. Her uneasiness was increased on first sight of the house which Cobb had built for himself and which, in memory of a great scholar of the past, he had called Selden Castle. Ruth had heard something about Selden Castle, but nevertheless was not fully prepared for what she saw.

It was indeed a castle that James Melton Cobb had built for himself in Clapham—but a castle that bore also many features of an ordinary suburban house. A crenelated outer wall had been built, but it was less than five feet high. The drawbridge entrance had been constructed to cross a moat not more than two feet wide. The house itself, built in gray stone, was a medley of gables rising from purposeless battlements on the sloping roof, casement windows alternating with diamond panes, and circular towers—one at each side of the house—topped by great figures of lions, griffins and hippogriffs. Ruth stared at the house over the stone parapet, and wondered seriously if Cobb was mad. Then she pulled a bell opposite the drawbridge (next to it, set in the wall, was a slot marked *Letters for Selden Castle*) and heard peals sound within the house. A man in green livery, wearing green hose and a green hat with a feather in it, came out of the house. He was a small sandy man, and as he looked at her across the moat through a grille in the drawbridge she repressed an inclination to laugh. It was all Dickensian, she thought, and when he said, "What name?" she was reminded strongly of *Great Expectations*. What would happen, she wondered for a moment, if she extended the fantasy and said, "Pumblechook"? Would Cobb turn out to be Miss Havisham? She pulled herself together and said instead, "Miss Evelyn, from *Chess News and Views*."

"Quite right," said the sandy man, following his Dickensian role. With creaking sounds the tiny drawbridge was lowered. Solemnly she stepped across it. "Follow me," said the sandy man, and she walked six steps over a lawn to the nail-studded front door. He preceded her into a small, windowless room with a stone floor. "I will tell the master that you are here," he said, and was gone. It was chilly in the little room, and Ruth Cleverly shivered. She walked round the room to look at the pictures that filled the walls, and saw with surprise that they were not pictures, but letters. "Dear Mr. Cobb," she read. "Your detailed inquiries flatter my vanity, but I am sorry that I cannot answer many of the questions you ask about my early books." She looked at the signature, "Tennyson," and, fascinated, passed on to the next letter, which was from Robert Browning. The next was from John Ruskin, and the next from Christina Rossetti. What kind of man was it, she wondered, who hung his walls with correspondence?

"Come this way," said the sandy man in green. She followed him down an uncarpeted stone-floored corridor. They turned a corner, and gargoyles grinned at her from the walls. She had a feeling that there was something wrong about their progress along the corridor. What was it? The man in green stepped a little mincingly two or three yards ahead of her, and Ruth suddenly realized that although two pairs of feet were walking along this stone corridor, only one pair—her own—was making any sound. The explanation was simple; the little man was wearing green rubber-soled plimsolls, as she saw now that she looked down at his feet. They stopped before another nail-studded door, and she saw that a knocker was fixed to it in the shape of a mailed fist. A thin voice said, "Come," when the man in green knocked. "Miss Evelyn, Master," he said, and closed the door.

Ruth had thought herself beyond astonishment, but still she was surprised by the room into which she now stepped, not because it was in any way remarkable, but because it formed such a strong contrast to the Gothic gloom out of which she had come. She found herself now in a typical Victorian parlor—so typical, indeed, that it might almost have come out of an exhibition. A dark floral paper covered the walls, a large picture of a Victorian family hung over the fireplace, two wing chairs faced a comfortable fire, china knickknacks and little tables stood about everywhere. Beyond these Victoriana, casement windows looked out onto a neat garden, in which a small fountain played. She had an impression for a moment that the room was empty; then a figure popped halfway up like a jack-in-the-box in one of the wing chairs. At the same time she noted with horror that a board with red and white ivory chessmen was standing on a bamboo table between the chairs. "Come and sit down, my dear Miss Evelyn," the jack-in-the-box figure piped reedily. "And forgive me if I come only halfway, as it were, to greet you. Even in this warm weather my rheumatism is so bad that I am unhappy unless I have a fire. I do hope that you will not find it intolerably hot. Permit me to say how pleased—and honored—I am by your visit."

Ruth sat in the other wing chair and looked at Mr. James Melton Cobb. She saw a man with a face like a walnut, wearing a high white collar that was a little too large for him, and an old-fashioned cutaway coat. On another table lay a thick malacca cane and a box of candies. The eminent bibliographer was obviously very old—he might have been any age between seventy and a hundred; it was also obvious from his smile that he was very pleased to see her. Ruth Cleverly suddenly felt ashamed of herself.

"You will do me the honor of joining me in a glass of wine?" He limped over to a mahogany sideboard with the aid of the malacca cane, and raised a cloth which uncovered a decanter with two glasses and a box of biscuits. "It is not often that I indulge myself with a glass of wine during the morning," he said chirpily. "But then it is rarely that I have such a charming guest. This is a particular occasion." The sherry was golden and Ruth, overwhelmed with contrition, drank. Obviously this harmless and physically feeble old Victorian gentleman who was so pleased to see a figure from the outer world had had nothing to do with the death of Arthur Jebb. His physique, for one thing, made it impossible that he could have killed Arthur. What a cruel trick they were playing on him! And then something, some sharpness in the look that the old gentleman gave her over the sherry glass brought Ruth Cleverly up with a shock. Could it be that he was really an excellent actor? She put down her glass and said, "It—it's a very interesting house you have here."

"Castle," corrected Mr. Cobb with slight emphasis. "I like to think that my home, although simple, is a castle, as should be that of every Englishman. And for *us*, of course, Miss Evelyn, the word has another very real significance, has it not?"

"Of course," said Ruth. She did not know what he was talking about.

"Or do you prefer the more modern term—rook?" Mr. Cobb asked. Again something in his manner struck Ruth as curious, but she had remembered that a rook, or castle, was a chess piece, and she simply nodded, smiled, and took out a notebook she had borrowed from the office in what she hoped was a businesslike way. She peered at her host through the plain glass spectacles. "How long have you lived here, Mr. Cobb?"

"Fifteen years," he said, and she wrote that down. "I built this place as a refuge from the world. I provided it with a shell of romance—something strange and Gothic, almost Byronic in feeling. But inside, in the heart of the place, I made it comfortable. It was my fancy to build a castle of which I could be king—where no pettifogging people I did not want to see should interfere with me. No reporters." He struck his stick sharply on the ground, and then smiled. "I make an exception in your case." He took one of the candies from the box by his side, and then as an afterthought offered them to her. She refused.

"I know you haven't given an interview to a reporter about your literary activities for a long time," she said. "But you are still carrying them on, aren't you?" He nodded. "Is there anything special that you are working on now?"

The knotted old hands picked a chocolate, and the mouth snapped it. He nodded again. Ruth asked boldly, "Are you working on these literary forgeries that everybody is talking about?"

There was a pause. The old, thin hand detached another piece of candy with a faint rustle of paper. The mouth closed on it decisively. "Shall we discuss chess?"

Ruth felt a slight sinking sensation in her stomach.

Would it be well to reveal her true identity now? Somehow it did not seem to her that the time was ripe for such a revelation. She heard herself saying something on the line of what Basingstoke had told her.

"I am flattered, most flattered," Cobb said in his thin voice. He took a gold half-hunter watch from a waistcoat pocket, snapped it open, looked at it, and returned it to his waistcoat. He drew the bamboo table with the chessmen on it near to him. "Since receiving the telephone call from your editor—it was your editor, was it not?" he asked, looking up at her sharply.

Had Basingstoke called himself the editor? She could not remember. "Yes," she said.

"Since receiving that telephone call, I have naturally given considerable thought to the matter of bibliophily in relation to chess. There are some peculiarly modern gambits which seem to me to require the same nice exactness of thought, the same following of minor points to their logical conclusion, that is needed by the ideal bibliographer." His mouth snapped on another chocolate. "Take that very modern gambit, the Allgaier, for instance. You know it, of course?" He did not wait for an answer, but began to move the pieces on the board rapidly. "Pawn to king four," he said. "Black replies pawn to king four. Pawn to queen four. Does black accept or decline? To the player of the Allgaier that is irrelevant. He advances pawn to king's knight three to free his bishop. The pattern is built up. Bishop to rook three, advance the knight, queen to king two—every piece must play its part, every contingency must be provided for." His hands fluttered over the board, moving the chessmen. "A bibliographical training has been invaluable to me in playing such a gambit as the Allgaier. Do I make myself clear, Miss Evelyn?"

Ruth sat as if petrified. "Quite clear." In the distance, very far away it seemed, a bell sounded. Cobb listened to it with his head slightly raised, like a dog. Another candy popped into his mouth.

"I thought so," said the old man. The expression on his face changed to a cold, hard stare. He levered himself slowly to his feet with the aid of his malacca cane, and then a sudden sweep of the cane sent the chessmen rolling on the ground. "The Allgaier gambit, my dear Miss Evelyn, is not a modern one, and is never used today—a fact which anyone interested in chess would know. Nor does it bear any resemblance to the farrago of nonsensical moves that I was showing you just now." Ruth sat staring up at him, speechless. "Nor does *Chess News and Views* acknowledge the existence of a Miss Evelyn upon its staff, as I discovered when I telephoned them after I had had the opportunity of reflecting on the curious reason for your interview mentioned by the accomplice who telephoned me. Whatever game the two of you are playing—you and the man who wrote to me called himself Shelton—it is up."

Ruth stood up. She talked desperately. "Look, Mr. Cobb, we've been foolish, I know, but I had to get in to see you about those forgeries. A man's been killed, Mr. Cobb—murdered—and the forgeries have something to do with it."

"Get out of here," shrieked the little man. "I'm not going to talk to you. Go back to wherever you came from, and tell them that you got no change out of James Cobb."

"Look here, Mr. Cobb——"

"Get out—get out, and look out for yourself when you're outside." He waved the malacca cane threateningly, and his eyes glinted with malice.

There was no help for it. Ruth retreated until she reached the door, opened it, and found herself looking at the mailed fist of the knocker. Disconsolately, with a sense of utter failure, she retraced her steps along the stone corridor. The gargoyles grinned at her again, and she was passing the door of the little waiting room when it opened. Two men stood looking at her without friendliness, and with complete astonishment she saw the dark, greedy eyes of Inspector Wrax, and by his side the waving gray hair of Michael Blackburn. The inspector and Blackburn seemed equally surprised to see her. As they stood staring at each other they heard three cracks, not loud but distinct, as if somebody were cracking a whip. Anger and surprise showed in the eyes of Inspector Wrax as he began to run along the corridor.

Cobb lay among his Victorian knickknacks, staring at the ceiling. He had knocked some of them off a table as he fell, and they were scattered on the floor around him. He had been shot three times, once through the neck and twice in the chest, at pointblank range. No gun was visible in the room. Inspector Wrax took in these details, telephoned to Scotland Yard, and then said grimly to Ruth, "Now let's hear what you have to say." The sandy man took them to the bibliographer's study, another Victorian room which contained a great many books, and a great deal of mahogany. In a daze, Ruth told her story. Blackburn listened to it with the air of amiable condescension that he had shown toward her in his own house. The inspector was less amiable. His manner was a mixture of ice and fire.

"Do you know what you are, Miss Cleverly, you and your friends? You are stupid, blundering, interfering idiots. I came here to get the answers to all your questions—and now perhaps we shall never know them." He stared at her. "And for God's sake take off those ridiculous spectacles. A child could see they're fitted with plain glass." Ruth took them off. "You may be interested to know that your friend Shelton was found in the early hours of this morning, knocked on the head and tied up, in an old warehouse near the docks. He met one of the gang who stole that book from him, and let himself be led down to the warehouse like a lamb to the slaughter, instead of getting in touch with us."

"Is he badly hurt?" she asked, alarmed.

"His skull's too thick," said the inspector unsympathetically. "But he's managed to give the gang good warning, so that they've now no doubt gone underground. You've stuck your nose in to queer our pitch with Cobb. I wonder what the other members of your quartet are doing," he said grimly.

"How did he die?" she asked timidly.

"Somebody came in through the garden, and shot him three times at close range. He was murdered."

"Then he didn't kill Arthur—Jebb?"

"It doesn't look like it, does it?" the inspector snapped.

"And he wasn't the forger?"

The inspector did not trouble to reply, and it was Blackburn who said in his beautifully modulated voice, "I for one have still to be convinced that any forgeries have been perpetrated, Miss Cleverly."

"Whoever killed Arthur Jebb apparently didn't agree with you."

Blackburn's broad shoulders were shrugged slightly. "As for the suggestion that poor Cobb was this hypothetical forger, it's really too ridiculous to contemplate."

A kind of whirling started in Ruth's head, and she gripped the sides of the chair to keep herself upright.

"It may interest you to know," said the inspector, "that when I telephoned Cobb this morning I hinted that the subject of literary forgeries might be raised, and he told me that he had deposited a full statement regarding them with his lawyer some time ago. Then I asked Mr. Blackburn to come along with me, so that I could have the benefit of his advice." He looked somewhere between Ruth and Blackburn as he said, "The evidence in the statement at Cobb's lawyers may well give us the name of the forger."

"If there was any forger," said Blackburn, and the inspector agreed politely: "If there was any forger."

Round and round went the whirlpool in Ruth's head. She started to say angrily, "Of course there was a forger," but somehow the words failed her. She seemed to move straight into the whirlpool.

The inspector was holding a glass of water to her mouth, and looking at her with no particular expression. Blackburn was rather feebly chafing one of her hands, which he relinquished as soon as he saw that her eyes were open. She struggled into a sitting position and saw her own face in a mirror with a shock. She had quite forgotten the hair which was screwed into a bun on the back of her head. "I'm awfully sorry," she said. "I don't know how I could have been so foolish."

"Mr. Blackburn," said the inspector, "would you be kind enough to see Miss Cleverly home."

"That's not necessary," she said quickly. "I can move under my own steam." Somehow the thought of being left alone with Blackburn alarmed her. She got up, and sat down again rather uncertainly.

The inspector continued as though she had not spoken. "I shall be busy here for the next hour or two, but I should like to see both of you at Scotland Yard this afternoon. Would three o'clock be convenient? Good. And you Miss Cleverly, are you likely to be in touch with your friend Mr.—ah—Basingstoke?"

"He's telephoning me," Ruth said in a small voice.

"Doubtless to discover the success of your masquerade," the inspector said with satisfaction. "Tell him that I shall be glad if he will favor us with his presence also." A man wearing a bowler hat put his head round the door. "Ah, Dr. McManus, all ready for you." He got up. "Three o'clock, then."

Dutifully, Ruth and Blackburn echoed, "Three o'clock."

II

A clock on the wall showed two minutes past three. They sat grouped in a semicircle. Uncle Jack was on the extreme left of it, then Vicky sat next to Basingstoke on one side, with Ruth on the other side of him. Anthony was next to Ruth, with Blackburn on the extreme right. Ruth's hair was now in its customary state of disorder, but she still looked pale. Anthony's head was swathed in bandages, and he did not exchange a glance with Vicky. Blackburn looked bored, Uncle Jack impatient, and Basingstoke rather nervous.

Sunlight filtered into the room from a window placed high in the wall, and lent Inspector Wrax a mellow look. He surveyed them all with an air of mild benevolence which had not characterized his previous dealings with them, and when he spoke his voice also seemed to have lost official harshness. A man sat in one corner of the room with a pencil in his hand and a notebook on his knee.

"I should like to say that I appreciate your presence here this afternoon on very short notice. I have asked you to come here because I will admit frankly that I'm puzzled. This case involves specialized knowledge of a kind that isn't, thank goodness, often needed here. We have our own experts on forgery, but the kind of forgery that we're considering is such a curious one that it comes into a special field of its own."

"If there has been any forgery," said Blackburn.

"I shall be coming to that point, Mr. Blackburn." The inspector's voice was as mild as milk. "I have asked you to come along because you are, of course, an expert on literary matters."

Ruth was something like her usual assertive self. She said sharply, "He's an essayist, not an authority on the authenticity of texts."

With overwhelming benevolence, the inspector said, "You will have a chance to deal with that point, Miss Cleverly, and I need hardly say that you also are present as an expert on literary matters. Mr. Basingstoke, too, a simple policeman must regard in that light in view of his ability to discover inaccuracies in publishers' names. Mr. Rawlings and Mr. Shelton, who have had books stolen from them, are naturally interested in getting back their property, and Miss Rawlings could hardly be omitted, in view of the detective work in which she had already indulged."

Detective work, Vicky thought, and a procession of phantoms—beautiful spies, amazingly handsome detectives, oily-skinned but attractive villains—moved across the screen of her mind, so that she forgot temporarily her misery about the quarrel with Anthony. *What are you putting into that envelope, Miss Rawlings?* And she replied: *The cigar ash that proves your guilt.* Vicky Rawlings, at the wheel of the great Hispano-Suiza, driving along the gleaming metal road. *We're gaining, Vicky, we're gaining.* Slowly the lights of the other car came back to them. Nearer, nearer, along the narrow mountain road—and then when they were almost level the other car, out of control, hurtled over the cliff, down and down—but not before she had caught sight of the driver's face. Oblivious to the inspector's remarks, Vicky sat with her mouth slightly open and stared at the bare buff wall.

"The activities of you four young people have also proved—if I may say so without offense—embarrassing to us," said the inspector amiably. "Yesterday Mr. Shelton met one of the members of the gang that had stolen his first edition—I should say alleged first edition," he added hurriedly. "Instead of getting in touch with us, he preferred to attempt to take on the whole gang single handed, and got knocked out. This morning, also, when I asked Mr. Cobb for an interview he told me that somebody had invented a pretext for seeing him. The somebody turned out to be Miss Cleverly, who, through a plan concocted by the ingenious Mr. Basingstoke, was seeking information. Cobb was murdered this morning, shot three times at close quarters by someone who entered his house through the garden." He picked up a number of photographs from the desk. "Look through these, Mr. Shelton, and tell me if you recognize any of them."

Anthony looked at them. "By Jove, yes. There's the little man who called himself Flash. And there's the chap with the mustache who stopped me in the road."

The inspector passed his second photograph to Ruth. She nodded. "That's the man."

"His real name is Billy Nugent, and he is known as Billy the Toff," said the inspector. "The little man uses a number of names, and one of them is Flash Dixon. I recognized them from your description, Mr. Shelton, and I already had a search out to pick them up. It is almost needless to say that, having been warned by your visit, they have gone into hiding. It may now be some time before we catch up with them." He smiled at them with false amiability.

Anthony tapped the photograph of Flash. "Could this gang have committed the murders?"

"No. Billy the Toff handles all sorts of jobs, including particularly smuggling and receiving stolen goods, but while he wouldn't object to a little strong-arm work, he'd draw the line a long way short of premeditated murder."

"But you told us Jebb's murder was unpremeditated," said Basingstoke.

"You're so sharp you'll cut yourself," said the inspector. "My basis for saying that was that it appeared one of Jebb's crutches had been used to kill him. That wasn't in fact the case. Dr. McManus tells me that another weapon was certainly used, and probably the crutch was used only to strike blows after death in order to make it appear that the murder was not premeditated. There are faint traces in the washbasin where the murderer washed the actual weapon—perhaps a walking stick or something like that—and presumably took it away with him." He looked at them. "If he is wise, he's probably burned it."

Uncle Jack was fidgeting. "Look here, man, you're talking as if one of *us* might be this criminal."

"Frankly, that seems to me very probable," the inspector said coolly. "Let me trace the course of events, and perhaps add a little to your knowledge. Some time last week a copy of *Passion and Repentance* was stolen from Mr. Rawlings' home. On Tuesday another copy of it was stolen from Mr. Shelton. But that is not all. Other copies of this book have been stolen. The number of copies printed is not known, but it must have been small. With the help of Mr. Blackburn, and through sales records, we have been able to trace ten of these copies. Of this number seven have been stolen during the past eighteen months. Two others, one of which was Mr. Blackburn's, have been sold."

There was silence in the room. Ruth looked intently at the inspector, Uncle Jack's face was red with suppressed curiosity, Anthony's face looked vacant below the bandages that swathed his head, Basingstoke's scar was twitching slightly, Vicky sat openmouthed. "We have learned all this in a day and a half," the inspector said with an air of mock modesty. "And our researches are far from complete. The copies in question, however, have been stolen in five cases from private owners, and in two cases from libraries. It is not, of course, difficult for anybody to walk out of a library with a small book in his pocket, but the thefts from private owners come into a different category. It is almost certain that these thefts were the work of Billy the Toff's gang." His voice took on a note of dulcet sweetness. "Perhaps now, Mr. Shelton, you will understand why I feel little sympathy for your misadventures. Billy the Toff was certainly acting for somebody, and you have delayed our chance of finding out the name of his client. In the meantime, I commend this fact to your attention. At least nine copies of *Passion and Repentance* have been stolen during the past two years. No copies of the other alleged forgeries have been stolen."

"How do you know the names of the other books?" Blackburn asked.

"The answer," said the inspector, "is to be found in

the document which Mr. Cobb left with his lawyer."
He smiled round at them, and his eyes were bright.

Anthony's head was buzzing. Why was there such
tenseness in the air? And why was the white-haired
man looking at them all so watchfully? Now he was
speaking again, softly, and his body was taut like that
of a cat about to spring. "This document purports to
give the name of the forger."

"Well, come on, man. Tell us who it was," said
Uncle Jack. "Don't sit there making a damned fiddle-
faddle of it."

"I propose to read you the document which Cobb
deposited with his lawyer on July 19, 1922, nearly two
years ago. But before I begin to read, let me ask if
any of you know the name of Leon Amberside."

Vicky, Uncle Jack and Anthony shook their heads.
Ruth said, "Just know it, but I don't know who he
was." Basingstoke said doubtfully, "Wasn't he a Victorian bookseller? But surely he died some years ago?"
Blackburn said nothing.

"Mr. Basingstoke is right, as he is so often right.
Leon Amberside was a Victorian bookseller, and he
died some years ago. Mr. Blackburn, can you add
anything to that?" He paused, and added, again with
elaborate mock modesty, "As I told you, I am fishing
in waters much too deep for poor policemen. You see
how much I need your assistance."

Michael Blackburn looked puzzled. "Yes; I know
quite a little about Leon Amberside. I don't see,
though, that it can possibly be relevant to your investigation."

"Tell us what you know, Mr. Blackburn."

"I knew Amberside personally—or at least I met
him once or twice—when I was a young man. He was
a rather shady, but in his way remarkable figure,"
said Blackburn thoughtfully. He seemed to be sum-
moning up ghosts out of the past. "I don't know what
his antecedents were, but in the eighteen-eighties he
made a splash as a bookseller—and also, incidentally,
in a small way as a publisher. He had two or three

bookshops in Central London—one in Piccadilly, I remember, and another in Chelsea—where he sold fine art books and first editions. He was one of the few booksellers of that time who specialized in first editions."

"And his publishing?"

"He published the works of young writers, little-known poets and novelists. He produced them very nicely, and had quite a success for some time. He dealt in erotica, too—modern and classical. He was prosecuted for the importation of indecent literature into this country, and it was discovered that he did a considerable trade in that way. He was fined a very large sum, had to sell the bookshops, and his literary career ended. I don't know much of his life after that, but I know he drank a great deal, and was very poor. He had an invalid wife, I remember. I should think he died about twenty years ago." Blackburn stopped, and looked at Inspector Wrax. "Cobb was very friendly with Amberside."

"Precisely. What a pleasure it is to have a literary man by one's side, able to evoke the past with such dramatic skill. Well, ladies and gentlemen, I do not propose to keep you in suspense any longer. According to the document that Cobb left with his lawyer the name of the forger is—Leon Amberside."

They looked at him incredulously, and then all spoke together.

"Stuff and nonsense," said Uncle Jack.

"It makes my head ache," said Anthony.

"Then who's stealing all these copies of *Passion and Repentance*?" asked Ruth.

"Does Cobb say that the things Jebb was investigating *are* forgeries?" Basingstoke wanted to know.

Then Vicky said with a rush: "I know, Inspector, I know. Amberside isn't dead at all. He's a presence moving amongst us." She looked round wide eyed. "*Amberside is in this room.*"

The inspector coughed. "Let us not place too much strain upon our imaginations. Leon Amberside, my dear Miss Rawlings, is certainly dead. But let me read you what Cobb wrote." They were silent as he picked up a sheaf of papers from his desk. He said dryly, "You literary people will appreciate this, I think. It's quite a little essay in its way. Remember the date of this document—July 19, 1922." He began to read:

Certain occurrences during the past six months make me think it is advisable for me to put on record now, as protection for myself, the full details of my acquaintance with Leon Amberside, and of the way in which I have fulfilled his deathbed request of me.

There will be few in this generation who remember this erratic and gifted man. I met him first when I was a little-known and lonely youth in London; and he, at that time a known and reputable literary figure, was kind to me. He invited me to several "At Homes," often asked me to dine with him (guessing shrewdly enough that I had few good dinners at that time) and frequently gave me small bibliographical commissions to execute for which I was paid extravagantly well. Amberside was indeed an attractive personality, generous and charming, and possessed by that real love for books which is found in very few people in any age; but he was indiscreet in his conduct with women (his wife, unfortunately, was a sufferer from infantile paralysis, and a permanent invalid), was an irregular but heavy drinker, and was fascinated by erotic literature, like so many other literary men of his age. Had he been satisfied, like them, to acquire a library of erotica, he might have come to no harm; but his tastes were expensive and always outran his income, and the secret sale of such literature offered rich rewards. He was prosecuted, heavily fined, and many of his books impounded; and this prosecution, combined with his many debts, ruined him financially and morally. He drank more heavily, and it was even said that he used drugs.

During the last years of his life our relationship gradually changed. Some fortunate bibliographical discoveries freed me from immediate pecuniary worries, and enabled me to give up my occupation as bookseller. As my own position improved, Amberside sunk lower and lower, maintaining himself by means into which his friends did not care to inquire too closely. We never lost touch altogether, and I did what I could to help him; but that was not very much, for he showed little gratitude to those who offered him the assistance which he seemed to regard as his right. His drink and his drugs and his women combined with this touchiness to estrange his friends from him.

I shall not easily forget the night on which I received a note from him, saying simply, *For God's sake, come.* An address in Holborn was scrawled above these words. I went there at once and found Amberside lying in bed in a filthy basement room, coughing blood, while his latest mistress sprawled in a chair blind drunk. It was typical of the other side of the man that he had rented a country cottage for his wife, saw to it that she had a nurse to look after her, and that she wanted for nothing; also that he paid for the education of his son. He saw his wife once a month, and on those visits he did not drink; but when he returned to London he went back to the life of debauchery that had gained a hold on him.

I saw at once that he was very ill, and I wanted to call a doctor. That, however, was not why he had sent for me. Between bursts of coughing blood he lay in that dirty bed with his eyes bright and his cheeks hollow, and told me what he wanted me to do.

He was dying penniless; but he had, he told me, one asset. Various little-known or unknown first editions of minor works by Victorian authors had come into his hands from time to time, and these first editions could provide a small income for his

wife, and also allow his son to finish his education
at a good school. He had several copies of most of
these books, and it would be foolish to flood the
market; they must be disposed of judicially, in ones
and twos. I was in a position, he said, to handle
these books for him, as a bibliographical authority.
Would I do it and send the money, anonymously, to
his wife, saying simply that it was money left in
trust for her own use and their son's education, by
her husband?

I felt that I could not refuse to undertake such a
commission. Perhaps I should have thought about
it more closely: but what man of heart would have
done so, sitting in that little room with a dying
man by his side, and a drunken trollop muttering
in one corner? My prime desire was to call a doctor
to see if he could be saved, and Amberside would
not let me do so until I had given him my promise.
Then he sank back in the bed and said, "Now I
can die in peace."

I called the doctor, but he could do nothing.
The bleeding was from an internal hemorrhage,
and it gradually lessened. I thought he might
recover, but the doctor shook his head. Amberside
asked for a priest—he was a Roman Catholic and
seemed satisfied when one came and gave him abso-
lution. I remained with him through the night. He
fell asleep, breathing at first in great gasps, but
then more easily. Just after half-past five I saw that
his eyes were open, and he was looking at me
curiously. He tried to speak, but a great fountain of
blood spurted from his mouth, and after one con-
vulsive heave he was dead. He was only forty-five
years old. He died on the morning of January 10,
1904.

The first editions he had referred to were stored
in a room Amberside had reserved for his use at a
firm of printers. I collected the books, and examined them at leisure. A complete list of them is
appended at the end of this statement. I saw that

they would indeed, as Amberside had suggested, be extremely valuable collectors' items if they were sold over a period of time, and I wrote anonymously to Mrs. Amberside to tell her that she could expect a minimum of two hundred pounds a year from a trust that her husband had left for her.

I wondered where Amberside had obtained these books, but no thought entered my mind that they could be anything other than what they pretended to be—genuine first editions. Amberside was a man with such a wide circle of acquaintances, and a man so well known in the book trade, that he would very naturally have been approached by anybody in possession of such a collection. Moreover, several of these books were already known—Amberside had placed them on the market in ones and twos during the preceding five years. I pondered over the best way to dispose of them. I was anxious to have no personal connection with the sale of the books, because of my former status as a bookseller, which, in my position as a bibliographical authority, was not a thing which I wished to be remembered. On the other hand, if I employed any well-known bookseller to dispose of them for me it was certain that before long rumors would go round the trade that I had a stock of various first editions. I should have found such a rumor highly distasteful, and it would have lowered the price of the books.

I compromised for a few months by giving a few books to various booksellers. Then I was put into touch with a certain Mr. Jacobs, a bookseller who traded under the name of Lewis, issued occasionally a small but select list and, I was assured, was absolutely to be relied on in confidential matters. From that time on I employed Jacobs, and found the arrangement a satisfactory one. Every three months I sent a substantial sum of money to Mrs. Amberside, and once or twice I visited her as a friend of her late husband. She wanted for nothing, and within the limits of her affliction she was contented. She was particularly pleased that her son, who was named Leon, like his father, was able to carry on his education.

This procedure continued for several years. A complete record of the books sold and of sums of money paid to Mrs. Amberside will be found appended to this statement. Like many chronic invalids, she lived for a long time, even though the last years of her life were marked by the tragic death of her son. He gallantly volunteered for service during the war, and was posted "Missing, believed killed" in 1916. Mrs. Amberside died two years later; and in a sense her death was a relief to me, not only because it relieved me of the burden of a heavy trust, but because for the last two or three years of her life it had been necessary for me to make up some of the money I sent her. The reason for this was that the number of what I may call "Amberside first editions" already on the market had caused a considerable drop in prices. When Mrs. Amberside died, I was some hundreds of pounds out of pocket because of the money I had sent her. It seemed to me then (and I must confess it seems to me still) that I had a moral right to recoup myself for this money from the remaining Amberside first editions. It is not for me, however, to debate this point of ethics, except to observe that I surely had a better title to the remaining books than anyone else. Young Leon Amberside was presumably dead, and the nearest relative was a very distant cousin. I am not concerned, however, to defend, but only to explain my conduct. I continued, after Mrs. Amberside's death, to dispose of these first editions through Jacobs.

In January of the present year, 1922, I was approached by a man named Jebb, who made certain allegations about the genuineness of several of these first editions, and asked if I could give him any information about them. He had been in touch with Jacobs, and asked him the source of his copies, and Jacobs, quite rightly, had refused to supply it. With singular pertinacity Jebb had also traced back some of the copies I had sold through other booksellers soon after Amberside's death, and he hinted, in a manner that I found altogether impertinet, that he thought I should make some explanation. Our correspondence was distinctly acrimonious, and it ended by my telling him that I did not recognize his authority to ask such questions.

Nonetheless, I was perturbed. In the course of our correspondence, Jebb gave me his reasons for believing that several of the Amberside first editions were forgeries. They were technical reasons connected with printing and paper, which I need not mention here in detail, but they seemed on examination to be exceedingly cogent. I was unable, also, to trace a single case in which an association copy of one of these books existed—that is, a copy given away, or inscribed, by the author. I was moved to a thorough examination of the Amberside first editions, guided by what Jebb had said. As a result of this investigation, I am now convinced that all, or almost all, of the Amberside first editions are forgeries.

Was I criminally careless in my failure to discover this before? I cannot think so. How could I imagine that such a man as Amberside would proceed to create a first edition by the simple expedient of having a book or pamphlet printed with an incorrect date, and with no publisher's name, or a false name, attached to it? The steps by which the man Jebb had been led to his conclusions are, indeed, more like those of a police detective or a laboratory chemist than of an accredited bibliographer. These vulgar investigations of type and paper are hardly a bibliographical task—although in the "scientific" world of the future toward which we seem to be moving the merits and demerits of

literature may well be established by subjecting it
to the scrutiny of an analytical chemist.

A fortnight ago I received another shock. Jacobs,
the bookseller, had, it seems, made some investigations of his own in the matter. He wrote to me,
hinting very crudely at some of Jebb's conclusions,
and suggesting that in any case any of the books I
had sent him were forgeries I should indemnify
him against possible complaint by his clients, and
loss of good will in his business, in the sum of
£250. He was not, he said, easy in his mind regarding the matter, and if he could not be indem-
nified, he felt that he should consult the police. In
other words—blackmail!

I am bound to say that Jacobs did not know his
man. I wrote him and said that I regarded his
letter as an attempt to obtain money by threats,
and that if I received any further communication
from him of a similar nature I should hand it to
the police myself. I have heard nothing more from
him, nor do I expect to do so.

But now I am faced with the question—what is to
be done? My own conscience is clear in the conviction that I have acted throughout like a man of
honor. But what course is open to me? If I make
known the full details of this transaction, I shall
disturb the market in first editions, I shall make
many people some hundreds of pounds poorer,
and—worst of all—I shall do a mortal disservice to
the memory of my friend, Leon Amberside. For
these reasons, and not because of any personal fear
of consequences, I have decided to remain silent.
On the other hand, even though I am still consid-
erably out of pocket, I cannot reconcile my conscience to the idea of marketing more of these
books. I have therefore destroyed this day the remainder of the stock of what I must now call the
Amberside forgeries.

I write this statement in case, at some future
time, the question of blackmail arises again, or the

egregious Jebb makes some public statement in the yellow press. I hope that nothing of the kind may happen, and that this document will be destroyed unopened at my death. I feel it necessary, however, to place on record this statement of my own actions and motives, and of the way in which I have discharged the trust placed in me by my friend Leon Amberside, when he died eighteen years ago.

JAMES MELTON COBB.

July 19, 1922

"There follows," said the inspector calmly, "a list of the books and pamphlets which he refers to as the Amberside forgeries, together with a collection of notes of sales of books from Jacobs and jottings by Cobb to the effect that he had withdrawn so much money from the bank on such and such a date, and sent it to Mrs. Amberside. He has kept the registration slips to Mrs. Amberside, but, without research into Cobb's banking account, which we haven't yet had time to undertake, it isn't possible to confirm that part of his story. The question of money, could however, have been checked easily if Cobb were alive—and since he made this statement to protect himself I think we can be quite sure that he did send money to Mrs. Amberside. And now I shall be happy to have your reactions."

"Dammit, man," said Uncle Jack, "I can't see what you wanted to have this long powwow for. If this chap Amberside was the forger, that clears up the whole thing, doesn't it?" He beamed round on them, and then said, "Except where my damn book is, of course."

"There is a matter of two murders, Mr. Rawlings," said the inspector, and Uncle Jack gasped.

"By Jove! So there is. Completely forgotten about those. Seems to me the murders and forgeries must be damn well separate. Nothing to do with each other. How's that, eh?"

"Rather a coincidence that one of the murdered

men was on the track of these forgeries, and that the other was putting them out."

"I dare say you're right," Uncle Jack agreed cheerfully. "What's young Sherlock got to say?"

Basingstoke said in his rich voice, "Since you've gathered us all together, Inspector, you presumably want us to talk." The inspector's small dark eyes stared at Basingstoke. He said nothing. "Can we be sure that this statement is genuine—I mean that it *was* deposited with Cobb's lawyer nearly two years ago?"

"No doubt about that. He's a most respectable solicitor, and certainly wouldn't be a party to any crooked business."

"Grant that, and even so we have nothing more than Cobb's word for believing that it's true. There's a smarmy righteousness about the whole statement that's very objectionable. Why shouldn't Cobb have been the forger himself, faking up this story in his own defense?"

"You forget that he made payments to Mrs. Amberside. There's no doubt about those, although, of course, Cobb may have been lining his own pocket at the same time. Cobb and Amberside may have been engaged in the forgeries together."

"That's possible," said Basingstoke with apparent reluctance. His scar was twitching slightly. "Another point—what about the bookseller Jacobs. What's his answer to the charge of blackmail?"

"He denies it, of course. Hardly likely that he would do anything else. He told me precisely the story he told you and without documentation we can't disprove it. He refuses outright to give the name of the man for whom he was acting in buying *Passion and Repentance*."

"Don't see we're any further on," Ruth Cleverly said. "Except that poor Arthur was right. This all seems a red herring—may be true, may be false."

The inspector transferred the stare of his hot eyes to her. "I don't think we can say that. You're expressing doubts because some of the things that Cobb said can't be proved. But that's only because he's dead, and there's no doubt Cobb made this statement for his own protection *while he was alive.* In fact, he was going to produce it to me. I don't say every word of it is true, but I do say that he was convinced he could use it to protect himself."

Vicky came out of the cloud of fictitious events in which she had been immersed, to a recognition of her responsibilities as a member of the Rawlings family. "I suppose Grandpa Martin's book *is* mentioned in that list of forgeries attached to Cobb's statement?"

Inspector Wrax looked like a cat that sees a mouse emerge from its hole. "The list of books attached by Cobb as the Amberside forgeries includes some thirty-five works by Victorian authors. *Passion and Repentance* is not among them."

They stared at him. "But—but that's impossible," said Basingstoke.

"Not impossible," Ruth said. "The old rat left it off for reasons of his own."

Michael Blackburn stood up. His anger was a little theatrical, but fine. "I am not prepared to stay here and listen to the memory of my dead friend being traduced." He stopped, uncomfortably aware of the inspector's inimical eye.

Very gently, the inspector said, "I think you'd better sit down, Mr. Blackburn. I told you that I should have something to say about the question of forgery, didn't I?" Blackburn sat down. "*Passion and Repentance* is not on the list of what Cobb calls the Amberside first editions, but nonetheless it is a forgery. Don't get up, Mr. Blackburn. You can talk when I've finished. As I told you, we're a little out of our depth in specialized matters of this kind, but we can still keep our heads above water. I have had the 1860 edition of *Passion and Repentance* which was in the British Museum examined by experts——"

"What experts?" Blackburn asked sharply.

"Paper experts. Most of the things that Jebb told

these young people struck me as highly disputable, but one thing he talked about seemed to afford a fair test, and that was the question of paper. The experts who have examined this 1860 edition are prepared to stand up in court and testify that the paper used in it was a mixture of esparto grass and chemical wood. Now, since chemical wood wasn't used before 1874, that proves, to the satisfaction of a simple chap like myself, that this edition of *Passion and Repentance wasn't* printed in 1860. In other words, it's a bibliographical forgery."

They sat silent. Then Blackburn muttered something inaudible. Basingstoke tilted his chair back and said, "Now we know, then. But when you've got it, what have you got? What does it mean?"

"I hoped you would be able to tell me that. What? Has nobody got anything to say? Mr. Shelton, not upset, about the loss of your hundred guineas? Miss Rawlings, no more bright ideas? Mr. Rawlings, have I stirred no childhood recollections?"

Uncle Jack said impatiently, "I told you I can't remember my father talking about it. What more do you expect me to say, man?"

Blackburn seemed the most surprised of them. "But what about James Cobb's authentication of the book— that story he told me?"

"Ah, what indeed!" said the inspector. He waited for them, but nobody spoke. He stood up. "Perhaps I have given you enough to think about. If nobody has anything to tell me"—nobody had—"the meeting is adjourned."

When they had gone Inspector Wrax sat looking thoughtfully at the calendar on his desk, and then picked up a telephone and asked for Sergeant Thynne. "Any news from Italy, Sergeant?" he asked, and frowned at the sound of the sergeant's squeaky voice. The voice sounded not only squeaky, but injured. "Only negative, sir. They're doing their best, but it's not an easy job you know, getting information that——"

He cut short the flow. "Any link with Cobb? Or any trace of a man leaving Cobb's house?"

"No, sir. He was lucky; nobody seems to have seen him."

"Billy the Toff?"

"Give us a chance. We've only had it a few hours."

"Jacobs?"

The sergeant brightened. "Got a clean bill of health for the last twenty years. Been a bookseller all that time. Can't trace him back before that, some say he came to England from overseas."

"Keep at it. Let me know as soon as you get anything, and don't wait for confirmation. I want the news as soon as you get it."

"Yes, sir." Sergeant Thynne ended on a squeak. Inspector Wrax sighed and ruffled his fine white hair. Then he pulled a pad toward him and began to write.

III

That evening John Basingstoke went to see a young friend who lived in Pimlico, in one of the many once-fashionable but now seedy streets that shoot off from the main stem of Warwick Street. The young man lived in a vast dungeon-like basement room at the bottom of a big black Victorian house. The room was windowless, and extremely high; it received light through a large glass skylight which extended beyond the back of the house, and was protected by wire netting against the stones and sticks of small boys passing by. This room, which contained a bed, four chairs, a table, a cupboard, and some books, was kept by the young man with quite extraordinary neatness. He was a common law clerk in a lawyer's office, but his interest in criminology extended far beyond his routine visits to the courts and the uninteresting statements that he took from bored witnesses. It was this interest that brought Basingstoke down the winding area steps to see him tonight.

The two young men had met (although "young" is perhaps too inclusive a word to apply to both of them indiscriminately, for Basingstoke, who was in his late twenties, judged himself to be at least five years the older of the two) in a public library where their hands reached for *The Trials of Neill Cream* at the same time. They passed to conversation, and Basingstoke was struck by some quality in the young man's mind, perhaps his obvious persistence in working toward any given end, or an unspoken assurance of his own ability, or a depth of reserve in his nature. Such qualities fascinated Basingstoke by their very unlikeness to his own character and outlook, and the two became acquaintances, if not friends. Basingstoke showed the young man his poems, and was surprised by the penetrative power of the criticism offered by one who had, as he confessed, no particular interest in poetry. It became his habit to call on the young man once a week, and to discuss with him many subjects, generally connected with current crime. Very often the young man had an explanation to offer of a criminal case of the day which seemed to Basingstoke ingenious, though generally it also seemed to him farfetched. It was in the hope of being given some plausible explanation of events which he found in many respects puzzling that Basingstoke called on his young friend this Thursday night.

Basingstoke found his friend eating a frugal supper of soup, made from the stock of mutton bones, followed by a salad with Brie cheese. He refused an invitation to join this repast, and while the young man drank two bowls of soup and ate bread and cheese and salad, Basingstoke recounted to him the remarkable events of the past four days. While Basingstoke talked, his young friend's eyes rarely left his face. They were eyes of a rather bright blue, and they enhanced the slight babyishness of the young man's smooth face, rosy cheeks, and carefully brushed fair hair. The eyes watched Basingstoke during most of his recital, and he was disconcerted, as he had sometimes been before, by something impersonal in their scrutiny.

When Basingstoke had finished talking, and had accepted a cup of coffee, the young man spoke.

"Interesting. I'd seen about Cobb in tonight's paper, but there's nothing to link it with the other business." He smiled, revealing very white and even teeth, and seemed to wait for his visitor to speak.

"There's one feature of this affair which nobody seems to have remarked but me." The young man looked politely curious. "I seem to be responsible for it all, in a way. *I* pointed out with my infernal knowingness that error in the publisher's name. *I* took them up to see Henderson the next morning. *I* made that ridiculous arrangement for Ruth Cleverly to see Cobb. My wretched curiosity seems to have been the moving factor in the whole thing. And yet, when I work it out, I can't see any chain of cause and effect. It's as though I'd put in hand without knowing it some criminal jaggernaut, and now I'm seeing it at work. I can tell you it's not pleasant."

"I don't suppose so." There was something impersonal about the young man's voice, as well as his blue eyes. "It does all seem to have started when you made that observation about the pamphlet being a forgery, doesn't it? And yet that can't really be so, because this man Jebb was already on the trail of literary forgeries, and had been writing round for a year or two about them to various people." Before Basingstoke could speak, the young man continued, in the kind of argument with himself which Basingstoke had seen him carry on before: "Wait a minute, though. You say *Passion and Repentance* wasn't on the list of Jebb's forgeries."

"Not according to Ruth Cleverly, who saw him. Jebb thought, from its appearance, that it was a forgery, but as I told you he said it wasn't from the same type fount as the others."

"And it wasn't included in the list that Cobb left."

"No. That's the extraordinary thing. If Cobb was the forger, the whole thing's crazy, because the murders were obviously committed to preserve the forger's secret. And if Cobb wasn't the forger, then it's even crazier."

"Not necessarily. I think it makes sense of a sort. But let's run over the course of events." He took a piece of paper, wrote for five minutes in a neat hand, and passed the paper to Basingstoke, who read:

Chronology

Last week. Presentation copy of *Passion and Repentance* stolen from Rawlings.

Monday. Shelton buys copy (not presentation) at sale. Basingstoke suggests it is a forgery.

Tuesday. Jebb confirms Basingstoke's view. Blackburn refutes it. Jacobs (bookseller) says that Cobb was the source of copies.

Wednesday. Jebb is found murdered. Leaves note about *Passion and Repentance* on his desk.

Thursday. Cobb is murdered. Leaves document revealing that Victorian bookseller Amberside was forger of many first editions (but does *not* mention *Passion and Repentance*).

That leaves out the thefts of copies of the book that have been taking place over the past two years. Does it seem a fair statement otherwise?"

Still studying his friend's handwriting with a frown, Basingstoke said, "Yes. But I don't see that it's any help."

"There are two or three suggestive points, but one thing stands out like a sore thumb."

"What's that?"

"*Passion and Repentance* isn't connected with the other forgeries."

"My dear chap." Basingstoke began to laugh, but was checked by his friend's cherubic seriousness.

"I will go further, and say that the murders were probably committed, indirectly, to conceal that fact. Consider what Jebb said. All of the other forgeries were printed from the same type fount, a fount different from that of the forged edition of *Passion and Repentance*. Isn't that suggestive? Isn't it suggestive, too, that copies of this edition of *Passion and Repentance*—but not of the Amberside forgeries—have been stolen from libraries and private houses? And isn't the simple and obvious explanation why Cobb left it off his list just that it didn't belong there, and that he never thought of it as a forgery?"

"What about the bookseller? He said the copies he sold came from Cobb."

"Perhaps they did—and their source is an entirely different one from that of the Amberside forgeries. Perhaps Cobb would have revealed that source, and that's why he was killed. Or the bookseller may be lying. But it's obviously a crucial point. Since your devouring curiosity has taken you this far, why not let it take you a bit further, and go and see the bookseller again tomorrow morning?"

"All right." The scar in Basingstoke's face was twitching. "But what could the motive possibly be?"

"That's obvious, too, in general though not in particular. It must be something connected with the Rawlings family."

"It could be, I suppose," said Basingstoke slowly. "Yes, by God, it could." Basingstoke's young friend watched with some amusement his growing enthusiasm. "Look here. What about this? There's an important secret hidden in just *one* copy of the book. That's why all the copies are being stolen—because whoever's after it doesn't know which copy it is. Hence the thefts. It must be something really rich and romantic, like a secret code. Jebb and Cobb were killed because they knew the secret, or were just about to guess it. Doesn't that seem plausible? But what can the secret be?" He got up and began to walk about the huge room, while the young man sat placidly at the table, turning a slightly ironical glance upon his excitable friend. "What about this? Old Martin got rich through an Australian cousin leaving him money. Until that happened he hadn't much, had he? Supposing that Australian cousin had a nearer relative who should really have inherited?"

"He could have gone to law about it."

"Then under English law he wouldn't inherit, anyway. And I don't see how you can tie all that up with the thefts of the book."

"A secret code—code making a will leaving someone else the money," said Basingstoke hopefully, and laughed as he saw his friend's face. "Don't you think I've got something, though?"

"Perhaps. You realize that if what you say is anything like right, Rawlings may be in danger?"

"Cæsar Rawlings? Or Edward?"

"Cæsar. If there's someone who is the rightful heir to the Rawlings estate—or who believes he is, which for our purposes comes to the same thing—he'll presumably be concerned to dispossess the present incumbent, by any means." He paused, and added thoughtfully, "Short of murder."

"Why short of murder? I should have thought murder——"

The young man's rosy face showed a trace of impatience. "No, no. A fine thing it would be to have the man in possession murdered and then, in a couple of weeks' time, Mr. Y. turning up, saying, 'I am the heir.' It would arouse suspicion at once. How much is the estate worth, by the way?"

"Vicky—Victoria Rawlings—says something near a hundred thousand pounds."

The young man's lips puckered in a noiseless whistle. "And who's the heir to it all?"

"Nothing there, I'm afraid. Uncle Jack has a son named Philip, who'll inherit."

The young man seemed gravely to contemplate the

possibility of Philip Rawlings' involvement. Then he cleared away the supper plates from the table and rinsed them under a tap in a little kitchenette. "We may be altogether wrong. I should like to know the meaning of that drawing Jebb made on his blotter." His voice trailed away, and when he spoke again it was on an apparently unrelated subject. "Has anybody studied the text of *Passion and Repentance?*"

With his face distorted in laughter, Basingstoke slapped his knee. "I wondered when you'd think of that. I've been doing that very thing, at odd times for the past day and a half. I can't help feeling there must be a secret in those damned poems or somebody wouldn't be so keen to get hold of them. I must have read those forty sonnets a dozen times, and I've compared the text in the British Museum copy, which is the 1860 edition, with the standard one which appeared in 1868. They're identical. And all anybody can get out of the poems themselves, it seems to me, is that the first twenty are full of blood and lust concealed in decent Victorian metaphor, and the last twenty are rather sickly and repentant. Of course, if there's a secret hidden in one single copy it wouldn't be revealed in the text."

The two men sat silent, one untidy, dark and eager, the other neat, blond and placid. A moth whirred round the naked electric lamp high above the table. Outside in the street they could hear the tread of passing feet, and the indistinct sound of voices. "What did that drawing look like?" the young man asked, and Basingstoke sketched roughly on a piece of paper the man's profile, enclosed in a kind of medallion. The young man studied it.

"It *doesn't* look like anyone involved in the case?"

Basingstoke shook his head, and said facetiously, "Perhaps it's the missing heir."

"Perhaps."

"I seem to have set you thinking." Basingstoke got up to go.

The young man smiled a little apologetically. "I've

never seen crime at such close quarters before. It fascinates me. Do let me know any further developments. I really have got some ideas, if I can sort them out."

"You've put some into my head too. I'll see that bookseller again in the morning, and let you know what happens."

The last thing Basingstoke saw before he closed the door of the basement dungeon and ran up the area steps was his friend's young blond head bent over the sketch he had made of the drawing left on Jebb's blotter.

IV

With the marks of tears dried on her face, Vicky Rawlings sat at her writing desk that Thursday evening, writing in her big red book.

The misery I've suffered, dear diary, these past twenty-four hours, is something that can't be put down but only experienced. I read somewhere, not long ago, that the degrees of misery and happiness are the same for everybody—that one person gets the same feeling out of listening to vulgar Mendelssohn that I do out of hearing exquisite Beethoven, and that a shop girl who has a row with her young man suffers just as much as George Sand in her love for Chopin. Well, *I just don't believe that's true.* It simply can't be true. I *can't express* how miserable I've been since I had that row with Anthony.

Of course, one doesn't *show* these things as a shop girl would, no doubt. Outside I've been as cold as ice—or I hope I have—but inside, what a raging fire! Don't tell me that any shop girl could have felt the same thing. And *he*, at the conference called by that beastly inspector, he was really like a dummy in the chair, with his silly head all swathed in bandages. I don't believe there are any feelings under that hard head. Oh, I could have *wept*! In fact I simply ignored him, but it was humiliating that he should ignore *me*. I thought when it all ended he would be certain to talk to me, but instead he was buttonholed by Uncle Jack and talked to him in a nasty, sly way. I don't know what it was all about, but they both seemed very pleased with themselves. I just left, without looking back. When I see Uncle Jack, I shall give him a piece of my mind.

To think that all this can happen over such a thing as *cricket*—that cricket can ruin two people's lives. It does really seem wicked that such a thing can be—and shall I confess to you, dear diary, what I would never admit to anyone—that I have never *seen* a big cricket match—though, of course, I played the wretched game at school. I simply feel that it is a wretched, common game, and my feelings are never wrong. Sensitiveness in such matters, and true refinement, is everything.

So I left Anthony talking to Uncle Jack, and that nice Basingstoke (he is really *not* repulsive, I find, but I will tell you, diary, in a moment what I do think about him) talking to the sluttish Cleverly girl, and came home alone by train. I was on my own in the carriage, and I began to *think*. The inspector had been beastly to me when, after he read the wonderful statement by that man Cobb (a voice from the dead, as you might say) I said that Leon Amberside might be in the room with us—but afterward they all looked surprised and foolish when I asked him if *Passion and Repentance* was on that list of Cobb's, and he said it wasn't. So I was right over *that*. Now, the thing that struck me in the train was this—Leon Amberside, the father, is dead, but what about Leon Amberside, the son? The boy who went to the war and was presumed to be killed. Supposing he *wasn't* killed. Supposing he's come back—to take revenge on Cobb? Cobb had as good as stolen money from young Leon

Amberside, and he might have kept much more
money than he admitted in the statement.

I hadn't got all this straightened out in my mind
properly, and I didn't quite see how Anthony's
book came into it, but I did see a kind of figure—
fighting in the war and wounded perhaps "presumed killed"—coming back unknown to anybody
to take a terrible revenge. And when I thought of
that there suddenly came into my mind's eye a
picture of *that scar*. That terrible scar of John
Basingstoke's and the explanation he'd given me
about his father being a boxer which I'd believed
at the time. But, thinking of his queer sense of
humor—look how oddly he behaved to me when I
first met him—I wondered if perhaps that story was
another of his jokes. After all, nobody could really
have a name like Basingstoke. Or could they?

Well, I was thinking these thoughts all the way
back home, and I wasn't at all prepared to find the
house turned upside down because brother Edward
had lost some drug or other, or thought he had. It
was something called adrenalin, or some such
name, and he was very mysterious about it, said it
could be dangerous in the wrong hands and all
that sort of thing. There was mother fluttering
about like an old hen, looking in all sorts of ridiculous places, among the boot brushes and in the
kitchen of all places, so that the new cook gave
notice—and there was Edward watching everything
gloomily and not trying to do anything himself, but
saying over and over again that he knew the adrenalin was in a certain place in his poisons cupboard,
and it wasn't there now. And he kept looking at me
queerly too, so that finally I asked right out if he
suspected *me* of taking it and he said hurriedly no,
of course not, and it turned out that he had in
mind John Basingstoke, when he was here to help
me look through those papers. I didn't see how he
could possibly have got at Edward's poison cupboard, and said so, but when I told him the stuff

would no doubt turn up, and was probably just mislaid, he was more annoyed than ever. He had the last word by saying again that my connection with crime was being talked about in Barnsfield, and was—bad for the practice.

Vicky felt suddenly extremely weary, and depressed. She put away the red-bound book with her usual care, and got into bed. A vision of Anthony with his head swathed in bandages was painfully before her, and her reaction to it was somehow not at all that of a grand lady. It was some time before she fell asleep, and as she lay in an uneasy doze two syllables formed themselves on her lips, and were repeated over and over. "Crick-et," she repeated. "Crick-et, crick-et."

V

"I was much delighted," Mr. Shelton said with a brown smile, "by your present."

"Present?" Anthony thought for a moment that his father was joking, and then he saw that the book held out to him had on its spine the words *Henry James*. "Oh. Very glad you liked it, Father."

"But I am sorry to see from your appearance that you have been in what we rather inexactly call the wars. Janet was anxious when you failed to return last night; and so," he added mildly, "was I. We were greatly relieved by your telephone call this morning which assured us that your injuries were minor. I gather that you trapped a gang of ruffians single handed, but were unable to deliver them into the hands of the police."

Anthony found himself, as always, petrified into silence by this badinage. At last he said sulkily, "My head aches," and sat down.

"My dear boy. Have you seen a doctor?"

"Yes. I saw the police doctor this morning and he says there's no damage done. Suppose the old skull's too thick." He added, with an obscure feeling of self-justification, "A whole gang of them set on me, cracked me on the head, and tied me up." His father was busying himself with a whisky decanter at the sideboard. "Seen a lot of the police today. Somebody shot that chap Cobb."

"So I saw from the evening paper." His father did not turn round. "Did the man get away?"

"Clean away. Bolted through the back garden."

Mr. Shelton squirted soda. "Have the police any clues?"

"Lord knows. This old man Cobb left a statement about a lot of things supposed to be forged by a chap called Amberside, but he didn't say anything about that little book I bought. Wish to God I'd never bought the thing."

"So do I." Mr. Shelton brought over two large glasses of whisky. "From every point of view."

Anthony drank some whisky. His head really was aching, and his perceptions were even less acute than usual, but he was aware of something odd in his father's tone.

"Have you ever considered, Anthony, where money comes from? Do you know the nature of my occupation, which provides you with a comfortable home?"

"Eh?" Anthony was altogether startled, and not at all capable of dealing with such questions, even though he had speculated on them himself not long before. "Why—something in the city. Stocks and shares."

" 'Something.' But you don't know what." Anthony shook his bandaged head in a doglike way. "I am a company director."

"Oh." Anthony was very little wiser.

"One of my companies—Antiguan Commercial Enterprises—ceased to be quoted on the Stock Exchange last week. Another, Brazilian Tractors Limited, dropped ten points. Yet another, the East African Mining Syndicate, dropped from eighteen shillings to ten shillings, and there are no dealings at the lower price."

Mr. Shelton's tone was conversational, and Anthony was deceived. "Oh, really," he said in a tone of polite disinterest, and his father's self-control snapped. Just for a moment his brown face was contorted with a rage that Anthony had seen only once or twice in his life. He leaned over the chair in which his son was sitting, and shouted at him.

"You don't understand what it means, do you, you dunderhead? Let me tell you, it means that just now I'm on the edge of ruin. Things may go right or they may go wrong in the next twenty-four hours—and if they go wrong there'll be no more Bentley cars and hundred-guinea books. I don't know what sin I've committed, but God gave me a son with a thick skull and nothing inside it, but perhaps you can understand *that*."

Anthony sat bolt upright as though an electric shock had been passed through him. Then in a tone not devoid of dignity he said, "Yes, father. I can understand that."

"And this is the time you choose to buy hundred-guinea books, to get yourself engaged to a doctor's simpering daughter, and, above all things, to get yourself mixed up in a murder case." He paced up and down. "Don't tell me that you don't see what that's got to do with it. You never have seen anything, and you never will. Don't you think it was useful to me when you got your Blue? Don't you understand that it would have given confidence to the rich fools I have to deal with if you'd been playing for Southshire and engaged to the kind of rich young woman who would have been dazzled by your appearance? Don't you realize that it's the finishing touch that now—at this, of all times—you should be mixed up in this murder case? But no, you don't realize anything."

Anthony sat staring up at his father. Under the white bandage, his great ox eyes were scared. "I'll

come and work with you, if you want me to, father. I
never thought I should be any use."

The storm of Mr. Shelton's anger passed as abruptly as it had come, and he was again a small brown
man in a neat blue suit. "I'm sorry," he said, and put
his hand on Anthony's shoulder. "I didn't mean to
say any of that. And I didn't mean it either. I only
wanted you to know how things stood, so that if there
does come any question—if things go wrong——" He
left the sentence unfinished, and crossed again to the
sideboard. "Have some more whisky, and tell me
more about Cobb and that fellow Amberside." Anthony told him, and the brown man listened with
keen interest. "Extraordinary," he said at intervals.
"Extraordinary."

Anthony's fingers moved round and round his
glass. He trembled for some moments on the verge of
speech, and then got up and moved toward the door.
"What you were saying earlier, father," he said, when
he had hold of the door handle, "about Vicky—and
our marriage—I don't think you need worry." Mr.
Shelton looked his surprise. "I think it's all off,"
Anthony said, and fled before he could be questioned.

FRIDAY

I

BASINGSTOKE'S YOUNG FRIEND, whose name was Bland,
sat up late on Thursday night, making notes on the
story that had been told to him. He went to sleep and
woke up thinking about it on Friday morning. He
thought about it while he washed, brushed his teeth
and ate a breakfast of toast, marmalade and coffee.
Then he washed up, meditating on literary forgery
and murder. He reflected with pleasure on the fortunate circumstance that he had taken this week for his
summer holiday. It had been spent partly in the
courts and partly in the theater (he believed that one
could learn a great deal about criminal psychology by
watching a good actor) ; and now his holiday allowed
him to visit the public library and return, within half
an hour, with a copy of the standard edition of
Passion and Repentance, and two or three books of
criticism which mentioned it. The sunlight shone
through the glass skylight and brightened one half of
the room; the other half was permanently in the
shade.

Bland read first of all the critics' view of the book,
which he found in general unenlightening. They
praised, or disparaged, imagery and meter—"vivid"
and "unhealthy" were words much used—but ad-
mirers and detractors were singularly uninformative
about the subject of the poems. "He writes with
power, and a frankness many will deprecate as unseemly, of his own marriage," wrote the Victorian,
R. H. Hutton; while a modern critic observed that
"The poems express continually and monotonously, in

metaphors restricted but powerful, the warring of Puritanism and sensuality in the poet's complicated nature. It is of no particular poetic relevance to remark that these sonnets obviously had their origin in the author's married life; and although human curiosity makes it inevitable that we should wonder just what facets of Rawlings' marriage drove him to rid his bosom of such perilous stuff, it would be both idle and impertinent to carry these speculations into uncomfortable detail." It might be impertinent, Bland thought with some irritation, but could hardly be called idle just at this moment of time. He turned to the book, and read the first poems in the series:

Adam to Eve: "This breast hard as an apple,
These slim, straight thighs, are built from dung and dirt.
The vitriol sucked from each tautened nipple
Runs in the veins of all whom life has hurt.
What is man born to but a long denying,
Who one day says, *I will be good forever*
And in an hour feels on him like a fever
The dark desire that leads to loss and sighing?"

And Eve to Adam: "Enter my strong arms,
Rest there at peace, and close those guilt-dazed eyes
That long have seen mirages of content.
Sleep, sleep; absorb my image and my scent,
Receive this benison of love that warms
The spirit to a human Paradise."

Poetry was at any time less congenial reading to the young man than accounts of famous trials, and he began to think the interpretation of poetry no less complicated. He read this first sonnet three times, and then made no more of it than that the poet considered love as something desirable but wicked, and that the female principle (represented by "Eve") lured men away from good toward evil. He sighed a little, and read on. In an hour he had finished the little book, and methodically began to make notes on it.

The notes, however, were really no more than an extension of Basingstoke's remarks on the previous evening. The first twenty sonnets might be called passionate and the next repentant, he reflected, although the repentance itself was both self-pitying and in itself highly passionate. It did seem, however, that the first twenty poems celebrated "sin" with a good deal of zest, in obscure metaphors, and that the last twenty expressed regret for sinning. When Bland had got as far as this with his notes, he put down his pencil in despair. Perhaps he was altogether wrong in thinking that there was some connection between the text of this book and the case. Or perhaps, after all, as Basingstoke had suggested, there was a secret attached to one particular copy. He ruffled the pages absently, and they opened at the twentieth sonnet— the halfway point, and the culmination of the poems of "Passion":

> Out of the sighs and anguish beauty comes.
> Or is it beauty? Can we give the name
> To what's begot in stealth and sin and shame,
> To lute of Lucifer and devil's drums?
> Look then upon this face, unearthly fair,
> And radiant with everlasting wrong,
> And wonder at what makes a poet's song,
> Grieve at the heavy burden humans share.
>
> For all, all share it: this small errant son,
> The germ of darkness and ecstatic joy,
> That tender mother cradling her boy,
> And most of all this lover of the sun.
> Who stretches arms to woman, not to God,
> Makes for his back a ripe and eager rod.

As he read and re-read these lines they changed from almost meaningless rhetoric into words weighty with a meaning that clarified the whole case: they

joined with the other sonnets and the drawing on
Jebb's blotter and the theft of copies of the book and
with many other facts to make a picture that was not
complete, but was within its limits clear. He sat for a
little while with his fair head above the book, thinking of what he had been told, and of what he had
read. Then he consulted a date and some details in
an old *Who's Who*, and an illustration in another
book on his shelf. It seemed that these were what he
had expected, for he nodded. He wandered aimlessly
round the great room, rubbing his finger on the tops
of books as if to assure himself that they were not
dusty, pulling straight the counterpane on his bed.
Then he slapped his hand on the table, said, "Of
course," picked up a trilby hat and almost ran out of
the dungeon room, slamming the door after him. In
the street he jumped onto a moving bus, changed
onto another, and booked a fare to Blackheath.

II

Vicky woke with a bad taste in her mouth, and a
feeling that something was wretchedly wrong. She saw
that she had overslept. The time was half-past nine.
In her misery and self-absorption on the previous
night she had forgotten to set the alarm.

Such a happening can lend a tone to the whole
day. Her sense of injury was not decreased by the
facts that the water ran lukewarm from the hot tap,
and that the haddock for breakfast was almost cold.
She made a poor breakfast, but sat on at the table
reading the paper, and had just found an interesting
item about the arrival in London of the King and
Queen of Italy, with the handsome Prince of Pied-
mont, when the telephone rang in the hall. As she
went to answer it, Edward popped his head out of
the dispensary. She took off the receiver, heard Anthony's voice and turned to Edward, who was hovering uneasily. "Oh—it's for you, is it?" he said. "Didn't
know you were up. Come in and see me when you've

finished, will you?" She nodded, and the baize door leading into his dispensary closed.

"Hullo," she said.

"Hullo, is that you, Vicky? This is Anthony." She made no reply to an observation so self-evident. "I just wondered how you were. If you got home all right, and all that."

"Perfectly, thank you. I came by train."

"Oh, that's good. Jolly good. But I say you should have waited for me, you know."

"You were busy talking to Uncle Jack."

"Oh, yes," Anthony said with noticeable constraint, and offered no explanation of that mysterious conversation.

"How's your head?" she asked, and he responded eagerly:

"Much better, thanks. Taking off the bandage to-day. Bit of a swelling, but nothing really." She almost heard a deep breath being taken, and then a kind of roar came out of the telephone. "I say, Vicky old girl, sorry about that spot of trouble we had. All my fault. Do forgive me. Can't we meet and have a talk?"

She heard him with delight, but it would never do to show it. She said airily, "I'd really forgotten about it—you were being so silly." It would never do to show him that she was anxious to see him. He could take her over to Uncle Jack's tomorrow. "I'm awfully busy today. What are you doing tomorrow afternoon? I could see you then if you like."

There was a stammer of dismay. "To-tomorrow afternoon. Well, as a matter of fact, Vicky, you see——"

"You're busy?" she said sharply. "Don't bother to explain."

"No, it's not—well, yes, I am busy but—it's something I can't put off. Tomorrow morning I could——"

"Don't put yourself to any trouble on my account. Good-by." She banged down the receiver and, without giving herself a chance to consider what she had done, charged through the green-baize door where

Edward was sitting, looking very worried indeed. "I've found the adrenalin," he said.

"Oh, have you? That's one trouble the less. Where was it?"

"That's the extraordinary thing," Edward said with gloomy triumph. "It wasn't in the poisons cupboard. It was on the shelf among all the other things—not at all where it should have been. I can't think how it got there."

"Perhaps you put it there yourself by mistake," she suggested, and he looked at her severely.

"Please don't be flippant. It might be very serious if this bottle got into unauthorized hands. The action of adrenalin stimulates the heart, and if administered to somebody whose heart was weak——" He held up a small bottle, and shook his head gravely.

"I suppose you've handled that bottle thoroughly, so 'that there's no chance of any fingerprints being found on it?" she said crossly. "Yes; I thought so. Can you remember how much was in it? Does any seem to be missing?"

"As a matter of fact," Edward said reluctantly, "there doesn't seem to be any missing at all."

"Then what are you worried about?"

"I don't know." Edward ran a hand through his thin hair. "Yes, I do. It's all your fault." She looked at him in surprise. "I've had one or two lapses of memory lately. They are quite brief, and so far as I can discover I act in a perfectly rational manner during them, but they are nonetheless distressing. I attribute them to worry about the practive, aggravated by this affair in which you've got involved."

"Nonsense," said Vicky briskly. "Anyway, you say the adrenalin's all there. Do you know what I should do about those lapses of memory, if I were you?" He looked at her inquiringly. "I should see a doctor." She went off into peals of laughter.

"I've asked you before not to be flippant. I feel a strong sense of responsibility. After all, I am head of the family."

"This branch of it." He looked at her again with apparent lack of comprehension, and she said, "Uncle Jack's the head of the family, if you want to use such phrases." He was still staring at her when the telephone bell rang again, and she said hurriedly, "I'll answer it." The voice that spoke to her was not Anthony's, but another that in its oily gratiness seemed unpleasantly familiar. After a moment she recognized it as that of Inspector Wrax.

"Miss Rawlings? I wonder if you can oblige me with a little information? Can you tell me the year of birth of the members of your family?"

"What?" She could not believe her ears.

With elaborate patience, the inspector repeated, "The year of birth of the various members of your family. Your father died three years ago, I believe."

"Yes."

"That leaves, then, your mother, your brother and yourself, your uncle, and—I understand your uncle has a son."

"Yes."

"If you can give me this information it will save some routine inquiries, and I shall be most grateful to you. Are you there, Miss Rawlings?"

"What do you want to know for?"

The inspector lubricated his voice a little. "It is purely a matter of routine. Of course, if you are unwilling to assist us——" He left the sentence in the air, and Vicky paused to consider.

"Why should I be?"

"Exactly," the inspector said heartily. "Why should you be?"

"My mother is fifty-four years old—that is, she was born in——"

"Eighteen-seventy," the inspector said. "Her maiden name was Muriel Parks, wasn't it?"

"I—yes, I believe it was."

"Don't you know?"

"Yes, of course I know. But what can my mother's maiden name have to do with this affair?"

"Nothing at all, very likely," said the inspector soothingly. "And your brother?"

"He was born in 1896—he's twenty-eight; and I was born four years later—I'm twenty-four this year. Uncle Jack is sixty-three—that means he was born in——"

"Eighteen-sixty-one."

"Yes, that's right. And his wife died ten years ago, just before the war began, when Philip was seven years old—so he was born in 1907."

"That's most helpful, Miss Rawlings. I'm very much obliged to you." He rang off before she had time to ask the questions that were at the tip of her tongue. Edward's head was poked round the baize door again. "Who was that?" he asked.

"The police inspector." She stood with her hand on the black telephone, as if she were mesmerized.

"And what did *he* want?" Edward asked pettishly. When she told him he was more annoyed than astonished. "Really, I do call that unwarrantable. He's prying into our private affairs. I trust you didn't tell him."

"Of course I did."

"You should have left him to find it out for himself." Edward fidgeted with a waistcoat button. "The whole thing is a calamity. People are looking at me in the street in a very peculiar way, and I can't say that I blame them. What did he want with that information?"

Vicky took her hand off the telephone. She had suddenly remembered Anthony's evasiveness. "How the devil should I know?"

III

The day was bright and warm when Basingstoke's young friend got off his bus at Blackheath station and walked briskly up Peaceful Alley. Within two minutes he was away from the brisk grocery and greengrocery shops of the village. Quiet Georgian houses with decorous front gardens lined one side of the road, confronted by equally subdued and respectable shops. Bland stopped before one of these, which bore the name *Lewis* outside in lettering of faded gold; this shop was more unobstrusive, even, than the rest, for its front shutters were closed. He rapped tentatively upon the shutters and heard a faint and curious noise inside, which he presently identified as the miaowing of a cat. He walked down a narrow alleyway at the side of the shop, and stopped before a green door, which was a side entrance to the bookshop. Outside this door he noticed, with a surprise, two quart bottles of milk. The green door opened onto a back garden and a path led through the garden to what was presumably the door of the small house which contained the bookshop. This door was open and from inside it the shadow of a man stretched out into the sunlit garden. The shadow, to be exact, was not that of a man, but of the lower half of a man, and it was cast, solid and seemingly permanent, with its vast legs extending down the asphalt path outside the door. The young man Bland stood with his hand on the latch of the green door, aware that there was something very wrong with this shadow, but unable to analyse his knowledge; until suddenly he realized that a man standing in a doorway, with the light behind him, does not throw the shadow of his feet but of his head, so that it should be an enormous head, and not enormous feet, visible outside this kitchen door. The man inside, then, was in some way defying the law of gravity, but as Bland came to that conclusion his attention was drawn from it by a sudden sharp pain in his left leg. He looked down, startled, to see a great blue Persian cat stretching against him, and staring up at him out of reflective amber eyes.

He pushed the cat down impatiently, and looked again toward the door, but now the shadow had disappeared. For a moment the space in the doorway was blank, and then it was filled by Basingstoke—a Basingstoke who held a clasp knife in his hand, and whose face was gray. He made a gesture to Bland, and the young man hurried across the garden. With a shudder, Basingstoke pointed inside the door and then stepped out into the garden, drawing into his lungs great gusts of air.

The room from which he had come was, as Bland had surmised, the kitchen. Unwashed dishes and plates lay in the sink; saucers were on the floor, but there was no milk in them; there was a strong and sickening smell of cats, and a buzz of flies; and sprawled over the stone floor of the kitchen was a body which the young man recognized from Basingstoke's description as that of the bookseller, Jonathan Jacobs. A white cat was licking at his face. Bland pushed away the cat, controlled his feeling of nausea, and bent down to look more closely at the bookseller.

His face was purplish in color, and his tongue hung out, swollen and discolored. A thin but strong-looking piece of rope was strung round his neck. He was wearing old flannel trousers and a corded dressing gown. Looking up at the ceiling, Bland saw a hook, of the kind that is often used for hanging meat, with a small piece of rope coming down from it. The man had been hanging, then, and it was his shadow that had shown so grotesquely through the doorway; Basingstoke (Bland remembered the clasp knife in his hand) had cut him down, standing on a chair to do it. It was this chair, presumably, that had been kicked away, Bland thought with a frown, when the bookseller hanged himself. At least there was no other chair in the kitchen. He bent down again by the bookseller, and his mouth made an O of surprise. He touched a small white patch by the man's ear, and examined the cups, teapot, and dishes in the sink carefully. Then he walked down the passage and into the room at the back of the bookshop, staring at the floor all the time. In this room it seemed that he found what he had been looking for. He straightened up, went out of the house, and joined Basingstoke, who was sitting despondently in the garden.

"I came to see him as you suggested, and found him like that," the tall man said. "It was awful. That damned kitchen was full of cats—all pawing at him. I think that was what really upset me. I couldn't let him stay up there like that. I had to cut him down."

"So I saw," said his friend, whose rosy cheeks and undisturbed manner presented a queer contrast to Basingstoke's almost distraught appearance.

"There's one consolation." Basingstoke looked toward the open doorway. "At least this ends it."

"How do you mean?"

"It's just as you said last night. He was a forger himself, obviously, and lied when he said he got the copies from Cobb. He knew the game was up." His young friend looked at Basingstoke with an expression that suggested a certain disappointment in his companion's mental powers, and said in his soft voice, "Oh, I don't think so. I mean, I don't think he committed suicide. It was rather a fragile rope, don't you think? It might have broken under the strain of the drop."

Basingstoke looked at him as if he had taken leave of his senses. "But—it didn't break."

"Because he was killed first, and then strung up there. When you hang yourself," he explained, and Basingstoke flinched a little, "you kick away the chair and drop, imposing a sudden strain on the rope. This rope might have broken, and I don't think he'd have used it when he had a good thick cord on his dressing gown. On the other hand, a murderer wouldn't worry about the rope in the same way." He smiled faintly, and added, "Or at least, not for the same reasons."

Basingstoke gulped. His face was showing a healthier color now. "That seems very fine spun."

Bland's hair gleamed like metal in the sunlight. "My dear fellow, there's no doubt about it. How long ago did you get here?"

"About twenty minutes ago."

"Very well. He died this morning. He had drunk a cup of tea before he died—the pot was still faintly warm, and so were the dregs in the cup. But he had put down no milk for the twelve cats he was so fond of. He died before the arrival of the milkman, then—because the milk is outside the door now. Would one expect a suicide, a self-condemned man, to take his early morning cup of tea? Well, possibly. Just possibly. But would he be in such a hurry that he would leave his beloved cats unfed? Surely not." He went on remorselessly. "And finally, surely he would not go so far as to shave in order to appear a presentable corpse? But Jacobs did shave this morning—there is a dab of cream just by his ear. No no, my friend, he was killed in that little room behind his bookshop—there are signs of a struggle on the linoleum back there—and then dragged into the kitchen and strung up."

Basingstoke looked at his friend with unfeigned admiration. "I say, you're wonderfully quick. But why should anyone want to kill him?"

"I think I know why."

Basingstoke laughed. "And you know who it was too, I suppose?"

Bland's cherubic face was grave. "I think I know who it was."

"Who?"

"The answer to that question may be inside, though I doubt it. But we ought to look."

Basingstoke's scar twitched. "I don't much fancy going in again." The young man made no reply, but stepped toward the kitchen door. Basingstoke followed unwillingly. They skirted the thing that lay on the floor, and Bland looked only cursorily at the bookshop and its little inner room. They went up a narrow flight of stairs into the three rooms on the first floor. One of them, obviously a lumber room, was crammed with odds and ends of the bookseller's stock. Another was a bathroom, and here Bland paused only long enough to point out the damp shaving brush. The third room had been the bookseller's bedroom, and here Bland paused on the threshold.

Basingstoke was about to enter and put his hand on the iron bedstead, when his friend checked him sharply.

"Don't do that. If there was anything here, it has been taken. I don't see any signs of disorder, but I'll swear that this room has been searched, and there may be a crop of fingerprints. We'd better inform the police." With a glance at his friend and a slight smile, Bland said, "I think we shall both of us be in for an unhappy half-hour—you for cutting down the body, and me for being here at all. You say the inspector's unpleasant?"

Basingstoke was given no chance to say what the inspector was like, at that time, for as they walked out of the garden through the little green door they met him coming down the passage. He glared at them and said to Basingstoke, "What are you doing here?" but without waiting for an answer to that question, asked two more. "Where's Jacobs? Why isn't his shop open?" When Basingstoke told him what had happened, the inspector stood staring at him as though he could not believe his ears. Then he went in and looked at the body. His expression was not pleasant. "What the devil did you cut him down for?" With savage mockery, he asked, "Did he make you feel sick? Well, let me tell you, *you* make *me* feel sick with your theories and conclusions. Who do you think had your precious book at the time you were telling Jacobs all about it?" He gave a kind of snarling snort. "*He had it himself.* What do you think of that, Mr. Basingstoke?"

"Had it himself?"

"Those crooks who knocked out your friend Shelton were doing the job for Jacobs, and passed on the book to him afterward. He certainly made a monkey out of you."

"You mean to say that he deliberately put me onto the track of Cobb, knowing Cobb wasn't the forger?"

Bland said quietly, "It's because Jacobs knew the identity of the forger that he was murdered."

Inspector Wrax's hot eyes passed over Bland, and he said to Basingstoke, "What the devil's this? Something out of Sunday school?"

"He's a friend of mine. I've told him something about the case."

"Oh, you have." He addressed Bland for the first time, as he said, "And what makes you talk about murder, young man?" Bland told him and, to Basingstoke's surprise, the inspector listened. At the end of the recital he grunted, and said, "I suppose you call yourself an amateur detective?"

"No. I call myself a clerk on holiday."

"And I suppose you think you've solved this case?"

The young man's smile was cherubic. "Yes."

The inspector glared at him. "Take my advice, sonny. I don't say you're not clever. You may be the orignal boy wonder, for all I know or care. But keep out of this." He pointed a threatening finger. "I've got my plans laid, and I don't want them messed up by a schoolboy amateur Sherlock." His glance ranged to include Basingstoke. "By a *couple* of amateur Sherlocks. Understand?"

They said they understood.

IV

When Inspector Wrax put down the telephone after speaking to Victoria Rawlings, he had no idea of going to Blackheath. He sat at his desk and stared with his hot, dark eyes at a spot on the opposite wall. Then another telephone on his desk rang, and when he lifted the receiver he heard Sergeant Thynne's voice, more squeaky than usual with excitement. "We've got Billy the Toff, sir. Picked him up in Limehouse."

The inspector took it calmly. "Good. Any news from Italy?"

"Give us a chance, sir." That appeal was the sergeant's stock in trade. "Do you want Billy in now? He's a pretty tough customer, and smart with it."

"Oh, is he? Send him in."

When the youngish man with the dark mustache was brought in, the inspector was writing at his desk. He looked up and said, as though his visitor were paying a social call, "Ah, Nugent. I don't think we've met before, but you've probably heard of me. My name's Wrax." Then he settled down again to writing in a notebook.

Equally conversationally, the man said, "I've done nothing wrong."

With a smile, Inspector Wrax said, "What would you say to robbery with violence?" The youngish man said nothing. "Doesn't appeal to you? Then shall we say—accessory after the fact?" His voice did not change in tone as he said, "You've done it wrong this time, Nugent. You're mixed up in murder."

"Not me," said Nugent confidently, and stroked his small mustache.

The inspector looked at him steadily, and under the gaze of those strange eyes it seemed that Nugent's confidence wilted just a little. "You're a pretty smart boy, aren't you? And you've got a nice little organization. I've admired it from a distance for some time. Ever heard of a man named Jebb?"

"Saw a piece about him in the paper. Somebody knocked him on the head."

"Somebody knocked him on the head," Inspector Wrax echoed. "Ever hear of a man named Cobb? Somebody shot him," he said in mimicry of Nugent's tone. He smacked his hand on the table. "And you're mixed up in it, Nugent."

"You know that's not true, Inspector. My boys had nothing to do with any of that."

"What about the book you stole from Mr. Shelton?"

"Never heard of him."

"Or of Mr. Rawlings either, I suppose? Or of a little book called *Passion and Repentance*?"

"Don't know what you're talking about." Nugent was looking much less happy.

"Shelton says you assaulted him—twice."

"No."

"Robbed him of a valuable book."

"I'm not a reading man." Nugent touched his mustache.

"You *are* smart," said the inspector admiringly. "I suppose you were more interested in his diamond ring."

"We never took a ring off him," Nugent cried. He stopped. The inspector was showing his teeth in a laugh. He added sulkily, "Or anything else."

Inspector Wrax was twisting a small piece of metal in his hands. He spoke persuasively. "Look here, Nugent. This won't do you any good. Shelton recognized your photograph, and so did his girl friend. They'll identify you. You can't wriggle out of it."

"If I knew what you were talking about," said Nugent, "which I don't—I'd say it was a different thing from murder. Don't see any connection."

"You can take my word for it that there *is* a connection. Those books you pinched had something to do with the murder of two men. Just let me tell you the way it works out for you. You won't mind me doing that, will you?" The smile on Inspector Wrax's face was benevolent, but the dark eyes under his beautiful white hair were hot.

"Say what you like," said Nugent. "It won't hurt me. I'm keeping my mouth shut. I had nothing to do with any murder, and you can't prove I had."

"Perhaps not. But I'm telling you now, Nugent, that if you keep your mouth shut I'll book you for accessory to murder as sure as my name's Sam Wrax." Nugent looked into the inspector's eyes, and then away. "And you know what they say about me—I never book a man on a charge without making it stick. Believe me, Nugent, I shan't mind one little bit making it stick in your case. If a man's against me—I break him. I think you'd be foolish to keep your mouth shut, but, of course, if you want to, that's your privilege." There was a sudden snap as the inspector broke the piece of metal he had been twisting. He showed it to Nugent with a whimsical smile, and tossed it into a wastepaper basket.

"Well?" Nugent's voice was slightly hoarse.

"Your other course would be to answer some questions. If you do that, I'll do what I can for you. I make no promises, Nugent, but I'll say this. If nothing fresh comes in, we'll be able to forget the murder charge, and I might be able to induce Shelton to drop the other."

The inspector saw with interest that beads of perspiration had formed round Nugent's mustache. The hand that came up to wipe them away was trembling slightly. He said, "I had nothing to do with any murder, and I'm not a nark. You'll get nothing out of me."

The inspector pressed a bell on his desk, and stood up. The corners of his mouth were drawn down, and his eyes were gleaming. "I'm charging you as accessory to the murder of Arthur Jebb, Nugent, and don't look for any mercy from me, for by God you won't get it." Nugent wiped his face with his hand again. A detective-sergeant opened the door, and the inspector made a violent gesture. "Take him away. Charge him as accessory to Jebb's murder." He turned his back.

"Wait a minute," Nugent said faintly. The inspector swung round, glared at him, and then said to the detective-sergeant, "Get out." When the door had closed he sat on the edge of his desk with his face inches away from Nugent's, and said, "Your boys took that copy of *Passion and Repentance* off Shelton, didn't they?" Nugent nodded. "And you were responsible for the other thefts from public libraries and private houses, weren't you?" He nodded again. The inspector's voice was not loud, but bitter. "All right. You're not a great reader. Who were you working for?"

"Jacobs," said Nugent. Inspector Wrax stared at him. "A bookseller—Jonathan Jacobs. Keeps a shop out at Blackheath."

Inspector Wrax walked slowly round his desk and sat down behind it. "If you're codding me, Nugent, you'll be in worse trouble than you are now."

"I'm telling the truth, Inspector." There could be no doubt of the man's earnestness. "Some of my boys knew this Jacobs from years ago. Sometimes he's come in on screwing a joint, see, but they didn't like him too much because he was a bit milky."

"He hasn't got a record," the inspector said sharply, and Nugent waved a hand in a nervous gesture.

"Not in this country, maybe. This boy of mine knew him in the Cape a matter of twenty years back. He was a queer cove then, by all accounts, always spouting books, and when he came over here he gave up the game and opened a shop—a bookshop."

"Was it a cover for something?"

With disgust Nugent said, "From what I heard, he ran it straight. I never heard his name, though, till this boy of mine said he wanted us to do a little job for him. It was easy as kiss your hand—knocking off a book from a private house—and he could easily have done it himself, only he was too milky. Anyway, we did it, and I passed over the book myself. Only time I saw him. We did a few more jobs for him afterwards, houses and public libraries. Queer they were, because it was always the same book."

"Passion and Repentance?"

Nugent nodded again. "I don't know about the passion," he said, "but I'm bloody well repenting now."

"Did he tell you what he wanted them for?"

"He said he had a crazy rich old gentleman who wanted to make a corner in them. Sounded to me like he was sprucing, but it was none of my business."

"He never gave you a hint who he was acting for?"

"Not a smell. I only met him the once. After that he telephoned, gave me the dope, and we went to work. There was nothing to it. Like taking chocolates from a baby."

"What about the copy you took from Shelton?"

Nugent clicked his teeth. "Somebody slipped up there. It was a copy of one of these books that had come up for sale. Jacobs got on the wire and said he wanted it all done legal—send along one of the boys and buy it for up to a hundred nicker, which should cover it easy. But it didn't. Then Jacobs told me he was going to make a bigger offer. That was no good, so he told me to get it any way I liked. I did that, and he had it Tuesday evening."

So when Jacobs was talking to that half-smart Basingtoke and the Rawlings girl, the inspector thought, he was stringing them along good and proper. "What else?"

"That's all there is. I don't know more than a baby what it was all about, or anything about this Jebb and Cobb you're talking about."

The inspector pressed the bell again. When the sergeant came he said, "Take him away."

"What's the charge, Inspector?"

"Grievous bodily harm."

"But, look here——" Nugent said, and the inspector gave him a hard stare.

"What do you want, Nugent, jam on it? I told you I'd see what I could do with Shelton, and I will. You can thank your lucky stars I'm a man of my word."

"I want to see my solicitor," Nugent said, in a kind of wail.

"See who you like, but if you know what's good for you, you'll stay in jail. It's going to be the safest place for you in the next few days."

The inspector rang through to Sergeant Thynne, who had no more news. "How did you get on with Nugent?" the sergeant asked.

"He was a half-smart bastard," the inspector said amiably. "I'm going down to Jacobs' bookshop at Blackheath. I'll be surprised if I don't add him to the bag."

But the inspector was surprised.

When the inspector let them go, the two young men returned to Central London. Bland seemed uncommonly cheerful, while Basingstoke was sunk in a profound gloom. In the railway carriage, Bland asked what his friend was doing with himself. "I'm going to old Jebb's funeral," Basingstoke said. "Ruth Cleverly asked if I'd like to be there, and I feel in a kind of way that I should. And tomorrow I've half-promised to go down to Millingham and see Vicky's uncle. I don't think I shall, though." He sighed. "I'm sick of this business."

"Have you lost your sense of curiosity?"

Basingstoke looked out of the window, and his scar twitched. "As I said last night, I feel that if it weren't for my damned curiosity all this might not have happened."

"You're wrong there." Bland shook decisively his-well-brushed fair head. "It's difficult philosophically to attribute a beginning to any happening——"

"Oh, philosophically. Do you think I'm talking about philosophy?"

"But in an immediate practical sense you only lighted, as you might say, a fuse which was already laid. Somebody had to light it some time, and it was a coincidence that it happened to be you. You might as well blame Shelton for buying the book."

Basingstoke said, with a snort worthy of the inspector, "Don't you think I do that every day? I hope I never see that lumbering ape again. I hope I never see any of them again." He turned his full face to Bland, and bent toward him, pointing to his scar. "This thing is a wretched disfigurement, isn't it?"

Bland did not move away. "If you let it be."

"There are times when I envy everybody who doesn't carry about with them a mark like this, everybody who's shaped to a fairly reasonable physical pattern. 'Oh, why was I born with a different face?'

But I don't think I should mind if I'd been *born* with a different face. It's having it thrust on me that makes it hard to bear."

Bland made no comment. He knew the story that Basingstoke had told to Victoria Rawlings. Presently he said, "That might be a theme for a novel. Comparison of the effects of physical and emotional maladjustment. Sometimes the most dangerous disfigurements are inside you—one can pay a great deal for presenting a perfectly harmonious front to the world."

"What the devil do you mean by that?" Basingstoke stared at him curiously.

"I was suggesting a theme for a novel. Don't you think the contrast might be worked up quite effectively? The battle between two men, one of them physically and the other mentally disfigured, for a woman. Which of them gets her?"

Basingstoke had his long legs stuck out, staring at them. "Not much doubt of that."

"It depends which of them gives up," Bland said with emphasis, and Basingstoke looked at him with renewed interest. "You understand, I'm talking about a novel."

Still staring at his long legs, the scarred man said, "Do you think I should go down there tomorrow?"

"It sounds very interesting. In fact I should like to go myself. And I should like to meet Miss Cleverly. Couldn't you take her along with you?"

"All right, all right. I don't suppose old Rawlings will mind if you both come along with me." He relapsed into his inspissated gloom, and then said, "How does this man Jacobs' death affect it all? It seems to me like a jumble perpetrated by a homicidal maniac. Is that what you think?" Bland shook his head. "Do you mean to say that there's some logical sequence in all this?"

"Given the murderer's point of view, quite logical."

"Well, I can't see it," said Basingstoke complainingly, but his friend did not enlighten him, and they hardly spoke again before they parted at Charing Cross.

Why had he come here? Basingstoke wondered, as he walked slowly among rows of marble urns and graves ornamented by white stone chips, to the spot in the middle distance where a small group of people was standing. Thinking half-consciously of the scene he had left that morning, the man hanging, horribly, in that small kitchen among the unwashed plates, he stopped and stood staring at a stone which commemorated the death of a boy of twelve. Underneath he read the words, *He rests in the bosom of the Lord.* Why do they accept it, he thought, as he joined the group standing with bowed heads round a brown box that was being lowered into a hole in the ground, why do people accept the fact of death with such unseemly and inhuman placidity, dreaming still that it is their sole link with an imaginary benevolence, instead of regarding it logically as the last indignity making us one with the kingdom of the pig and the dog. He lowered his own head dutifully, but took the opportunity to look round as stones and dirt rattled on the box, and saw with pleasure Ruth Cleverly's small face, white and strained, and then with a shock of surprise noticed Anthony Shelton's fair curls beside Blackburn's elegant figure. When it was over he stepped across to Ruth and took her hand. The smile she gave him was a mockery of her usual gaiety.

"I'm very sorry to be late," he said, but her hand waved his sorrow impatiently away. He followed the direction of her glance, to where men were filling up the hole in the ground. "It's a poor end we come to, isn't it?" he said.

"A poor end and a sad one, for him." She spoke without her usual brusqueness. "He had so little out of life. All he wanted was bound up with that book, and then somebody took it away. Like taking a toy from a child."

He looked round at the mass of marble, and his

shoulders gave a shrug that was almost a shiver. "I thought there might be no one you knew here, but I see I was wrong."

"That snake," Ruth Cleverly said bitterly, looking at the retreating back of Michael Blackburn. "Why was he here with Shelton?" They were standing alone by the grave now, and the men who were filling it in stared at them. Again Basingstoke felt inclined to shiver. "Shall we go?" he asked, and without answering she turned and they walked together down the formal and well-kept paths toward the neat iron gate. With his hands in his pockets and his shoulders slightly hunched, Basingstoke brooded over his own problems. "Do you believe that when we die we're gone?" he asked, and pushed out his lips. "Pfft. Like a light."

"Don't know," said Ruth Cleverly. "Never thought much about it. I suppose, like most people, I believe in—something." She glanced back over her shoulder. "Anyway, I'd like to. Why?"

"I saw someone dead this morning. It started my mind moving in all sorts of queer ways."

"What——" she began, and then they both became aware of the two tall figures standing at the gate. Anthony smiled awkwardly and shyly, but Blackburn nodded to Basingstoke and spoke, gently and apologetically, to Ruth:

"My dear Miss Cleverly, I want to say how sorry I am for my outburst yesterday. I was overwrought, but it was really unpardonable. Do forgive me."

With no change in her white-faced grimness, Ruth said almost absently. "That's all right." Then she added with a flicker of dislike, "Nice of you to come. I didn't know you thought so much of Arthur."

"I hope my presence may be taken as a token repentance for harsh words I've spoken in the past. But really it's our young friend here"—his long hand rested on Anthony's sleeve—"who's chiefly responsible. I asked him to lunch, and it was his suggestion that we should come on here."

Three pairs of eyes looked at Anthony—Blackburn's benevolently, Basingstoke's with awakened curiosity, and Ruth's almost blankly. He blushed, and seemed to feel the need of explanation. "I don't know—I just seemed to feel that—well, hang it all, it was all through me in a way that it happened, wasn't it? I mean to say, if I hadn't bought that thing to give to Vicky——" He left the sentence unfinished, and plunged on. "And I did see the chap—with you, Ruth—Miss Cleverly—the day before he died. I thought it was only decent—mark of respect and all that——" He lapsed into silence.

Somebody else, Basingstoke thought, with a feeling of guilt to expiate. He felt for the first time almost warmly toward Anthony, and quite forgot that a little while before he had called him a lumbering ape. "I was saying the same thing myself this morning, on my own account, to a young friend of mine who knows about this case—that I felt responsible in a way for these three deaths because I'd really started off the hunt. And if it's any consolation to you, he said that I'd only lighted a fuse which was already laid."

"What?" said Anthony.

"He meant that the roots of it all went back a long way," Basingstoke said with some irritation.

Blackburn picked an imaginary piece of cotton off his elegant dark-blue suit. "Did you say—three deaths?"

Watching them all, Basingstoke said, "A man called Jacobs was found hanged this morning." He learned nothing from their expressions, and added, "He was the bookseller who made you an offer for your copy of the book, Shelton. Miss Rawlings and I went to see him."

"Good Lord, yes," Anthony said. "The chap Cobb sold all those books to. What an extraordinary thing."

Blackburn was stroking a long upper lip. "When you say he was found hanged, I take it you mean that he committed suicide. Doesn't that seem to give grounds for thinking that he may have—ah—laid the fuse?"

"My young friend," Basingstoke said slowly, "seemed to think that the death was made to look like suicide. That really he was murdered."

"Your young friend seems ubiquitous," Blackburn observed politely.

"Wrax believes it," Basingstoke said with rather unwarranted boldness and watched them carefully as he added with spurious hesitation, "Wrax says that Jacobs was the man responsible for the book thefts."

Anthony's brows were bent together, as he tried doggedly to find his way through this maze. "But— why should anybody kill *him*? If he was responsible for it all?" Basingstoke made no reply, and the four of them stood silent by the cemetery gates in the hard sunlight.

"If we're going to Lord's today, my dear Anthony," Blackburn said gently, "we'd better go."

The young man roused himself from a kind of stupor of thought. "I suppose we'd better. Can we give you a lift?" Ruth Cleverly shook her head, and the Bentley whirled away in a cloud of dust. When it had gone she said with decision, "That snake's got something to do with it all."

"Your feelings do you credit. It's unpleasant to see him fawning round young Shelton. But I'm sure you're wrong. He's only an elderly dilettante with a penchant for youth."

They walked along the road, like Mutt and Jeff. Her lower lip was thrust out rebelliously. "I've chucked my job. What do you think about that?" She did not wait for a reply, but added, "If I hadn't chucked it, it would have chucked me. Henderson as good as told me they didn't want anyone who mixed themselves up in such unsavory affairs. I told them I was going to Arthur's funeral, and left as of this morning."

"In that case, if you've no commitments, I can ask you to tea."

"I don't want anything to eat, but I'll drink a cup of tea with you. I'm a fool to do it, though. The last cup of tea we had put me at the top of the list of police suspects."

"I don't think you're there now." They went into a genteel teashop, and sat down. Still with a vivid recollection of that scene at Blackheath, he said, "If this man Jacobs was murdered, I don't think you'd have had the strength to lift him so that he was hanging. It wasn't pretty."

"Did you find him?"

"I cut him down." He crumbled a scone. "Did old Rawlings ask you down to see him tomorrow?"

"Yes; when I saw him yesterday. But I don't intend to go." She took a piece of thin brown bread and butter and smeared jam on it.

"Why not come down with me?" She stared at him, and he turned his face away.

"Don't do that," she said sharply. She made a gesture toward his scar. "Don't be so damned sensitive, shying away like a horse. Nobody will mind it, unless you make them." She leaned over, touched it lightly with her fingers. "You're a fool about it. Things like that don't matter."

His smile was crooked. "I wish I could believe you. A friend of mine told me the same thing this morning."

"Your ubiquitous young friend," she said in a parody of Blackburn's mellifluous tones. She took another piece of bread and butter.

"He's really quite remarkable. He thinks he knows who's behind all this. He'll be there tomorrow. Do come down. You can't start looking for a job until Monday morning."

"Will you promise not to turn away your face?"

He looked at her and felt a melting of the core of hardness inside him, the slow quiescence of the tiger of pride. "I promise," he said. They laughed together.

SATURDAY
MORNING

I

ALL OF MICHAEL BLACKBURN's actions were informed
by a sense of the importance of ritual, and he treated
breakfast seriously because it began the ritual of the
day. To the left of his plate the daily newspaper must
be folded; in front of him the jug filled with cream
for his porridge or cereal; to the right the rough-cut
marmalade, the honey and the sugar. Such a particu-
larity of arrangement was essential to his well-being
in the early morning.

This morning all was as he wished it. The coffee
brought by the maid was of exactly the right strength,
and heated to a temperature that permitted it to be
drunk immediately without the least sensation of
scalding on the tongue; the porridge was thick, yet
perfectly smooth and consistent; when the toast came,
each piece was warm and done to the same shade of
medium brown. Yet Michael Blackburn's forehead on
this morning was marked by two small perpendicular
ridges of worry just between the eyebrows. He looked
with much less than his usual interest at the record of
cradles, orange blossoms and graves in *The Times*,
and read his assorted letters with indifference. His
mind turned to the past and to death: to the miserable end of the reckless, dissipated and generous man
called Leon Amberside, to the sudden and terrible
death of his old friend James Cobb, and to the fate of
the little cripple whom he had snubbed. These
thoughts were not pleasant, and yet he was sorry to
be disturbed from them by a telephone call which
proved to be in invitation from his friend Stuart, or

Porky, Henderson to spend a week end at his country cottage with some really amusing people. He refused this invitation with a sharpness that left Henderson injured and unhappy, and expressed disinterest in the news that Ruth Cleverly was no longer a member of the publisher's staff. When Blackburn returned to his breakfast, the coffee had lost some of its vital warmth, and two pieces of toast had hardened a little. He left them untouched, looked at his watch and adhered to the ritual of this disturbed day by going up to see his mother.

She received him equably in bed, where, neat and exact as he liked to see her, she sat propped by pillows reading *My Friend Prospero,* by Henry Harland. He wandered round the room, picking up and putting down a piece of Staffordshire pottery, adjusting a picture on the wall, fiddling with a trinket box. At last she said in her cool, old voice, "Is anything the matter, Michael? Anything to do with that boy you took to Lord's yesterday?" He turned round with a look of surprise, and she said pleasantly, "I have my own ways of finding out things. He seemed a nice boy, but stupid. He is very handsome. Where does he come from?"

"His father is a rather shady company promoter. In financial difficulties, I believe."

"But that is not what is worrying you? It is something to do with that boy, though, is it not? About the people who came to tea on Tuesday."

"Yes." He passed his fine hand wearily over his fine forehead. "I have a presentiment of something unpleasant impending. James Cobb's death distressed me."

"It does seem scandalous that people should be able to walk into other people's houses and shoot them and walk out again," she said placidly. Her old eyes were remarkably watchful. "Where are you going today?"

He made a slight, irritable gesture. "Down to a

place called Millingham. This afternoon. Young Shelton's playing cricket down there."

"Don't do anything foolish, Michael."

"Of course not." He came over to the bed, kissed her thin veined hand and patted her cheek. Then he looked at his watch, said, "It is time for you to get up," and left her. He wandered downstairs, stopped uncertainly before the door of his study, went in and took a book from the shelves. He sat down and began to read it. The book was his own collection of essays, *Sesame Without Lilies,* and he opened it at the biographical essay dealing with Martin Rawlings, called "A Turbulent Boy."

II

Anthony heard the buzz of the lawn mower, looked out of his bedroom window and saw his father solemnly propelling the machine up and down the lawn. It was the one form of physical exercise in which Mr. Shelton indulged, and with a kind of scared affection the young man watched the small figure driving the mower with relentless efficiency in regular and unwavering lines. Mr. Shelton waved cheerfully to his son, and Anthony ran lightly down the stairs and out into the garden. His father rested one arm on the mower and smiled.

"Hullo," he said. "I didn't see you last night."

"No. As a matter of fact, I had dinner with a man called Michael Blackburn. Literary sort of chap. I expect you've heard of him."

"Yes," his father said meditatively, and added, "Well?" The word was an amiable question.

Anthony smiled nervously. The words he had on the tip of his tongue simply failed to come out. "How's the old garden?"

"There are some troublesome worm casts." Mr. Shelton looked slightly perturbed. "There was something you wanted to say?"

"Yes, Father." Muscles at the back of Anthony's

neck strained with effort. "I may play for Southshire this season, after all." His father's brown face showed a pleasure, apparently unalloyed. "But I wondered about—Brazilian Tractors—and the East African Mining Syndicate—and——" He had looked up the names laboriously in the paper.

"My dear boy, don't let that disturb you. That's all over."

"Over?" Anthony was bewildered. "But on Thursday night you said that you were—on the edge of ruin."

"That was Thursday night. I said also that things would go right or wrong in the next twenty-four hours. This is Saturday morning. I'm happy to be able to say that things didn't go wrong."

"But I don't understand."

"The operations of financiers"—his father chuckled —"may be beyond the comprehension of even the most talented fast-medium bowler. A financier is in effect a juggler, and he needs the most delicate sense of balance. He is keeping three balls quite comfortably in the air, and—presto—a fourth is added to them. He manages to absorb it into his trick. But then another is added—and another. And now he must exercise the most exquisite care, because an error involves not merely the fall of one ball, but the failure of his whole trick. On Thursday night it seemed that all the balls might fall to the ground. Now, lo and behold, the juggler has mysteriously recovered his sense of balance, and is again performing his trick with the utmost apparent ease."

Anthony's bewilderment was very little decreased. "But that sounds awfully dangerous."

"Life, as a fine novelist once observed, is a bazaar of dangerous and smiling chances. Whether we encounter them through the urgent physical battles in which you have recently been engaged, or through the mental struggles which are more suited to my years and physique, seems relatively unimportant. Accept my assurance that you need have no further worries." In the same breath, his father continued, giving the mower a meditative push, "What worries *me*, I confess, is your choice of a dinner companion."

"Michael Blackburn? But he was awfully nice to me."

"I don't doubt it."

"And—I'm going to play cricket this afternoon, and he's coming down to watch."

"That indicates a praiseworthy enthusiasm on his part for our English field sports. Your life, of course, is entirely your own affair, but Michael Blackburn is in some respects a dangerous companion." He pushed the lawn mower backward and forward again. "What has become of—ah—Vicky?"

"We had a row—on the telephone." Anthony looked like a large and sulky baby. "She wanted me to take her somewhere this afternoon, and I couldn't because I'm playing cricket."

"M-m. It happens that I am free myself this afternoon. Would it be possible for me to accompany you?"

"Good Lord! Of course, Father. I didn't think you'd want to."

"My capacity for physical exercise, taken vicariously, is considerable," his father said. He looked at his watch and gave the mower a final push. "It is nearly eleven o'clock. I think the rest of the lawn can fittingly be left to the gardener."

III

Vicky spent the morning in a state of gloom. She attempted to make notes in her diary, but found herself too depressed to do so. Then she sat down and wrote the first page of a story about a young woman whose life was ruined by her inability to be faithful to any young man. She rushed downstairs to answer two telephone calls, but they were both from patients of Edward's. When she tired of the story she wept quietly for a few minutes, and then returned to reading the newspapers with particular care, to see what information they contained about the death of Jacobs. She had learned of this on the previous evening, when Uncle Jack had telephoned in high excitement. He read out to her with gusto the heading in his evening paper, *Bookseller found hanged in Blackheath*, and a short and obviously official paragraph that followed, to the effect that Mr. Jonathan Jacobs, a bookseller, of Peaceful Alley, Blackheath, had been found hanged on his own premises that morning. There was no addition to this meager news item on Saturday morning; but, like Uncle Jack, Vicky assumed that this was the end of the case, and that the death of the bookseller was an acknowledgment of guilt. She said as much to Edward and her mother.

"As far as I'm concerned," Edward said, "it's one more disgraceful feature of a disgraceful affair. The family won't be able to hold up its head in Barnsfield after this."

Muriel Rawlings said to her daughter, with an air of gentle reproof, "Your father would never have cared to be connected with such an affair, dear."

"Do you suppose I care to be connected with it?" Vicky snapped. "It's not my doing."

Edward tapped impatiently on the table. "My dear girl, you speak as though you hadn't rummaged through family papers in the attic with that extraordinary man, and then borrowed my car without so much as a by-your-leave to go goodness knows where."

"I borrowed it to go to see Uncle Jack."

Edward put his hand to his chest. "It is too bad of you to make me excited in this way. It is bad for my heart."

"And Uncle Jack said he hoped we would all go over this afternoon. If you're not going, Edward, I'd like to borrow the car again."

Her brother popped two tablets into his mouth. "Where's Shelton? I haven't seen him round here for the past day or two."

"I don't know or care where he is."

"Oh." Edward stopped sucking the tablets and stared at her. "Well, you mustn't expect me to interfere in lovers' quarrels." He added hastily, "But I might be able to drive you over myself. It will be inconvenient, of course, but I can come back if there's anything urgent. And really I suppose we should bury the hatchet with Uncle Jack. Will you come too, Mother?"

"I have my household affairs to attend to," Mrs. Rawlings said with dignity. "But you may give your uncle my kind wishes."

IV

Uncle Jack had taken his morning exercise—fencing in the garden with his son Philip. He had been called away from it to receive a telephone call which brought him news of major importance.

"Rawlings," a voice said. "Deeds here. Got some bad news."

Uncle Jack grunted. Colonel Deeds was, or regarded himself as, the feudal squire of the village of Sellingham, five miles north of Millingham.

"Wilkinson's poisoned his foot."

"Sorry to hear it," Uncle Jack said. His red-apple face was undisturbed.

"He's right out, I'm afraid," said Colonel Deeds. "No use at all."

Uncle Jack gave another grunt that was perhaps an inadequate vehicle to convey both sympathy and an acknowledgment of the seriousness of the case. "Pity. Great pity." There was a silence.

"Going to make things a bit uneven," said Colonel Deeds.

"Oh, I don't know."

"Wondered if you could help us out at all."

"No chance of that, I'm afraid," said Uncle Jack immediately. "Had a job myself, y'know."

"Heard you were pretty strong. One or two new

faces, someone told me. All our boys are local, of course."

"Ah," said Uncle Jack, with no particular sound of encouragement.

"Shouldn't think of askin' in the ordinary way, but it's a blow. Struck down, as you might say, at the last minute. No denying it's a blow."

"See what I can do," Uncle Jack said curtly. "Great pity about Wilkinson. Ring you in a few minutes. G'by."

He sat down heavily in front of the desk and stared at a sheet of paper, on which were written eleven names. They were the names of the Millingham cricket team to play Sellingham that afternoon on Millingham village green. The rivalry between the two villages was considerable, and the two teams were never confined strictly to village inhabitants. It was understood, however, that if not inhabitants, the players should be relatives of inhabitants, or if not that, relatives of relatives. It is axiomatic, however, that when once an inch has been allowed an ell will be taken, and it had been customary for several years past for Uncle Jack and Colonel Deeds, as the cricketing despots of their respective villages, to try to enlist the support of any good players who could be regarded as connected, even remotely, with the villages. The Millingham team had once included an England batsman who had been lured to Millingham to stay with the owner of a local brewery, and had then been induced to play, rather against his own will and to the vividly expressed indignation of Colonel Deeds. He had, however, been hit on the arm off the third ball he received from Wilkinson, the Sellingham fast bowler, and had thrown away his wicket in the same over. It was this Wilkinson, a bowler of no especial subtlety or accuracy, but a mainstay of village green cricket, who had poisoned his foot.

Uncle Jack sat staring at the list of his team while caution, rather than chivalry, warred in his mind with desire for victory. It was clear that Sellingham's position must be acute, or Deeds would not have asked for the loan of a player. It was clear also that Deeds knew something of the plans that Uncle Jack had laid for a Millingham victory; and he was quite capable of making an unpleasant scene by questioning the credentials of one or another player, if his request was refused outright. What, then, was to be done? It was out of the question for any of the seven genuine local Millingham players to transfer their allegiance. That left Norman Summers, a former Blue who lived in Millingham several years ago, and was at present in the village on the visit to a friend, Alec Johnson, a doctor acting as a *locum* for a local practitioner who had sometimes turned out as a fast bowler for Southshire, Bill Debenham, a nephew of the local brewer, and—Uncle Jack sighed as he came to the fourth name on his list. It was a name, certainly, which had a very slender right to be there, but that right would not have been questioned had Sellingham been able to field a strong side. As it was, Deeds would certainly be unpleasant—that remark about new faces foretold a little of the wrath to come. And it was probable that, with Sellingham fielding a weak team, a little magnanimity could be afforded. Uncle Jack shook his head sadly and with a thick, blunt pencil crossed out the name of Anthony Shelton, replacing it by that of the village greengrocer. Then he went to the telephone and talked to Colonel Deeds.

V

Ruth Cleverly lay in a hot bath and thought about John Basingstoke, his disorderly dark hair and his long, lean and awkward body, and his mixture of shyness and sophistication. He believes I'm terribly practical, but he's wrong, she thought. She looked at her monkey face in a mirror without much affection, and stuck out her tongue. She began to wash herself all over with a sponge.

The thing is, she said to herself, shall I marry him? For they had gone to a cinema on Friday night, to see a film made by Charles Chaplin, called *A Woman of Paris*, with a new actor named Adolphe Menjou; and then they had eaten dinner together (a dinner, incidentally, which he had lacked money to pay for), and beween the entrée and the joint he had asked her to marry him. It was when he had said that he was unable to pay for the dinner that she had asked what they would live on.

"If you're in love with me that doesn't matter."

"You're quite sure that *you're* in love with *me?*"

"Oh yes. I couldn't be mistaken. That was why I went to the cemetery this afternoon, although I didn't know it at the time."

"Why don't you get a job?" she asked, and he stared at her.

"I write books," he said with a kind of offended dignity.

"I didn't ask how you'd keep me in cigarettes. You forget I worked for your publisher until today. I know how many copies your poems sold. And, anyway, I haven't noticed you writing any books in the last few days." She leaned across the table and took his lean hand in her stubby one. "I'm sick of living from hand to mouth, John. It's all right when you're twenty, but later on it's no fun. And what should we do but live from hand to mouth?"

"In a year or two——"

"And what should we do for that year or two? I can look after myself, but I don't want to have to look after you as well in the interests of high art."

Then he looked hurt, and was upset. They split the cost of the dinner.

Ruth Cleverly splashed the bath water violently. Why did I have to put it just that way, she thought, a way that was certain to upset him? Why couldn't I do it tactfully? She got out of the bath, enveloped herself in an enormous towel and dried herself with quick, impatient rubs. And above all, she thought as she finished drying herself, *am* I going to marry him, anyway? Because, appearances to the contrary, I'm not a practical person.

During the course of this mental soliloquy she had not once thought about his scar.

VI

Basingstoke missed the last train to Barnsfield on Friday night, and stayed with his young friend. Bland, whose passion for personal neatness was mixed with an amiable tolerance of the disorderly habits of others, made up a bed for him on the floor of his dungeon out of an old sleeping bag, a pillow and a blanket. Although it was after midnight when Basingstoke arrived, he saw that a light was shining through his friend's skylight, and Bland told him that he had just returned from a lecture on "The Psychology of the Criminal," given by an American penologist visiting England. Basingstoke, who felt tired and discouraged after dinner with Ruth, quickly went to sleep in the sleeping bag. He woke to the smell of frying bacon, and saw that the table was laid with a gay check cloth for breakfast. Bland's face was flushed as he turned from the gas stove.

"You had an air of abstraction from earthly things last night. I hope you're prepared to eat a light snack this morning."

The light snack was quantities of scrambled eggs and bacon, with hot toast and a great deal of milky coffee. "You live awfully well," Basingstoke said, his mouth half full. "Bacon and eggs for stray visitors. I can't think how you do it on your salary."

"These things are a matter of organization. I earn two pounds ten shillings a week. My rent is ten and sixpence—which perhaps explains why I live in this curious room. I smoke and drink very little, not because I have any prejudice against tobacco or alcohol, but simply because such things are bound to be luxuries for me. If I ever become involved with a woman, I shall make sure that she doesn't want to eat at the Ritz." He shrugged his shoulders. "With such tastes, it's possible for me to provide bacon and eggs not for stray visitors, but for my friends."

"And are you happy, living like that?"

"Don't let us become involved in metaphysics. Which of us is happy? And what is happiness? What song did the sirens sing?" When Bland smiled he looked no more than sixteen years old. "Am I right in deducing that you have fallen in love with someone who demands the Ritz?"

"Not altogether." Basingstoke told the story of his proposal. "It's no use laughing at me. I'm perfectly serious."

"She doesn't mind about your scar?"

"She says she doesn't."

"Then why not do what she says, and get yourself a job?"

"Do you mean sitting in an office all day and adding up rows of figures? I couldn't do that. I don't want to be tied to anything that affects my freedom," he said rather pompously.

"I had the impression you were interested in the Rawlings girl."

"Good Lord, no. She's good looking, but hasn't a brain in her head." Basingstoke sat picking his teeth. "It would be nice to get hold of some money. You still believe you know who's responsible for all this?"

"Yes."

"I can't get that damned man hanging up in the kitchen out of my mind."

"I'm not surprised," Bland said, and added as the other looked at him, "I can't get him out of my mind either. The inspector's been cautious. There's nothing in the papers beyond the bare official statement that Jacobs was found hanged on his own premises, and that it's probably suicide."

Basingstoke read the papers, while Bland dressed with his customary care. When the two young men went out Bland stopped by the postbox, and took a long and bulky envelope from his pocket. "In case of accidents," he said, and dropped it in.

VII

Inspector Wrax sat at his desk staring at the photostat of a document which he had received that morning. It was what he had expected, and now that he had it the warmth faded from his eyes, and left them lusterless as pebbles. He sat meditating at the desk, chewing savagely the end of a pencil. The telephone rang, and he heard Sergeant Thynne's squeaky voice.

"I think we're on to something, sir. You know the milkman?"

The inspector bit through his pencil, and spat it out. "I can't say I've had the pleasure."

"I mean, sir, you know there was some milk left outside Jacobs' house? We've got hold of the milkman, and he says when he was delivering he noticed a man coming out. That was about eight o'clock, and he didn't get a proper sight of the chap because he wore a trilby hat and had a scarf wrapped round his face—as if he had a bad tooth, see. Now, we've traced him further. He took a ticket from Blackheath up to Charing Cross—ticket collector remembers a man with a scarf who didn't speak very clearly."

"Any identification? Short or tall, dark or fair?"

The sergeant coughed. "The milkman said he was a bit above medium height, and the ticket collector thought he was short. But we're still trying to pick him up from Charing Cross."

"What about Cobb's house? Still nobody who saw anyone leave there?"

"Not yet, sir. But we're still trying."

"Yes," said the inspector. "Go on trying." He put down the telephone, and said aloud, to the wall, "But the case is closed."

SATURDAY AFTERNOON

THE EXTREME LACK OF confidence with which Edward Rawlings handled a car was perhaps partly responsible for the falling-off in his practice, for some of his patients may have felt that one so inept with a mechanical object might be no more skillful with stethoscope and hammer. He regarded his car rather as an animal that had a life of its own, quite independent of the attempts made by its driver to control it. Nevertheless, he recognized that the use of clutch and steering wheel had, in an unaccountable way, their effect on the animal's conduct, and was very careful not to let them get out of control. His top speed on a good, straight road, with nothing in sight, was twenty miles an hour, and he slowed down on turning corners so that the car almost stopped. He earned the reward of such care in a puncture when they were ten miles from Millingham, and he mended it slowly and with a great deal of fuss. It was a hot afternoon, and by the time Edward had finished he was red and sweating. "This kind of thing is bad for my heart," he said as he got back in the car.

"Speaking of hearts, what about that missing stuff? Did you find out anything more about it?"

Edward looked embarrassed. "As a matter of fact, I did. It was all Mother's fault. She *will* come into the dispensary to ask what I want for lunch—really a most disconcerting habit. I questioned her closely, and she agreed that in the course of such a conversation she had seen me take a bottle *out* of the poison cupboard and put it on the shelf, and take a bottle *off* the shelf and put it in the poison cupboard. Do I make myself clear?" He looked solemnly at his sister.

"Perfectly. And don't you remember anything about it?"

"Nothing whatever. Isn't that an appalling thing?"

"I shouldn't worry," said Vicky unfeelingly. "If you don't go a little faster, the car behind will ram us, and then you probably won't remember anything at all." Edward pressed the accelerator a little, and shuddered sympathetically as the car leaped forward.

When they reached Uncle Jack's house half an hour later, Mrs. Holroyd opened the door. "Mr. Rawlings has gone," she said, and they stared at her. "He said I was to give you this note." She hesitated between them, and gave it to Vicky. Edward stood with his lips pursed in disapproval, while she tore it open. The note said, in Uncle Jack's dashing hand:

DEAR VICKY—and Edward too, if you come—I promised you a surprise. Come down to the green and see what it is. Meant to take you down myself, but had to rush off.

Delighted to see you both. Edward—please don't give me a depressing view of my health.

Your loving uncle.

"Whatever is Mr. Rawlings doing at the village green?" Vicky asked, and the woman looked at her pityingly.

"He's gone to the cricket."

"Cricket," Vicky said with disgust when the door was closed. "I don't want to see cricket."

"I knew all this would be a complete waste of time." Edward stood kicking the car wheel despondently, in a way that made her feel perversely annoyed.

"Now that we're here we may as well go down to the green," she said sharply, and climbed into the car again. As they drove toward the village, her mind moved into fanciful thoughts of Uncle Jack making a will in her favor. *Vicky, my little girl, you are the only one amongst us who is fitted to carry on the torch lighted by your grandfather. At my death this house will be yours, with all that's in it. See that within these walls the flame of arts is kept burning.* What alterations would have to be made to the house? She was brooding on them when the car jolted to a stop and Edward said, "Here we are."

Millingham Green was not unbeautiful at any time, and was looking its best on this fine May afternoon. The green itself was large and triangular, and it was ornamented by two marquees, each with a flag fluttering above it. A good deal of bunting was strung about for no obvious reason. Deck chairs were placed round the marquees, and on another side of the ground were several benches on which old men were sitting, many of them smoking pipes. A dozen cars were parked at intervals round the green and perhaps a hundred and fifty people were watching the men who performed a complicated ritual in the middle of it.

"Rather pretty, isn't it?" Edward said, but Vicky did not hear him. She was gazing with parted lips at the scene before her, a scene as intricate and carefully designed as a ballet. The bowler stepped up and as he did so some of the men walked forward. Smoothly his arm swung over and the little ball was projected into the air. It thudded gently against the bat and rolled toward one of the walking men, who gravely picked it up, looked at it, and returned it to the bowler. The bowler walked back, ran forward and again his arm swung over smoothly. The whole thing had, Vicky felt (although she would not have phrased her feeling in quite those words) the repetitive and incantatory quality of all primitive art; and it had also the small novelty and variation of such art, for as she watched, the batsman swished violently at the little ball, it rested in the thick gloves of the sinister crouching figure behind him and several of the flanneled men bayed like dogs to the blue sky.

The swisher stood hesitantly for a moment, a brave man prepared to meet his fate. Then he turned on his heel and strode away, as a figure in a white coat lifted a finger. On the benches there were murmurs, shaking of old heads and knocking of almost equally old pipes.

"Pleasant enough here," Edward said grudgingly.

"It's *wonderful*," said Vicky. It will be remembered that she had never watched a cricket match before. "Why, there's Uncle Jack," she cried, standing up in the car. Two or three people on the green turned round to smile at her benevolently and on the field a red-cheeked figure, silk scarf tied loosely round neck, waved a friendly hand. The new batsman was tall and broad shouldered, and he wore a cap of many colors. He had no immediate chance to show his abilities, for over had been called and Uncle Jack himself took the ball at the other end. It was apparent from the way in which he gripped the ball in his hand and tossed it into the air, that he was a bowler of much guile. The batsman pranced down the pitch with his head in the air and missed the ball completely. Again the dogs bayed to the sky and the fierce little man ran toward the marquee, swinging his bat cheerfully.

"Eight men out," Edward said. He pointed to a wooden board on which a boy was hanging three rows of numbers. They read 110—8—15. Vicky stared at it, and asked what it meant. "It means that the side batting has scored a hundred and ten runs with eight men out, and that the last man out made fifteen runs." Edward looked at his sister with his eyes screwed up. "You seem very interested. I thought you didn't like cricket."

"*This* kind of cricket is quite enchanting," Vicky said, making an unspoken reservation about all the other kinds she had not seen.

Still with his eyes screwed up, staring out at the green, her brother said, "I understand now why you were so keen to come down."

"Why?"

"There's Shelton batting."

"*Anthony.*" She realized suddenly the identity of the tall and strangely familiar figure in the many-colored cap. She realized also, with a rush of relief, the reason for Anthony's reluctance to tell her where he was going that afternoon. "If only I'd known," she murmured to herself. She felt like singing.

The other batsman had scraped a single, and now Anthony faced Uncle Jack. He stood comfortably, erect and graceful, waiting to receive the ball. Uncle Jack trotted up and tossed the ball into the air as usual. It looked remarkably innocuous but somehow Anthony managed to miss it, and the ball hit the three sticks behind him. Vicky put a hand to her mouth as he walked out. "Oh. Does that mean he's finished?"

"Yes; he's out, I'm afraid. Here's that chap Basing-stoke. What the devil's he doing here?"

Basingstoke had with him Ruth Cleverly and a friend whose name, when he was introduced, turned out to be Bland. Vicky was too much upset by the sight of the small boy putting up on the wooden board figures that read 111—9—0 to pay much attention to these newcomers. When her attention wandered from the cricket, however, she saw that Basingstoke looked more cheerful than usual, and that his young friend, who was dressed with clerkly neatness and tidiness, allowed his impersonal blue eyes to rest on her for a little longer than seemed necessary. She noticed also that Ruth Cleverly was looking much smarter than usual, in a blue silk dress. They had come down, it seemed, to have tea with Uncle Jack and he had told them (what he had kept from Vicky) that a cricket match would be part of the entertainment. Edward greeted them all with a kind of suspicious gloom, and while they stood round the car talking the players walked slowly off the field in the direction of the marquee. Presently Uncle Jack came briskly over to them, followed by a young man recognized by Vicky (although she had not seen him for two or three years) as his son Philip. Uncle Jack was looking very pleased with himself.

"Something like a day, isn't it?" he chuckled. "Something like a day. How are you, Edward? Not looking too well—trust a doctor not to be able to prescribe for himself. And you, my dear." He kissed Vicky heartily on the cheek. "Told you I'd have a surprise for you, didn't I? Surprise for your young man, too—didn't tell him I'd asked you to come over. Doesn't know you're here yet. Did you see me bowl him out, eh?" He turned to the others. "Miss Cleverly, delighted to see you, very much delighted. Allow an old man the privilege." He kissed her on the cheek. "And you, young Sherlock, how are you? Brought your assistant with you, I see."

"As a matter of fact, he *is* interested in that affair, but I'm really *his* assistant," Basingstoke said in his rich voice. The glance that Uncle Jack gave them from under his thick brows was remarkably keen, but he made no comment. Instead, he gestured toward the young man by his side. "Want you to meet my son Philip. Come down specially to score all the runs, now that I've got them out." He gave a dig to Vicky. "Unless your young man gets *him* out."

"Uncle Jack, why is Anthony playing against you?" Uncle Jack wiped his brow with a handkerchief and looked rather angry.

"Lent him to the other side, my dear. Long job to explain. Should really be playing for us."

"But he doesn't belong to your village."

Uncle Jack snorted.

Philip Rawlings said hastily, "I say, shouldn't we go and have some tea?"

"Of course, of course," said his father. "Arranged the tea interval now. Let's go over." He took Vicky's arm as they walked toward the marquee. "Haven't had a chance to speak to your young man alone yet. Just had time to tell him he was playing for Sellingham. Understand you don't approve of this game."

"I love it," she said enthusiastically.

"Oh." Uncle Jack was rather disconcerted. "Good for you. His father's here," he added as an afterthought.

Inside the marquee plates of bread and butter, jam, watercress, radishes, scones, buns and cakes were laid on long tables at which the players sat. There were smaller tables for visitors, and Uncle Jack steered them to one of these, said "Back in a few minutes; help yourselves," and disappeared. Two people were sitting at the table already and Vicky, when she sat down, saw that one of them was Mr. Shelton and the other Michael Blackburn. Mr. Shelton's brown face creased into a smile as he saw Vicky. She sat down next to him.

"What a pleasant surprise for us. I thought you were very much opposed to cricket."

"Not *village* cricket, because it *looks* so lovely," she said rather desperately.

"My dear—um—Vicky, I am delighted to know that so profound an exponent of the modern idea in most things should tolerate an old-fashioned sport upon the village green. I fear that Anthony did not altogether distinguish himself with the bat. Will you have some watercress?"

She champed watercress, listened abstractedly to the conversation around her, and watched Anthony's fair head bobbing sideways at the other table.

"You know Miss Rawlings, I believe," Mr. Shelton was saying to Blackburn. "She and Anthony are to be married very soon." Blackburn's head was bent over his plate as Vicky turned round, quite startled. Mr. Shelton gave her a prodigious wink, and then Anthony was standing beside her, looking godlike and boyish at once.

"Vicky! What are you doing here?"

Dabbing at her eyes, she said, "Uncle Jack asked me to come."

"Vicky," Mr. Shelton said with a gentle cough, "approves of village cricket. In time, perhaps, she may be won to sympathy with more august aspects of the game."

"I say, that's jolly good." A vast smile split Anthony's face. "I *am* glad to see you. You didn't say, you were coming, and I didn't like to tell you I was. I say, though, have you had some tea? Will you look after Vicky, Father?"

"I shall look after you both," said Mr. Shelton.

"There's been some mix-up. Your uncle asked me to play for his team, but now it seems I'm playing for the other side. Do make sure Vicky has a deck chair, won't you, Father? I've got to go out and field now."

"Good luck, Anthony," Blackburn said.

"Thanks." Bending his head to kiss Vicky awkwardly on the cheek Anthony repeated, "I *am* glad to see you," and went away. There was, indeed, a general exodus from the tent, and they followed it, settling themselves in deck chairs in time to see Sellingham take the field, followed by Millingham's opening batsmen.

"There's Phil, and Norman Summers with him," Uncle Jack said and chuckled. "Beautiful bat, Norman. Ought to make a lot of runs—unless your young man does some damage." Anthony was out of practice, however, and his first over was an unhappy one. The batsmen scored off every ball, and a hush fell on the little group in deck chairs. Mr. Shelton's face might have been cut out of brown rock, and even Uncle Jack's glee was mixed with embarrassment. "Pity," he said, and sat down in a chair beside Basingstoke. "Rotten affair, that chap Jacobs."

Basingstoke had been engaged in an earnest conversation with Ruth Cleverly. Now he turned round. "I found him," he said, not without a touch of bravado. He waved a hand past Ruth, where his rosy-cheeked young friend sat leaning forward, intent on the cricket. "Bland here was with me at the time."

Without looking away from the cricket, Bland said, "I came a few minutes afterward. It wasn't pleasant."

"Horrible," said Uncle Jack with relish. "Strung up

like a pig in his own kitchen. Suppose that's the end of the story, eh?"

He addressed himself to Basingstoke, but it was Bland who replied. All of them seemed to listen with attention as he said, "The police seemed not to think so, but you never can tell what they really believe. The information they gave to the newspapers afterward was very scanty."

"Like to know if that damn Jacobs got hold of my book," Uncle Jack said irritably. "Oh, that's too bad. He's taken Shelton off." Anthony had indeed been taken off, after his one unhappy over. Uncle Jack rose from his deck chair, as if about to protest, and then sat down again. Conversation died. They watched rather uneasily, as the score mounted through the thirties and the forties. Vicky was distressed. "Won't they let him bowl again?" she whispered to Mr. Shelton.

"Later, perhaps. I'm very glad you came this afternoon, so that I could tell you that I have changed my view about the necessity of—um—a long engagement." She blushed. At her other side Edward was saying something to Uncle Jack about indigestion. Mr. Shelton said, "I do hope that nothing will prevent—ah, Anthony's going to bowl again at the other end."

Colonel Deeds was speaking to Anthony, and had given him the ball. Anthony went back and marked carefully the spot at which he would begin his run. Quietness seemed to hang over the green. Vicky watched expectantly.

"I say," Edward said petulantly, "I think it's going to rain." Anthony ran up and bowled. His first ball broke sharply and hit Summers' wicket. Vicky clapped her hands.

"One for sixty-two," Uncle Jack said. "And thunder about." They turned to look where a heavy cloud was coming up behind the marquee, and as they did so a man came out of the tent. He had an envelope in his hand, which he gave to Uncle Jack. "Found this on the floor of the marquee, sir, when we were cleaning up. It's addressed to you."

"To *me*." Uncle Jack looked at the envelope with some distaste. "Right you are, Saunders." He tore it open and read the contents with a frown on his face. Then he looked at the envelope again.

"Oh, well bowled," said Mr. Shelton. Anthony had bowled the incoming batsman. There was a spatter of applause from the benches. Uncle Jack sat down and passed a hand over his forehead.

"Bad news?" Edward asked.

"Bad news for somebody, but not for you, Edward, my boy." He tore up the letter into small shreds and sat with his chin on his hand, watching the cricket.

Anthony was now bowling really well, and he began to skittle out the batsmen. He was aided by the pitch, which showed the cracks and bare patches that lend what is called a sporting character to so many village wickets. When the score board showed five men out for eighty runs Uncle Jack went out to bat. His bright eyes flickered over the visitors in their deck chairs and he grinned unexpectedly. "Hope I come back safe and sound."

Uncle Jack trotted to the wicket and took guard. There were still five balls to Anthony's over. The first of them was good length, pitched on the wicket. Uncle Jack strolled out to it and lifted it over the bowler's head for four. The next was shorter and he made a kind of circular mow which was not within inches of the ball. He mishit the third ball and the batsmen ran two.

The cloud was overhead. One or two heavy drops of rain fell. Basingstoke said, "We'd better get under cover," but Bland seemed not to hear him. He was staring out onto the darkened cricket field.

The next ball was Uncle Jack's glory. It was a good length, and rose sharply. He went down on one knee and tried another mow. This time it connected, and the ball sailed high into the air and landed among the benches where it was finely caught and thrown back by one of the old men with pipes. The umpire signaled six runs.

Rain was falling now quite heavily. Mr. Shelton got up, put his coat round Vicky, and they joined the little crowd that had clustered at the entrance of the marquee. Only Bland sat in his deck chair as if mesmerized as Anthony came up to bowl the last ball of the over.

Perhaps the ball slipped from his hand, or perhaps it was a reversion to his wretched opening over. Anyway, the ball was a very short one. Uncle Jack advanced on it with bat raised threateningly, but somehow failed to play a stroke. The ball rose sharply, like the preceding one, and struck him on the forehead. He crumpled up on the ground. The rain fell thickly in heavy drops. Anthony ran up to the figure on the ground and bent over it. The other players crowded round them. A motorcar drew up at the side of the green and two men jumped out of it. Bland stood up and shrugged the rain off his shoulders.

The two men were running now. The foremost of them was Inspector Wrax, his dark eyes hot and angry. Bland turned to meet him in the rain. His young face was set and grave. He said to the inspector, "You are too late." The players were carrying Uncle Jack off the field. The cloud above them was suddenly split by lightning. There was a roar of thunder. The rain came down in splinters.

SATURDAY
EVENING

A THIN LIGHT FILTERED through the partly glassed roof of Bland's dungeon and illuminated his neat hair, as he took from a cupboard two tumblers, a chipped mug, and a decorated wineglass. He added to them a toothbrush glass, produced two bottles of beer and, gravely and carefully, poured the beer into the five receptacles, which were raised and lowered by his guests. Basingstoke's young friend rubbed his nose reflectively and said, in a voice not entirely free from smugness, "You're sure you want me to talk about it?"

Anthony rushed in before any of the others could reply, "Absolutely, old man. Basingstoke says you just sat here in this——" he was about to say "hole," but altered it quickly to "room"—"and solved it all on the spot. I think its wonderful."

"I still don't know what it was all about," said Ruth Cleverly.

Bland drained his toothbrush glass and set it down on the table. "And yet it was all obvious, and you would have seen what it was about if you'd not been thinking about a great international gang of forgers. You had all the clues in your hands, but you put a wrong interpretation on them. The evidence in the poems alone was enough to tell you the meaning of the case, and there were two clues which led straight to the murderer."

Basingstoke turned his scarred face. "Evidence in the poems? I've read them a dozen times, and I didn't see anything at all that could possibly have a bearing on the case."

"That's because you weren't looking for the right thing. And yet on Thursday evening you were nearer than I to grasping the truth. I said that the crimes must have something to do with the Rawlings family, and you suggested that the Australian cousin who left Martin his money might have had an illegitimate son who regarded the money as rightly his. I scoffed at the suggestion, but it wasn't far from the truth, except that we had our characters a little mixed. It was Martin Rawlings who had an illegitimate son."

Vicky said with a gasp, "Not—Uncle Jack?"

"Certainly Uncle Jack."

"But—he *was* the murderer, wasn't he?" Bland nodded. "But I don't understand. Why should he have wanted to harm anyone—he had the inheritance."

"The object of the murders wasn't to gain an inheritance, but to keep one. Let me tell you things as they happened, or more or less as they happened.

"Martin Rawlings was a wild young man and, as we can see from Blackburn's essay on him, very little indeed is known about his life in Italy. Blackburn says there that he disappeared for long periods at a time—and after one of these disappearances he turned up with a wife and a son. The very form of that phrasing should make one sit up and take notice. In fact, Cæsar Rawlings was born in April 1861, and Martin Rawlings was married in June of that year. In other words, Cæsar was born illegitimate."

"How do you know all that?" Ruth Cleverly asked.

Bland's smile was guileless. "I didn't. I deduced it. But Inspector Wrax, with whom I had an uncomfortable but not unprofitable interview, made certain of it by checking on the details with the Italian police. He suspected Rawlings, but wanted to wait until he had positive proof before he took action. He waited too long.

"After their marriage Martin and Maria had another child—your father, Miss Rawlings. And it was after that—probably in 1865 or 1866—that Martin Rawlings wrote *Passion and Repentance,* which was first published in 1868. Common sense should, indeed, tell anybody, that such poems must have been written *after* his conversion to Catholicism and not before—their whole tone is that of a convert, although a rather unorthodox one. In 1876 Martin Rawlings died and, thanks to the fact that he had not made a will, his elder son Cæsar inherited the whole estate. The brothers quarreled bitterly, and as Miss Rawlings told John her father refused to accept any financial assistance from his elder brother, although it was offered."

Vicky nodded. Her mouth was slightly open. Bland raised an admonitory finger.

"Cæsar Rawlings wasn't an habitual criminal—or perhaps he would have been a better one. There is no reason to suppose that he knew himself to be an illegitimate son, and the wrongful inheritor of the estate, in his youth. It is more likely that he discovered it when, as a young man, he went on a tour of Italy and visited those places where his father had lived. When he did so, no doubt he visited the little village where his father and mother were married, examined the register—and saw with shocked surprise that he had been born a bastard. At some time, at any rate, he discovered it, and must have pondered what, if anything, he should do about it. It's possible that if he had been on good terms with his brother, he would have suggested to him a division of the estate. In view of the enmity between them, however, the question didn't arise. As soon as Cæsar Rawlings made known the circumstances, he placed himself at his brother's mercy, for he was holding an estate to which he had no shadow of a legal claim. I'm right in thinking, Miss Rawlings, am I not, that such an appeal to your father to divide the estate wouldn't have been looked on favorably by him. Eh, Miss Rawlings?"

Vicky came to with a start. "Dad was always very bitter—against Uncle Jack, and against grandfather Martin because he hadn't made provision for him."

"Cæsar Rawlings, anyway, did what many men would have done, and decided to hold onto his inheritance. And then one day it must suddenly have occurred to him, as it occurred to me, that the story of his illegitimacy was set down plainly enough in his father's poems.

"Most of the critics were baffled by the exact meaning of *Passion and Repentance,* and in fact didn't trouble themselves to examine its literal meaning closely. But it's perfectly plain that the poems describe in metaphorical language the poet's sinful production of a child, and his repentance of that act." There were gestures of protest from Basingstoke and Ruth. "Perhaps I should say that this meaning is plain once you are looking for it. It is made very clear in one of the sonnets,[1] which begins 'Out of the sighs and anguish beauty comes' and talks of 'What's begot in stealth and sin and shame' and of the 'small errant son' who was 'the germ of darkness and ecstatic joy.' Once the meaning of this sonnet has been understood it illuminates all the others, and one wonders how it was possible to miss a theme which is so obvious—Adam feeling for Eve 'the dark desire that leads to loss and sighing,' the reference to 'Bitter, fruitful, all too fruitful days,' 'the record of past sin' joined to such phrases as 'Walking found your body like a fire, And neither of us recked a reckoning.' It's all, when you look for it, clearly set down that Martin Rawlings had a child whose creation was an act of 'stealth and sin and shame,' a sin of which he repented now that he had become a Catholic. Cæsar Rawlings read the poems with this knowledge of their meaning, and it must have brought him out in a cold sweat. If ever his brother should read them in the same light—if any damned good-natured friend should do so, and tell his brother about it—a few

1 See p. 178.

investigations need only be made in Italy, and he would be dispossessed of his fortune. And then what seemed a bright idea occurred to him. Nobody had ever troubled in the past to attach a precise meaning to the poems—could he prevent anyone from doing so in the future by making it appear that they were written *before* his own birth in 1861? Then any inquisitive soul who became curious about them and got an inkling of the truth would find that apparently his dates were all wrong, and give up in despair. But how could that be done? Simple—publish an edition of the poems dated a year before his birth, so that they must refer to events before that time."

"Then Uncle Jack was the forger?" Vicky said. "But he was never much interested in books."

"He never professed much interest, but when you went to see him with John he said casually that he had collected first editions in his youth. He let slip the fact that he knew Jacobs by saying that he had bought his own first edition of *Passion and Repentance* from him. Finally, in an access of foolishness, he showed you the copy of the book that Cobb had given his father, and told you that he had known Cobb when he was a child. It may have been Rawlings' acquaintance with Jacobs that put the whole idea in his mind. Wrax has discovered that Cæsar Rawlings got to know Jacobs in the South African War, when he was an officer and Jacobs was in his regiment. Lord knows how or why Jacobs got into the army, but once there he was involved in a jewel robbery. Rawlings made Jacobs return the jewels and let him go, but he forced him to write out a confession, which Wrax found in Rawlings' safe."

"You didn't know any of *that*," Ruth said.

"It wasn't possible or necessary to know the exact relation between them. Both of them had been in South Africa and the other circumstances of the case made it certain that Rawlings must have been Jacobs' 'client.' But I'll deal with my own thought processes later, and tell the story as Cæsar Rawlings saw it.

"Some time after Cæsar Rawlings came back from Italy, he conceived this idea and carried it out, printing a very few copies of *Passion and Repentance* with the date 1860 on them, and marketing them through Jacobs. No doubt he told Jacobs a story about finding them in some odd corner, which appeared perfectly plausible. He put on the booklet the name of the publisher who was no longer in business—making the slip that John's keen eye observed—and he must also have taken or sent one or two copies of his 'find' to Cobb. Cobb gave it his authority as a bibliographical discovery and, when approached by Blackburn for information connected with his biographical essay, cheerfully passed on the story Rawlings had told him. Cobb also presented one of the copies Rawlings gave him to the British Museum. So the bibliographical 'find' was firmly established.

"In the meantime Cobb had made a find of his own in the books left to him for disposal by Leon Amberside. Whether he guessed that those pamphlets were forgeries or not, he saw immediately that they were worth a good deal of money, and he was confronted by the same problem as that which confronted Rawlings, although for different reasons. How could he dispose of the books without spoiling the market? He was put in touch, he said in that interesting document he left, with a certain Mr. Jacobs, who was absolutely to be relied on in confidential matters. It is a good guess that the person who put him in touch was Cæsar Rawlings.

"Well, no inquiring literary critic or other busybody worried about the meaning of the *Passion and Repentance* sonnets—or if they did they were put off the scent by Rawlings' forged edition. Years passed. Rawlings married, had a son, his wife died. His right to the inheritance was never questioned. He probably put the whole affair of the book which he had forged in a panic out of his mind. But then one day out of the blue he received a letter from Jebb, who spread his discoveries far and wide, in spite of his talk of the necessity of keeping them secret. He gave a courteous rebuff to Jebb, but he realized the danger of these inquiries. The forgery which had been designed as his protection might now be his undoing, simply because Jebb was on the track of some other forgeries. If it were discovered that this book was forged, his own connection with it might be made known, and all sorts of awkward questions would be asked. He began to collect all the copies he could lay hands on, using for the purpose his old friend, Jacobs. The bookseller got in touch with one of his old criminal associates and Rawlings got back a number of copies—some of them by robbery, others by purchase. It was expensive, but less expensive than dispossession.

"That was the position when, on Monday, Shelton bought a copy of the book and John here suggested that there was something wrong about it, on the evidence of the publisher's name being incorrect. Rawlings had given instructions that it should be bought for him, and must have been furious when he found that it had slipped through his fingers. He foolishly increased the offer, through Jacobs, to an extent which was suspicious in itself, and when that was refused had Shelton knocked over the head in order to get the copy away from him. That was a stupid thing to do, and it was stupidly carried out—it would have been much more sensible to arrange a robbery in which the theft of the book was only an incident.

"His panic was increased when Miss Rawlings came to see him on Tuesday with John, and you told him your suspicions. He put you off with a story about being robbed of a copy of the book himself—a story containing a fairly palpable flaw, which I'll come to in a moment. He sent you to see Jacobs, got in touch with him while you were on the way there, and told him what to say. Jacobs made very fair fools of you both, and told you that he had obtained his copies from Cobb."

"Do you mean to say," Vicky asked, "that when we

went in the shop that man Jacobs knew who we were?"

Bland coughed. "Yes."

"Well," said Vicky, "I never heard of such a thing."

"The two of you sealed Jebb's death warrant, unknowingly, when you told Rawlings that Jebb was being consulted. It would be quite easy to show by his tests of paper alone that the book was a forgery. On Tuesday evening he went up to London, telephoned Jebb, and no doubt said he knew of the investigations and had some important information. He saw Jebb, killed him, and destroyed his papers. That wasn't very difficult."

The corners of Ruth Cleverly's mouth were pulled down. She looked as if she were going to cry. Basingstoke leaned over and patted her hand. The young man went on without looking at them.

"Perhaps he was safe now, then? But he very soon saw that he wasn't, and that his move in telling Jacobs to put you on to Cobb was not clever, but crassly stupid. He had thought that you wouldn't be able to obtain access to Cobb, and that the affair would die down. He hadn't reckoned that you would be involved in the police investigation, and tell the police the whole story. When you did, he knew that he was finished unless he could silence Cobb, for although you might not be able to induce Cobb to talk, the police would certainly do so. Cobb would tell them immediately that it was not he, but Cæsar Rawlings, who had passed on those copies to Jacobs. He should have thought of all that before he put you on to Cobb's trail, but he didn't. He was fundamentally a very stupid man, although he had a good nerve for action, like other stupid men. He silenced Cobb. And he was lucky—he got away. He must have had a bad time when that statement of Cobb's was being read, for fear that his name should be mentioned. It wasn't, but something happened that was almost as bad. Wrax had discovered that the book was forged. Nobody at the time, not even Wrax, realized the full implications of that discovery.

"By now, however, he was above his neck in trouble, for he was in the hands of Jacobs. Jacobs knew everything—he was party to the thefts, and knew where the forgeries had come from. He was in an ideal position to levy a little blackmail. I realized on Thursday evening, when John was telling me his story, that Jacobs was the key to the case, because he plainly knew the true origin of the books. When, on Friday morning, I understood that Cæsar Rawlings was the murderer, I knew that Jacobs was in danger. I went down to Blackheath, but I was too late. Rawlings had strangled Jacobs, and made a clumsy attempt to make his murder look like suicide." He sighed. "That's all, really. Thirsty work talking so much. Have some more beer."

"But," Vicky asked, "what did he do it all for? We didn't want his money. At least——" She hesitated.

"Your guess is as good as mine, but remember that he had enjoyed a property, and the use of money to which he had no right, ever since his father's death. Remember that he had a son, whom he obviously loved. I don't think you need look further for a motive. And remember also that, from his point of view, the first steps he took were mere peccadilloes. He hoped that he would be able to get the books back by theft and purchase, and if he had done so from his point of view there would have been no trouble at all. It was only your inquisitiveness, and Jebb's infernal nosiness—as he considered it—that made him tell a pack of ridiculous lies, and finally take the irrevocable step of murder."

Anthony was frowning. "I still don't see how you knew he was the murderer on Friday *morning*."

"The poems, darling," Vicky said airily.

"Yes; I can see it's awfully clever and all that, to have seen what those things meant, but I mean they weren't evidence, were they?"

"They were sufficient to convince me," Bland said

"that Cæsar Rawlings was probably an illegitimate child, and once I had realized that, everything else fell into place. But there were two pieces of quite concrete evidence which led direct to Cæsar Rawlings. One of them was the evidence of the book that wasn't there. Cæsar Rawlings had lost his copy of the early edition of *Passion and Repentance*—or said he had. And there was something very special about that copy—Rawlings told you, John, that it was *a presentation copy*. That was one of those inspired pieces of authentication in which he specialized, and which turned out to be extremely foolish. As Jebb said, the existence of association copies, given by the author to his friends, is one way of helping to determine the authenticity of a doubtful edition. And this, curiously enough, was the *only* presentation copy of this book that was ever mentioned. Now, when the inspector discovered by paper tests that the book was a forgery the question should have arisen—although nobody asked it—how could a presentation copy exist? The answer was, of course, that we only had Rawlings' word for its existence, and that the very fact that he had been trying to authenticate a forgery was damning evidence against him.

"Once the book had been shown by Wrax to be a forgery, also, the question arose: what of the authentication of it by that story told in Blackburn's essay? That story was either a true authentication or a deliberate lie. Blackburn referred it back to Cobb as authority for it, but who was Cobb's authority? Isn't it obvious that it must have been either Martin Rawlings or his son? And since—as was shown by the fact that the book was forged—the story was a lie, the person who told it must be the forger.

"But there was one piece of evidence that was quite damning. Jebb kindly left the name of his murderer on the blotting pad." He went over to a bookcase. When he came back he was laughing as he showed them an illustration. "Is that the face in your medallion?"

"Why, yes," Anthony said. "But what——"

Basingstoke was laughing too as Bland took his hand away and showed them what was written underneath it: *Julius Cæsar. Profile of the bust in the British Museum.* "It wasn't hard to guess what Jebb had in mind in making this symbolical drawing of his visitor, Cæsar Rawlings, when you remembered the nature of the drawing he made earlier in the day—Ruth amidst the alien corn."

"What fools we were." Basingstoke stroked his chin ruefully. Bland protested.

"The essential thing, unless you were in command of all Inspector Wrax's apparatus of investigation, was to discover the meaning of the poems. Once that was done, lots of little things fell into place—including, by the way, Rawlings' knowledge of facts about Jacobs' death, which he couldn't have got from the newspapers. On Saturday afternoon I dropped a little note in the marquee, so that Rawlings should know that he was finished. He had some pills on him, and used them when he was at the wicket. A cricketing death," Bland said solemnly.

It was almost dark in the great room. "Poor Uncle Jack," Vicky sighed. "I always liked him. He was very nice to me."

"He was a murdering rat," Ruth Cleverly said.

Basingstoke got up. "I must be going." He looked at Ruth.

"All right. I'm coming too."

"I'm going to look for a job," Basingstoke said to Bland with a straight face.

Vicky advanced with her hand held out. "So we're the heirs to the Rawlings fortune—though we shall come to an arrangement with Philip, of course. And it's all through you. You must come to our wedding. Anthony and I are going to be married next week." Anthony muttered something.

"I shall be delighted," Bland said. "Where are you spending your honeymoon?"

"Anthony is playing for Southshire on their

northern tour," Vicky said serenely, "and, of course, I shall be with him."

"One more thing," Basingstoke said. "What was in that note? It must have been something awfully potent to induce him to take poison."

"I simply told him what I knew," Bland said, and smiled.

"But why didn't he try to—dispose of you—as he had of the others?"

"Because I also told him that I'd taken the precaution of writing out my story and posting it to Inspector Wrax. You saw me do that on Saturday morning."

They were standing on the steps now, outside his dungeon. The sun was dying in a blaze of red and gold. "You think of everything," said Vicky. "You ought to be a detective. I mean," she added hurriedly, "a policeman."

"Perhaps I shall be," Bland said, "one day."

THE END: BUT PLEASE TURN OVER

POSTSCRIPT

IT WILL BE OBVIOUS to those of my readers interested in bibliography that the bibliographical "discoveries" in my book are derived from that most ingenious piece of literary detection, *An Enquiry into the Nature of Certain Nineteenth Century Pamphlets*, by John Carter and Graham Pollard. I have taken the liberty, in my story, of anticipating by a few years some of Messrs. Carter and Pollard's conclusions. This purely fictional anticipation was rendered necessary by certain changes in the English law of inheritance, because of which my story had to be set in a year before 1925; no reflection is intended upon Messrs. Carter and Pollard's original researches—by which I have been propped, indeed, as by a pillar.